ARE YOU READY?

NEW YORK TIMES BESTSELLING AUTHOR

KAYLEE RYAN

Cover Design: Lori Jackson Designs
Cover Photography: Michelle Lancaster
Special Edition Cover: Emily Wittig Designs
Editing: Hot Tree Editing
Proofreading: Deaton Author Services, Jo Thompson, and Jess Hodge
Paperback Formatting: Integrity Formatting

KAYLEE RYAN

ARE YOU
READY?

PROLOGUE

T HERE ARE MOMENTS IN LIFE that define us. Moments that tear your soul open and make you bleed, and moments that fill your heart with so much love and joy, it feels as though it might burst.

I never thought I'd be living in both of those scenarios at one time.

Let's start with my heart being filled with so much joy, so much love, that it feels entirely too large for my chest. Hot tears coat my cheeks as I stare down at my daughters.

I'm a mother.

I never imagined that I'd be a mother four weeks before my nineteenth birthday, but here I am, holding my twin girls in my arms. My pregnancy was a result of one of those tear-your-soul-out moments—the kind you want to push to the back of your mind and never think of again.

Six weeks later, you're standing in the upstairs bathroom that you share with your twin sister, staring at a positive pregnancy test. That, too, was a moment—one that altered the course of my life in a matter of weeks.

You'd think that would be enough, right? That the hand I was dealt was filled with enough tragedy, but the universe had other plans, telling me to hold its beer. When three weeks after finding out I was pregnant, my father was diagnosed with stage four pancreatic cancer.

Fuck cancer.

Fuck the universe.

The last year has been a whirlwind of emotions.

Pain.

Anger.

Heartbreak.

However, as I stare down at my daughters, the love I feel for them, no matter how they came to be, overwhelms me. It holds me captive, just as the weight of their tiny bodies in my arms does.

My heart is bursting with love, but also tearing to shreds from pain. You see, my father is also in this hospital. He's one floor below me. His cancer is taking him away from us. He's been here for weeks under the care of the hospice unit. They told us two weeks ago, he had days to live, yet he's still here. He's still hanging on, and I'm pretty sure the two tiny humans in my arms are the reason why.

He wants to meet his granddaughters.

"How you hanging in there, Momma?" My twin sister, Brogan, enters the room. She's wearing a smile, but it doesn't mask the sadness. Two events causing two very different emotions at the same time.

"Tired."

"You should get some rest." She comes to sit next to me on the bed, running her index finger over each of the girls' foreheads. "They're beautiful, Briar."

"Thank you." I choke up. From the moment I found out, I knew there was no other outcome. I was going to be a mother, and boy, was I shocked when, at eight weeks, the doctor insisted I have an ultrasound. I thought there was something wrong with my baby. Little did I know it was because he thought he heard a second heartbeat, and he was right.

"Have you decided on names for these little angels yet?" Brogan asks.

"Yeah, I think so."

"Finally," she says dramatically. "You've been holding out on me this entire time. Let's hear it."

"Brogan, meet your nieces, River and Rayne."

"Aw, I love them. They remind me of...." Her voice trails off.

"Dad." I nod, my voice cracking. "Me too. He always loved to go to the river behind our grandparents' place to fish, and he insisted that the fishing was better if it was raining. "You think he'll understand?" I ask.

"I'm certain he will." She nods, but I can see the hesitation in her eyes. Our father has been in and out of consciousness for the past week, so it's anyone's guess whether he will be awake to meet his granddaughters.

"I need to see him. They need to meet him," I tell her.

"Okay. Let me get a nurse. You're going to need a wheelchair and permission."

"Yeah, they're not stopping me."

She nods. "I'll be right back."

Brogan has been my rock my entire life, but the last year, she's been my saving grace and my sanity. I never could have done this without her. She held my hand during labor and told me how great I was doing. Her support has never wavered. I know she feels bad about that night, but that's in the past, and it's not her fault.

A knock on the door pulls me out of my thoughts. "Hey there, Momma," my nurse, Lisa, greets me. "I hear you and those gorgeous girls want to take a little stroll."

"Yes, please." My eyes mist with tears.

"Let's take these two and get you in the chair." She takes River, and Brogan takes Rayne, placing them in their beds while Lisa helps me out of bed and into the wheelchair. "I'm going to push you, and we're going to let Auntie push the girls in one bed. How does that sound?"

I nod, because I know if I try to talk, words will get lodged right along with the knot of emotion swelling in my throat.

The elevator ride to my father's floor is quick, and before I know it, we're knocking on his door before Nurse Lisa pushes me inside, followed by Brogan with my daughters. My dad's eyes are closed, and he looks so peaceful.

"I'll leave you to it. Just let a nurse know when you're ready to come back and I'll be here to get you."

"Thank you, Lisa."

She gives my shoulder a gentle pat and leaves the room.

"I don't know how to do this." My voice cracks.

My sister, my best friend, pulls a chair up to sit next to me. "I want him to be here with us, but I also don't want him to be in pain anymore," she confesses.

"They'll never know him," I say as tears break free. "He's the greatest man I know, and I know he would have loved to spoil them rotten." I glance over at my sister. "We're all that they have."

"We will be everything those two little angels need, Briar. There will never be a single day that they don't know how much they are loved. We've got this."

"I love you, sister."

"I love you too." Brogan leans over and hugs me.

"My girls," a croaky voice speaks.

We both wipe at our cheeks and answer, "Hi, Daddy," making the three of us laugh.

Dad swallows hard. "Babies?" he asks, his voice gruff.

I smile. "Happy and healthy," I tell him. Brogan stands, picks up one baby, and hands her to me. I can tell from the purple hat, it's River, and she holds Rayne.

"So beautiful," he rasps.

"Their names are River and Rayne," I tell him.

"I always loved my time at the river," Dad muses. "And the fish always bite better in the rain." One side of his mouth kicks up in a smile as I lose my battle with my tears. They flow freely over my cheeks.

He gets it. I didn't have to tell him, because my father is the greatest man I'll ever know. He's the only man I'll ever love, and the only one who has ever held my trust. My heart aches knowing we're losing him, but he's not living. Not lying here in this hospital bed. It's selfish of me to want to keep him here when his body is failing him.

"I promise they'll know you. They'll know you were an amazing father and that you would have spoiled them endlessly," I say, my voice cracking through my tears.

"So proud of my girls. All four of you," Dad says weakly. He closes his eyes, and we sit here with him, talking to him as if he's in the conversation until it's time to go back to my room and feed the girls.

At the time, I didn't know that was the last time I'd talk to my father, but the memories we've made will last me a lifetime. Brogan and I will keep his memory alive, not only for us but for my daughters too.

FORREST 1

T HE QUIET OF THE SHOP surrounds me as I work on my sketch. The last client left a couple of hours ago, and so did everyone else. I stayed behind to work on a mock-up for a new client I have coming in a few weeks from now. It's a large, intricate back piece that's going to take several sessions, and I want to make sure I hit every detail.

Besides, it's not like anything is waiting for me at home. My big ole house is empty now that my sister, Emerson, married one of my best friends and co-business owners of Everlasting Ink, and moved out. I'm not a fan of the quiet. In fact, it's downright lonely. Sure, my sister, best friend, and baby niece, Lilly, live next door, but that's their home. Not mine.

And yes, one of my other best friends and co-business owner, Legend, and his wife, Monroe, live across the street. I know I could knock on their door as well, and they'd happily invite me in. It's nice having them so close, but it's still lonely and too damn quiet.

Standing, I place my hands on the small of my back and stretch. Glancing at the clock that hangs over the door, I see it's past eight. My stomach growls, reminding me I haven't eaten since lunch.

I make quick work of cleaning up my area and locking up the shop before heading home. The drive is short, and the house is dark when I pull into the driveway. I can see the soft glow of light from Emerson and Roman's house next door. Glancing in the rearview mirror, I see the same from Legend and Monroe's.

I know that I'm welcome at either place at any time, but this is their family time. I won't intrude on that. Emerson invites me over every single night for dinner. I take her up on it sometimes, but not often. She worries about me living here alone, but she shouldn't. She has her husband and her daughter to focus on.

I could have gone out with Lachlan and Maddox tonight, but honestly, the random hookups and nights out at the bar don't do it for me anymore. I blame Roman and Legend for opening my eyes to what healthy, happy relationships look like. I'm envious of them, and I want what they have. Something tells me I'm not going to find it at a bar. Who knows, maybe I will, but I'm just not feeling it.

I get the same invitations from her best friend, Monroe, and Legend to their place across the street. Again, I accept sparingly, because it's not their job to keep me fed or entertained.

With a heavy sigh, I turn off my truck, grab my phone and keys, and head inside. Flipping on the lights, I kick off my shoes and make my way toward the kitchen. I don't really feel like cooking, so I scrounge through the fridge. The leftover Chinese I picked up on the way home two nights ago will have to do.

I don't even bother heating it up. Instead, I stand at the island and scarf it down as I flip through the mail. Most of it is either junk mail or bills, nothing enticing. Tossing the junk mail in the trash, I set the bills aside to handle tomorrow, before turning off the lights and heading up to take a long, hot shower and go to bed. It's been a long, exhausting day, and I'm more than ready for it to be over.

Tomorrow, it's my turn to host our weekly Sunday get-together, and for a little while, this big old house won't feel so lonely.

The house smells incredible, but that could be because I'm starving. Last night's leftover Chinese didn't satisfy me, and this morning, I had a banana with my coffee and immediately started cooking. It's my week to host our Sunday lunch, dinner, or whatever you want to call it. It's something we've done for a while now. It used to always be here, at my house, but now that Roman and Legend have bigger houses that have room for our group, we take turns.

This is my week, and I made a huge pot of chili. I have cornbread and peanut butter sandwiches to go with it. I like both, so I made both. I can have two bowls, one with cornbread and another with a peanut butter sandwich. I'm a growing man, and I need fuel. Besides, I know the others like it both ways as well, and we don't have to choose, so why should we?

The front door opens and voices carry to me in the kitchen. We don't knock; well, we do now at Roman's and Legend's because they're both married, and honestly, I don't need or want to see what happens behind closed doors. I shudder at the thought. That's my little sister, and her best friend, who might as well also be my little sister.

Yeah, definitely knocking.

"Uncle Forty!" my sister calls out.

I smile. I love being an uncle, and I'm about to get my niece fix. "In the kitchen," I call back. I quickly wash my hands and turn to see Emerson and Roman enter. Roman is carrying my niece, Lilly, who's smiling widely as she babbles in her daddy's arms.

"Please tell me you made your chili," Roman groans. He sniffs the air and nods. He doesn't need me to answer him, but I do it anyway.

"Yep." I lean over and give my sister a one-armed hug, quickly pulling away and holding my hands out for Lilly. She grins and leans into me, letting me take her from her dad's arms. "There's my favorite girl." I kiss her cheek, and she snuggles into me, resting her head on my shoulder.

"I see how it is. I father your niece, and you can't even say hi to me," Roman jokes.

"Hey, Rome." I smile down at Lilly, rubbing her back. "Lilly, Daddy is jealous of you," I say sweetly, running a soothing hand up and down her back.

"I'm his sister, and I barely got a one-armed hug. It was more like a quick lean in with a pat on the back," Emerson adds.

"Sounds like your mommy is too," I tell my niece. She lifts her head and places a wet, sloppy kiss on my cheek. "Aw, I love you, too, Lills."

"Where is everyone else?" Roman asks.

"I'm not sure," I reply as I bounce Lilly in my arms, making her giggle. The door opens and heavy footsteps fall.

"Aw, man, I wanted to beat you here so that he wouldn't be a baby hog," Maddox complains, as he and Lachlan enter the kitchen.

"Hand her over." Lachlan opens his arms, and I spin to keep Lilly away from him. She laughs, and Lachlan grunts. He follows me, walking in a circle until I relent and hand her over. "Did you tell Forrest I'm your favorite?" he asks my niece, snuggling her close.

"We all know that I've got the favorite uncle title in the bag," Maddox tells him.

"Won't be long and you'll have another one to fight over," Legend says, walking into the room. His words have all of us going quiet. Everyone but his wife, Monroe.

"Legend!" Monroe tries to scold, but she's laughing. "We were going to wait."

He shrugs. "They're family."

"I know, but it's still so early," she says, her voice soft.

I watch as Legend wraps his arms around her and pulls her into his chest. His lips press to her temple. "Everything is going to be just fine," he says, soothing her.

"So, I guess the cat is out of the bag." Emerson laughs.

I'm not surprised that Emerson knew. She and Monroe have always been tight. I glance at Roman, and he doesn't look surprised, which means he probably knew too. I guess that's his right as the best friend's husband.

"I guess so." Monroe sighs.

"We're pregnant," Legend says with a smile and much more enthusiasm. He pulls his wife into his arms and places a kiss on the top of her head. He's smiling so widely that I fear his face might crack. Monroe's smile matches his, and happy tears shimmer in her eyes.

We rally around them, offering them hugs and congratulations. I'm so damn ecstatic for them. Legend is a great guy, but Legend with Monroe, he's on another level. The same way Roman is with my little sister. I guess the love of a good woman can change your life. Not that I would know anything about that personally. I'm an outsider looking in, but my friends have never been happier, so there has to be something to it.

One day, I'll have what they have.

I hope.

"We need three more," Maddox speaks up.

"Three more of what?" Roman asks.

"Babies. One for each of us." He points to where Lachlan is holding Lilly. "The competition is fierce around here."

The room erupts in laughter. He's not wrong. Technically, by blood, I am Lilly's only uncle, but you don't have to share blood to be a family. Everyone is in this room. They're my family. I would do anything for any of them, and yeah, I happen to agree. We need more babies around here. I love seeing my best friends fall in love and start families. Call me sentimental, but it makes me happy to see them finding their forevers.

None of us have been keen on relationships. Me, because I was too worried about raising my little sister because our parents were... *are* deadbeats. Being ten years older, I did everything I could, including buying this house to give Emerson the stability that our parents failed to provide for her.

Now, here she is, married to my best friend, and a mother. She has a great job, which was a struggle at first. It was hard for me to convince her to let me pay for her schooling, but she eventually relented. The shop does really well, and I wanted to do that for her. I wanted to give her a shot at a real future outside of that rundown trailer we grew up in.

This house was for her, but now, it's just me living here all alone, and in moments like these, when it's filled with love and laughter, my heart is content. However, at night, it's silent and lonely. I can only hope that I find her. That I find the woman who will make me change the way I look at life, the way Emerson and Monroe have for Legend and Roman.

I know that when I find her, I'm going to fight like hell to keep her.

My mind goes back to the conversation we had before I found out about Roman and Emerson and was put on the spot, asking what my ideal woman would be. It's a short list, and it all comes down to being genuine. I want something real. Something that will last and stand the test of time.

"Let's eat!" Maddox says, grabbing a bowl from the counter and pouring out his chili. Within ten minutes, we're all settled around the table. Roman has Lilly in his arms, giving her small bites of his.

"I can't believe she's turning one already," Monroe says, watching Lilly eat bites of her dad's peanut butter sandwich.

"Time for another one," Roman replies.

"Maybe let's get her out of diapers." Emerson laughs.

"Lills, Daddy needs you to learn to use the potty so we can make you a big sister." Roman kisses her cheek, and she offers him a huge grin in return. Damn, this girl is too cute.

"Don't worry, she'll have a baby cousin in about seven months," Legend says proudly.

Monroe smiles up at him, and something a lot like envy courses through my veins.

"What are you all doing next Saturday night?" Roman asks.

"Nothing." I shrug. My life is quite literally boring as shit these days. Work and repeat. "What's up?"

"These two"—he nods toward Emerson and then to Monroe—"are having a girls' night. I'll have Lilly with me at the house. Thought we could all hang out."

"I'm in," I tell him.

"Me too," Legend agrees.

"Yeah, been a while since it's just been us guys," Lachlan says. "Count me in."

"Lilly will be there," Maddox reminds him, "and I'll bring the pizza."

"She's a baby. She doesn't count. She's not going to ride our asses about belching and cursing too much," Lachlan explains.

"Belching can slide, but she's picking up everything, so you'll need to watch your mouth," Roman tells him.

Lachlan waves him off. "I would regardless, but you know what I mean. Just the guys."

"Are we cramping your style, Lachlan?" Emerson teases.

"No." He's quick to shake his head as well. "Please don't be offended," he rushes to say. "It's just our family is growing, and it used to be just the five of us, and it's been a while since it's been that way. That's all that I'm saying."

Emerson smiles. "I know. I'm just giving you a hard time."

"We should be thanking you for planning a girls' night," Maddox chimes in with a wink to help lighten the heaviness of the conversation.

"Just the two of you?" I ask them. "Do you need a ride?" I know that my sister is an adult and married with a baby, but I'll never stop taking care of her. It's who I am.

"No, but thank you. We're all set. Besides, preggers over there"—she points to Monroe—"can drive me if it comes to that."

"We've invited a couple of girls we work with," Monroe adds.

"Are they hot?" Maddox asks.

"Very." Monroe nods. "Although, I've never met Maggie." Monroe looks to Emerson.

"She's very pretty," Emerson announces.

"So—we're crashing girls' night?" Maddox asks hopefully.

We all laugh at him. "What happened to glad it was just the guys?" I ask him.

"That was all this guy." He points to Lachlan.

"I mean, pretty girls...." Lachlan shrugs. "Plans are made to be broken."

"Stop." Emerson shakes her head. "You are not crashing girls' night. We're hoping to make this a tradition. If you all want to plan a guys' night, go for it."

"We're having one," Legend reminds her.

"I mean, when you won't have Lilly. You can curse and belch until your little hearts are content," she teases.

"Maybe." Roman doesn't sound convinced. I'm not surprised. Lately, if my little sister or their daughter aren't involved, it doesn't hold his interest.

"Can we talk about Lilly's birthday party?" Lachlan asks.

"We can." Emerson nods. "What's up? You're going to be there, right?"

"Oh, I'll be there. I just want to make sure no one else bought what I did."

"I'm sure whatever you bought is perfect," Emerson assures him. "You don't need to buy her a gift. Just being with us to celebrate is enough."

Lachlan looks appalled. "Not buy her a gift? What kind of Sam Hell nonsense is that?" He points to his chest. "Favorite uncle title to maintain."

"I bet my gift is better than yours," Maddox chimes in.

"Doubt it." Lachlan crosses his arms over his chest and smirks. He thinks he's got this in the bag.

"Yeah? Well, I bought her—nope. You know what? I'm not going to tell you so that you can top my gift. We'll reveal them at the party."

Legend reaches over and takes Lilly from Roman. "Little lady, you might be the most spoiled little girl on the planet." He kisses her cheek, and she giggles.

"Come here, sweet girl. Listen," Monroe says, once Lilly is in her arms. "These men, they're big teddy bears. Your mommy and me, we know how to work them. Take notes, kiddo. Use this to your advantage."

Emerson snickers with laughter, while the rest of us are smiling. She's not wrong. There isn't anything we won't give or do for that little girl, and as soon as Legend and Monroe have their baby, it will be the same way.

Our Everlasting Ink family is tight. We're closer than blood, and our bond is strong. I have no doubt that all of our current and future children in the group will be spoiled rotten, but more than that. They will be loved beyond measure.

That's just what we do.

After we finish eating, we move to the living room. I'm sitting in the recliner with Lilly sleeping soundly on my chest, and take it all in. Roman and Legend are wearing permanent smiles that never seem to leave their faces, and Maddox and Lachlan are giving them shit over it. The girls laugh it all off, and I couldn't think of a more perfect day. Well, maybe I could. I could have the love of my life here with me, and maybe, just maybe, it would be my own baby girl I was holding while she slept.

One day.

"HOW YOU DOING OVER THERE, Momma?" my twin sister, Brogan, asks me.

"Am I that obvious?" I glance at her in the passenger seat, where she's watching me.

"Pretty much." She grins. "Come on, Briar, you've known Monroe for a while now. The girls are going to be just fine with her parents tonight."

"I know." I exhale and glance in the rearview mirror at the girls. They're smiling and chatting happily with one another, just like they always do. Since we moved to Ashby two years ago, I've not had to leave them with anyone but Brogan. I know that's not realistic, but she's my only family, and I don't trust easily. Then again, neither does she.

"It's for a couple of hours, tops."

"Right." I nod as I turn into Monroe's parents' driveway. I met Heather and Eric Morrison earlier this week. I've seen them around town, and, of course, Brogan works with their daughter, Monroe. I do too. Kind of. I'm employed by the same company, but I work from home in medical billing. They're good people and were thrilled to keep the girls for a few hours. They insisted it would give them practice for when Monroe and her husband, Legend, start having kids.

Brogan and I have worked with Monroe since moving to Ashby, and she's invited us out and to her place several times, but we always decline. I'm sure the last thing they want is my twin girls running around like the silly, tiny humans they are during their backyard barbecue. And like I said, I don't trust easily. My ability to do so was torn away from me.

Monroe kept asking, never giving up, and here we are, going to a girls' night dinner with her and her best friend, letting her parents watch my daughters for a couple of hours. Something she insisted they would be thrilled over, and after meeting them, I know she was right. It still makes me nervous.

"We're here," I say brightly. The girls cheer from the back seat and rustle around to unbuckle their seat belts. A task they learned not long ago. They about gave me a damn heart attack when I was driving down the road and suddenly, they're both peeping into the front seat over the console. I immediately pulled over to the side of the road and read them the riot act. Of course, they cried, which made me feel like a shitty parent. However, I'm the only one they've got, and it's my job to keep them safe.

I might have made a detour for some ice cream to help with the sad faces. In case you didn't know, ice cream for three-year-olds is the cure-all.

After everyone is unloaded, and the girls have their backpacks strapped to their backs, we make our way to the door. Heather greets us with a wide smile before we can knock.

"My friends are here!" she says excitedly.

"We're sisters," River tells her.

"And we look the same!" Rayne adds, making Heather laugh.

"Did I hear we have twin sisters in the house?" Eric asks, stepping outside on the porch with us.

"My mommy and my auntie too!" River says, jumping with excitement. Brogan and I are fraternal twins, just like the girls, so we look similar, but you can definitely tell us apart. However, my daughters are still amazed by the fact that they are twins, just like their mommy and Aunt Brogan.

"Yeah," Rayne adds.

"Well, come on in. We're going to make pizza."

"We are?" both girls say at the same time.

"We sure are. Then we're going to watch a movie. Wait, do you like princess movies?" Eric asks, feigning concern.

"Yes!" they scream.

"Okay, girls, inside voices," I remind them.

"But, Momma, we outside," Rayne points out.

"Don't you worry, Momma. You go have some fun. We'll be here when you get back," Heather assures me.

I lower to one knee and pull the girls into a hug. "I'll be back in a few hours. Best behavior," I remind them. I was worried about them staying here since they've never really stayed anywhere, but they really hit it off with the Morrisons when we met earlier this week, and there are no tears in sight.

"We sleep ins our bed, right, Momma?" River asks. She's my inquisitive one. She needs to know when, what, where, and how. Whereas Rayne is happy to go with the flow.

"Yes, you will sleep in your bed. Mommy is going to dinner with some friends while you stay here."

"Okay." She nods, satisfied that I'm coming back for her.

I stand and address Heather. "Are you sure you don't mind watching them? I feel terrible even asking you to do this."

"Briar, we're honored. This house is too quiet with Monroe gone. I know she's an adult, but she moved back home after college, and with her gone again, it's too quiet," she says again. "We're thrilled to watch the girls. I'm happy to help out anytime you need me. When they say it takes a village, they're not wrong. Lean on us."

Hot tears prick my eyes. I miss my dad so much. I wish I could say that I miss my mother, but I don't remember her. I do mourn the loss of never having a mom in my life, but my dad, he was the best man, and we never went without and always knew we were loved. "Th—Thank you." I swallow hard. "I appreciate you so much."

"I have personal pan pizzas ready for cheese!" Eric calls out.

"Pizza!" the girls cheer and rush past Heather into the house.

"Well, that went well." Brogan chuckles. "They won't even miss us."

"Not helping." I glare at her.

"Come on." She tugs on my arm.

"Two hours, tops," I tell Heather over my shoulder, allowing Brogan to lead me to my car.

"Take your time. We'll be here." Heather smiles kindly and waves before walking into the house and closing the door. Brogan leads me to the passenger side of my car and opens the door.

"Get in."

I do as I'm told because my heart is breaking. "I'm leaving my daughters with strangers," I say as soon as she slides behind the wheel.

"They're going to be fine. We've known Monroe for a while now, and you toured the house, and the girls are happy. They didn't even care that we were leaving. It's all going to be fine," she assures me.

I know she's right, but leaving them with people I don't know very well still makes my heart race. I know I need to get over it. They're turning four soon, and then in another year they'll be heading off to kindergarten. I need to adjust to them not being with me or Brogan twenty-four-seven. Besides, I know this is good for them, to have other people in their lives.

Baby steps.

"I'm so glad we did this," Emerson says, smiling widely as she takes a drink of her beer.

"Right?" Monroe agrees. She glances over at me and Brogan, and then at Maggie, a nurse who works with Emerson. "It's nice to have some other ladies to hang out with. We're surrounded by men."

"I mean, they're sexy men, but yeah." Emerson shrugs.

"I'm going to need photographic evidence, or it's not true." Maggie points her finger at Emerson.

"Please hold." Monroe holds up her index finger, telling us to wait before grabbing her phone from the table. She taps the screen and grins, nodding. "This was from New Year's Eve," she says, passing her phone to Maggie.

"Damn." Maggie nods her approval and passes the phone to Brogan.

"Holy hell. You're complaining about hanging out with these guys? Really?" Brogan asks, handing me the phone.

I glance down at the screen, and staring back at me are five very gorgeous, very tattooed men standing side by side. I take in each of their features. They're all gorgeous, but one stands out in particular. His blondish brown hair is cut short on the sides, and longer on top. His eyes are dark brown, and if I didn't know better, I'd think I was the one he's looking at in this picture. His gaze is piercing.

"Wow," I finally say, reaching across the table and handing Monroe her phone.

"So, which one is yours?" Brogan asks Monroe.

"Legend. He's on the very far right," she says, nodding to the picture. She lifts her phone so that we can see it again. "The guy next to him is Roman, Emerson's husband, and the middle man is Forrest, Emerson's brother. Beside him is Lachlan, and then Maddox." She rattles off names I probably won't remember, but I do remember the name of the man in the middle.

Forrest.

"I feel so bad for you," Maggie says, smiling and shaking her head.

"They're great guys," Emerson says. "But it's nice to have this too. For so long, it was just me and Mo, and the rest of them. Hey, why don't you all come to Lilly's birthday party next weekend? You can meet the guys for yourselves."

"There are three of them and three of you," Monroe says, wagging her eyebrows dramatically, making us laugh.

"The girls would love that," Brogan tells her.

"Twin girls, right?" Emerson asks me.

"Yes. They'll be four in April. Wow, that's next month."

"Time flies," Emerson says. "I can't believe Lilly is turning one."

"It really does. Another year and they'll be going off to kindergarten," I say, voicing my earlier thoughts. "I'm so not ready."

"You have to bring them to the party. Lilly will love it. It's a small group and no other kids. My mother-in-law watches her, so no daycare kids or anything, and no cousins yet." She winks at Monroe, who smiles brightly.

"Are you sure? I don't want to intrude."

"Positive," Emerson says. "Lilly will love having other kids there. I'll grab your number from Monroe and send you the address. Brogan and Maggie, you'll both be there, too, right?" she asks.

"If the tattoo hottie squad is going to be there, I'm in," Maggie jokes. At least, I think she's joking.

Monroe tosses her head back in laughter. "Oh, wait until I tell them that you called them that. They're going to eat that shit up."

"They look badass," Emerson tells us. "However, you should see them with Lilly. They're really just a bunch of teddy bears."

"They're all in competition for the favorite uncle title." Monroe laughs. "That girl isn't even a year old yet and has all five of them wrapped around her little finger."

I smile, but inside my heart breaks for my daughters. They don't have a male figure in their life. Lilly is such a lucky little girl to have so many people around who love her. Picking my phone up from the table, I look at the message Heather sent about thirty minutes ago. It's of the girls smiling as they eat ice-cream cones.

Moving to Ashby was the right choice for us. And maybe, just maybe, I can let go of this inability to trust and allow more people into our lives. Tonight has been eye-opening in that regard. I'm glad I came.

"Thank you, Monroe. For inviting us and helping me find sitters in your parents for the girls. This was a lot of fun."

Brogan leans her shoulder into mine and I know she's happy. She has the same fears as I do, but her experience and mine that made us unable to open up and trust are vastly different.

"Always."

"It was nice meeting both of you," I tell Emerson and Maggie. "I really should get going. I promised the girls they'd be home to sleep in their beds, and it's well past bedtime already."

"Mom life." Emerson smiles. "I'll text you the address for next weekend. No need to bring gifts. She's blessed beyond belief. We just want your company."

I nod. It will be nice to make friends with another mom and compare notes. After another round of goodbyes, Brogan and I head to pick up my girls.

I stand with the girls on Emerson's front porch and ring the doorbell. The door opens to a smiling, handsome man covered in ink. I can't remember which one he is, and I don't get time to ask because River speaks before I do.

"We party!" she says excitedly.

The giant of a sexy, tattooed man laughs and kneels so he's eye level with the girls. "Well, if you came to party, you're in the right place." He holds out his hand to River. "I'm Roman. It's nice to meet you."

"My name is River, and I have a twin sister." She points at Rayne.

"I see that." He chuckles. "And what's your name?"

"I'm Rayne." She places her little hand in his, and he gently shakes.

"Our mommy and auntie are twins too!" River tells him. I swear that's her favorite line.

Roman peers up at me. "Roman, Emerson's husband," he offers helpfully. "I'm so glad you could make it." He stands to his full height but keeps his eyes on the girls. "How about you come inside, and you can meet my daughter, Lilly?"

Rayne peers up at me. "Can we, Mommy?"

"Of course. It's Lilly's birthday. Remember, she's smaller than you, so we have to be gentle."

"We will," they say together.

Roman smiles. "Come on in." He steps back and allows us to enter.

"Thank you. I'm Briar, and as you know, these are my daughters, River and Rayne. Thank you for having us." I hand him the pink and purple gift bag holding the gifts the girls picked out for Lilly.

"You didn't have to do that."

"We wanted to."

"My little girl is blessed." His smile is kind as he ushers us into the room.

"You made it!" Emerson calls out. She's standing at the kitchen island, slicing tomatoes. "We're grilling, even though it's cold outside. Have a seat. Can I get you something to drink?"

"No, thank you."

"Mommy, can we go play?" Rayne asks, pointing to where Lilly is playing with some blocks.

"Stay where I can see you."

"They'll be fine. Trust me, there are enough adults around here. They won't get into anything. My husband has kid-proofed every inch of this house. They're safe."

"That makes it nice not to have to worry so much. Can I help?" I ask her.

"I think I'm all set. This was the last part. I don't like to slice them too early because they get soggy." She wrinkles her nose. "Where's Brogan?"

"She worked today. They had a blood drive for Hoxworth, and she's exhausted. She was getting home right as we were leaving. I told her we would wait, but she said she just wanted to go to bed."

"Can't say as I blame her there. I'm sorry we missed her. I'm glad you and the girls came. Let me wrap up here, and I'll take you around and introduce you to everyone."

"Is Monroe or Maggie here?" I ask.

"Monroe is here, but she's not feeling well. She's lying down in the guest room. My guess is that Legend is with her. Maggie picked up a shift at the hospital. She works there just on an as-needed basis for extra cash, and they gave her a bonus, plus double time. She couldn't pass it up."

"Wow. Good for her, but I'm sorry she missed this."

"I know. I really wanted all of you to meet everyone, but at least you're here, and your girls. Let me wash my hands, and I'd love to meet them." She places a lid on the bowl of tomatoes and moves to wash her hands.

"Okay. We're all set. Maddox and Lachlan are manning the grill. Roman's parents are out there supervising. Roman and my brother are with the girls, at least my brother was in there with him." She links her arm through mine and leads me to the living room where the girls are playing.

"River, Rayne, come and meet my friend Emerson." The girls come rushing over to me.

"It's so nice to meet you," Emerson says, lifting Lilly, who just slowly toddled after them into her arms. "After we eat, we're going to have cake and ice cream."

"I wove to party," Rayne says with a wide smile, making us laugh.

"Rome, you met Briar, right?" she asks her husband, who's sitting on the floor in front of the couch next to where the girls were playing.

"I did." He smiles.

"And this is Lilly." She bounces her daughter on her hip, making Lilly giggle.

I offer Lilly my finger, and she takes it, smiling. "Happy Birthday, Lilly."

"And this is my brother, Forrest." Emerson walks to the front of the couch and smiles down at the two men.

Forrest.

The man in the middle of the picture from last weekend.

Emerson's older brother.

I school my features and smile at Roman, before turning my gaze to Forrest. Damn. The picture didn't do this man justice. I shift my stance as he studies me. "Hi." I wave awkwardly.

"Hey." He climbs to his feet and offers me his hand. "Forrest."

"Briar." I take his hand and the warmth of his wraps around me. His dark brown eyes stay locked on mine. There seems to be this... current of electricity that flows between us, and even though I know I should, I can't look away. His eyes have me held captive in their gaze.

"She's our mommy," Rayne offers helpfully.

I can feel my face heat. Any semblance of attraction he might have been feeling is surely wiped away, finding out I'm a mom of two. "These are my daughters, River and Rayne." I love my daughters, and they will always come first in my life.

I don't know what I was expecting, but it's not for Forrest to drop to his knee just as Roman did and greet them.

"Hey, ladies. I'm Forrest. It's nice to meet you."

"Why do you and him draw on each other? Mommy says that's bad," River asks.

Forrest's deep rumble of laughter fills the room, and it does something to me. The carefree sound is soothing.

"These are tattoos. See." He holds his arm out. "They don't wash off."

"Oh," River and Rayne say at the same time.

"Mommy, can we get one of these?" River asks me.

"No, sweetie. Not until you're older."

"We're almost this many." Rayne holds up four fingers. "Is that enough?"

"Not nearly enough," Forrest tells her.

Rayne's shoulders sag.

"How about we draw on some paper instead? If that's okay with your mom?" He glances up at me. "Sorry," he says sheepishly. "I should have checked with you before I said something."

"No. It's okay. They don't need to draw. We're getting ready to eat."

"It's no problem," Emerson says, speaking up.

Shit. I forgot she and Roman were even in the same room with us. "We have crayons and paper that Lilly uses. Well, tries to use. The girls are welcome to use them as well."

"Are you sure?"

"Positive," Roman speaks up.

"Food's done!" another male voice calls out, as what sounds like the patio door closing fills the room. Footsteps follow and two new men appear, faces I recognize from the photo, but I don't know who is who. "Em, you invited a gift for me?" the shorter, but only slightly of the two, says.

"She's mine," Emerson fires back. "This is Briar, and her daughters, River and Rayne. Ladies, this is Lachlan, and that one is Maddox. And that's my father-in-law on the grill. My mother-in-law is somewhere around here too."

"It's nice to meet you," I tell them.

"Damn, all the pretty ones are taken."

"Oh, she's not taken," Monroe says, joining us. "Hey, Briar. Good to see you."

"You as well. Feeling better?"

"I am. This is my husband, Legend."

"Nice to meet you."

"Where's Brogan?"

"She worked today and was exhausted."

"Wait. Who's Brogan?"

"My twin sister."

"There are two of you? Fuck," Maddox says.

"Language," Roman growls.

"Sorry." Maddox winces.

"Is your sister single too?" Lachlan asks.

"She is. So is Maggie," Emerson offers helpfully, "but she couldn't make it. This is our girls' night crew, minus Brogan and Maggie, of course."

"My mommy and my aunt are twins like me and sissy," Rayne announces.

"Twins?" Lachlan repeats, sounding as if he's pained.

"Yep," River and Rayne reply.

My daughters are not used to strangers, so I wasn't sure how they would act, but they don't seem the least bit intimidated by these men. Maybe because I'm here with them. I'm not sure.

"You gots lots of taboos too," Rayne blurts.

"Tattoos," I correct her.

"Mommy said we can't have them," River adds.

"Not until you're much older," Legend says, joining the conversation.

"Come on. Let's eat," Roman's dad says, placing a tray of grilled meat on the island.

Roman takes Lilly into his arms and bounces her on his hip, and she latches on to his hair with a gummy grin. My heart aches for my daughters, who are standing still, watching them together. Forrest moving pulls me out of my trance. He bends so that he's eye level with the girls.

"You ladies want a lift?" he asks them.

"What's that?" River asks.

"I can carry you to the kitchen," Forrest explains patiently.

"Yes!" They move to crawl all over him and before I can tell them to—I don't know what—he's standing with a twin on each hip, and moving toward the kitchen.

I'm rooted to the spot, watching them go. It's not until I feel a presence beside me that I pull my gaze away. I look to my left to find Monroe and to the right to find Emerson. It's just the three of us.

"What just happened?"

They both smile, but it's Emerson who speaks. "Welcome to the family."

I don't know what she means by that, but emotion wells in my throat. I choke it back. For far too long, it's just been me, Brogan, and the girls. For her to say I'm part of their family... is not what I expected, and my head is telling me to take a step back, but my heart, the one that yearns for more, wants to race full-speed ahead.

Forrest peeks his head around the corner. "The girls are all set up. Are you ready?" he asks.

I know he's asking us if we're ready to eat, but to me, it feels like more.

So. Much. More.

I DIDN'T KNOW IT WAS POSSIBLE to witness such longing on a child's face, but that's what I saw just seconds ago with River and Rayne. They watched Roman with Lilly as if their little lives depended on it, and their faces.... Damn, they both looked so sad that I had to do something about it.

I should have checked with their mom, but all I could think about was making them smile again, so I dropped down to their level and offered them a ride. Once I explained, the light in their eyes was vibrant once again, and the four tiny hands that were gripping my heart loosened.

I don't know if their dad is in the picture, and it's not my business, but something tells me he's not, and seeing Roman with Lilly was breaking their hearts. I couldn't stand another second of watching it play out like a movie script.

When we make it to the kitchen, I take the girls to the island where the food is set out. Roman still holds Lilly, so I don't want to put them down. Luckily, Monroe saves me.

"Girls, let's get you in a chair and I'll make you a plate." Monroe smiles at them as if she's known them all their lives.

"We want to sit with hims," the girl on my left says, wrapping her arms around my neck.

Damn, she's cute as hell. I really need to learn which one is which.

"Are you sure?" Monroe asks them.

They nod their little heads, and my chest swells.

"It's fine," I tell her. "You ladies can sit with me." I carry the girls into the dining room. The table seats ten, so luckily, my plan for them will work with the number of people here today. "How about here?" I place them both on their feet and pull out three chairs. "I can sit between you."

"Mommy can sit there," the twin I now know as Rayne says. I also note that her hair is a little lighter than her sister's. I keep that information at the forefront of my mind so that I can tell them apart.

"That sounds like a plan." Monroe gets them set up at the table, and I peek back into the living room, letting Briar know we're all set up.

"Mommy, sit here," River tells Briar as soon as she enters the room.

"You sit here," Rayne says, pointing to the chair they deemed as mine already.

"Why don't we let Forrest sit where he wants, and Mommy can sit with you?" Briar suggests.

In an instant, two little lips jut out in a pout, and I'm toast. "This seat is perfect if it's okay with your momma?" I glance at Briar and give her what I hope is a warm smile. I don't want to step on her toes, but these two little angels got me in my feels and no way do I want to be the cause of their pout.

Nope. Not me. Not today. Not ever.

Briar bites down on her bottom lip. It looks pillowy soft, and I'd love to test that theory, but I push the yearning deep and wait for her answer. "Are you sure?"

"I'm sure." I pull out a chair and help River sit, then do the same for Rayne. "You ladies, sit right here, and we'll be back with some food."

"Cake?" Rayne asks.

"Not yet. You have to eat all of your lunch first." Rayne nods and wiggles in her seat.

Placing my hand on the small of Briar's back, I lead her back to the kitchen. "What can I help you do?" I ask her.

"Oh, I can do it. I'll make them both a plate and then make mine."

"Nah, you make one and tell me what to put on the other, and we can do ours at the same time."

"You don't have to do that."

I lean in close and whisper in her ear, "I want to." Goose bumps break out across her skin, and I have to fight my grin. Good. I'm glad I'm not the only one feeling this—whatever it is. Reluctantly, I drop my hand from the small of her back, already missing the warmth of the connection between us, and grab two paper plates, handing them to her and snatching two more.

"All right, who do I have?" I ask, grabbing a hamburger and making myself a sandwich. Everyone is gathered around the kitchen, but I ignore them as I help Briar.

"Rayne, a hot dog, but I'll cut it up for her, and some mac and cheese will be good. Just a little, though. I don't want them to waste it."

"We have plenty," Emerson says from across the island.

"Hot dog and mac and cheese. Anything for the hot dog?"

"Ketchup."

"Got it." I make Rayne a plate, then make mine and head to the dining room.

"Rayne, this is yours. River, your momma is bringing your plate." I don't know why I feel the need to explain. I guess so River doesn't feel left out.

"Okay." River climbs to her knees and looks toward the kitchen, waiting for her mom.

"Now, Momma says we need to cut this up." I get to work cutting up the hot dog into small pieces. I don't want her to choke, and I don't know how big of bites a four-year-old needs or can have. It's been years since Emerson was little, and I was just a teenager who didn't think about those kinds of things.

Once I'm finished, I grab the ketchup bottle from the center of the table and give her a little pile, hand her a fork and a napkin, and take my seat between the girls, just as Briar sits down and hands River her plate. She has the same thing that Rayne does, and I smile when I see her hot dog cut up just as I did Rayne's. My pieces might be a little smaller, but the smile is because I didn't fuck it up.

"Rayne, let Mommy...." Her voice trails off when she looks over the top of her daughter's head to see her hot dog already cut up. "Thank you, Forrest." Her voice is soft.

"I got you. Have a seat. Let's eat." I wait until Briar is seated and takes her first bite before I take one of my own.

"You wike hot dogs?" River asks me before she takes a bite of hers.

"I do. I also like hamburgers." I take a bite of mine to prove my point. The girls chatter around the table, stealing the show. They talk about their Barbies, and how they want a Barbie house and a Barbie Jeep for their birthdays that they promise to share, because sharing is nice.

"How old are you going to be?" Legend asks them. Together, they raise their hands and hold up four fingers.

"Dis many," they say in unison.

"So you're old ladies, then," Maddox teases.

"We not old." They giggle, which makes Lilly giggle, and as I look around the table, every single adult has a smile on their face.

This is what it's about. Spending time with the people who mean the most to you, being in the presence of the innocence of the next generation.

After lunch, we all help clean up. Briar grabs a pack of wipes from the bag she brought with her and cleans the girls' hands and faces. I'm standing at the island in the kitchen, wiping the same spot on the counter over and over as I observe them. I'm aware that it's creepy as fuck, but I can't make myself look away from them. The three of them are so in sync with one another.

My staring could also be because Briar is a knockout. Her long brown hair and big green eyes are captivating. Her daughters look just like her, and it's definitely a sight worth taking in.

"Are you ready to watch Lilly open her presents?" Briar asks her daughters. They nod and scramble out of their chairs. I'm expecting them to rush toward the living room, but instead, they rush toward me. Dropping the rag on the counter, I turn toward them just in time. They slam into my legs, each wrapping their arms around me. On instinct, I place my hand on the back of their heads as they lean into me.

"We want a ride," River tells me. She releases my leg and raises her arms in the air. Rayne watches her sister and does the same.

Damn, these two are just too cute. Bending down, I wrap an arm around each of their waists, and they latch on to me like little monkeys as I stand and carry them to the living room.

"I'm so sorry," Briar says, trailing behind us.

"Nothing to be sorry for. I'll give these little ladies a ride any day." Once we're in the living room, I bend, placing the girls back on their feet, and resume my position from earlier in front of the love seat. The girls crawl up behind me and pat the cushion next to them.

"Mommy, sit with us," one of them says.

Briar steps around me and sits on the open seat. Legend is on the couch, with Monroe on his lap, and Maddox and Lachlan are beside them. Roman is in the recliner, sitting on the edge with his cell phone in his hand, ready to take pictures, while Emerson is on the floor with Lilly. Roman's parents are sitting together in the oversized chair. They, too, have their cameras at the ready.

"Girls, why don't you come and sit with me, so Forrest doesn't have to sit on the floor?" Briar suggests. Her tone tells me it's not really a suggestion.

"Forrest, sit with us," one of them says. I can't tell their voices apart just yet to know which.

I turn to look over my shoulder. "I'm fine here."

"Pwease?" Rayne says. She juts out that little lip of hers and I'm toast. How do parents do this? How do they say no? Does Roman know what's about to happen to him once Lilly starts talking more? He's screwed. Fuck. We're all screwed.

"All right," I agree, because... pouting little lips.

I move to the love seat and smile at the twins, then their mom. Damn, she's gorgeous. I wonder what the deal is? Where is their dad? How could any man walk away from the three of them?

"Present time!" Roman cheers and claps his hands. Lilly squeals and claps her hands just like her daddy.

Emerson places a present in front of her and helps her tear it open. It's a new doll from Roman's parents, from the looks of how his mom is gushing over how she had to buy it because the doll resembles Lilly. However, Lilly is more interested in the wrapping paper than the doll.

"Never fails." Briar chuckles softly.

"What's that?" I ask her.

She nods toward Lilly. "They always like the paper or the box that the gifts come in at that age better than the gift. These two were the same way." She smiles fondly at her daughters.

"We wike gifts, Mommy," River tells her.

"You do now," Briar agrees. "When you were one like Lilly is today, you liked the wrapping paper and the bows better. I have pictures to prove it," she says, bopping each of the girls on the nose with her index finger, making them giggle.

I have to tear my eyes away from them and focus on my niece. That's why I'm here to celebrate her first full year of life. Not to drool over my sisters new friend.

The girls start to get restless, as does Lilly. "Why don't we skip to cake, and Lilly can open the rest later?" Roman's mom, Sarah, suggests.

I can see the indecision on Emerson's face. "We get it, Em, don't sweat it. The little tyke is worn out, and we kind of went overboard." Everyone laughs but nods their agreement because I'm not wrong. We all spoil her rotten, and sure, no one-year-old needs this much stuff, but we can afford to do it, and I know for me, Emerson and I didn't have this growing up, and I wanted to make sure that my niece does. Sure, Emerson and Roman, and his parents, will make sure of it, but as her uncle, her blood uncle, I felt like it was my job too.

As for the rest of the guys, well, they claim uncle status as well. They should. We're family, regardless of blood, and Lilly is the first baby in the family. Apparently, we're going to be spoiling all the kids born into the Everlasting Ink family. I smile at the thought. I wouldn't want it any other way, and I know the guys feel the same.

"Are you ladies ready for some cake?" I'm asking the girls, but I love that Briar is included in that statement as well.

"Cake!" the twins cheer.

"We better go grab some before Maddox and Lachlan eat it all," I tell them. They gasp as if that's the worst thing they've ever heard in their lives, and my smile widens. "Let's go." I stand and offer them my hands. They quickly climb off the couch and don't hesitate to slide their little palms in mine. "You coming, Momma?" I ask Briar.

She swallows hard. "Yes." She nods as if she also needs to show me her answer before standing and following along behind us to the kitchen.

When we make it to the kitchen, Lilly is already in her high chair, and her small little smash cake, which is what Emerson called it, is in front of her. We sing "Happy Birthday," and Lilly smiles and claps. Before the song is over, she's already dipping her index finger into the icing and shoving it into her mouth.

All the adults have their phones out, taking pictures, and Lilly hams it up for the camera. She's the perfect mix of her parents. I can see both Roman and Emerson in her mannerisms.

"Who wants cake?" Roman calls out as he starts to slice pieces of the large birthday cake.

I stand back and watch as Monroe and Briar grab a piece of cake and some ice cream for the twins and set them up at the little picnic table I bought Lilly for her birthday. It's just one of the many gifts because I'm going for the "favorite uncle" status, after all. She might be a little too young for it now, but I thought it would be perfect for our summer outside cookouts. In fact, I need to order one for my place so she also has one there when she comes to visit.

Once everyone has a piece of cake, we sit at the dining room table. Briar sits on the edge of her seat and constantly checks on the twins, who are chatting away with each other enjoying their cake and ice cream in the corner of the dining room.

"So, Briar, you work with Mo?" Maddox asks.

"I do. My sister, Brogan, and I both do. I'm in billing, and work from home most of the time, which is helpful with the girls, and Brogan is a phlebotomist."

"And you're twins?" Lachlan asks.

"We are." Briar offers him a smile.

"And you're both single?" Lachlan clarifies.

"We are." Briar nods, and her cheeks take on a soft pink hue.

"And the other one?" Maddox asks.

"Oh, that's Maggie. She's a nurse who works with me at the surgery center. And yes, she's also single."

Lachlan goes to speak, but I shake my head, and he quickly closes his mouth. "This cake is great. Where did you get it?" I ask my sister. Lachlan gives me a "what the fuck" look, clearly thinking I've lost my mind, and I probably have, but I don't want him grilling Briar. She's already embarrassed if the pink of her cheeks is any indication.

I ignore him and pretend that my sister telling me about the woman she found in the town over from ours who made the cake is the most riveting conversation I've had in weeks.

"So you all work at the same tattoo studio?" Briar asks.

"We do." Roman nods. "We're building a new site out on the edge of town. The south side."

"That's right. I remember Brogan telling me about that." Briar glances at Monroe. "She said you told her that's where I should go to get my ink."

"Are you thinking about a new tattoo?" I ask her.

She turns to look at me where I'm sitting next to her. "I am. My first. I want something for the girls and my dad all in one."

It's on the tip of my tongue to tell her that I'll do it for free, just to spend more time with her, but my sister opens her mouth before I can.

"All five of them are extremely talented. When you're ready, you can't go wrong with any of them."

At least she didn't suggest one of the guys and not me. I'm already thinking about how I can tell Lyra and Drake that if a Briar calls, she's to be scheduled with me. "She's right," I tell Briar. "We can all help you. Do you need help with a design?" I might as well go ahead and toss my name in the hat.

"Maybe." She bites down on her plump bottom lip. "I have ideas. I just don't know how to incorporate them all."

"When you're ready," I say softly, keeping this part of the conversation just between us.

"Thank you, Forrest."

I nod and look up to see my sister watching me. I can't read the expression on her face, but it's gone before I can name it, anyway.

As the party dies down, I offer to carry the twins to the car for Briar. They're both tired and asking Briar to carry them. She's a tiny thing, so I don't see how she can. They're sitting on the love seat, while Briar stands before them.

I kneel so that we're at eye level. "Would it be all right if I carried you to the car?" I ask them.

"I can help," Lachlan offers.

"You don't have to do that. They're big girls now. They can walk," Briar says, more for the girls' benefit than ours.

"We got this." Lachlan bends down just as I am. "Who wants a ride to the car?"

The girls point at me, and something in my chest swells. I've just met them, but damn, these little angels have a hold on me.

"How about we race?" Lachlan asks. "River and me against Rayne and this guy." He points to me. I don't think he can tell them apart, but he does know their names.

"Can you go real, *real* fast?" River asks him.

"The fastest."

The twins look at each other and have some sort of silent communication before they're nodding. River crawls over Rayne to get to Lachlan, and lets him take her into his arms, as I scoop Rayne up into my arms as well. We carry them out on the front porch and down the steps.

"Ready?" Lachlan asks.

"Go!" the girls cheer, and we take off toward the car. We get there at the exact same time. "Tie!" they cheer, their melancholy from having to go home nowhere in sight.

"Thank you for that," Briar says, once we have the girls loaded into the back seat of her car.

"Anytime. You ladies be good for your momma," I say before closing the door. "When you're ready for that tattoo, give me, or any of us, a call." *Me. Call me.* That's what I want to say, but I can't for the life of me understand why it's so important to me that I be the one to ink her.

"Thank you," she says again, before climbing into her car and driving away. I watch until I can no longer see her, and hope like hell I'll get to see her again soon.

BRIAR

THE GIRLS ARE FINALLY ASLEEP. It only took three books, and the promise that they could have their own small birthday cakes for their birthday in a few weeks. I tried to explain that small individual cakes are usually just for first birthdays, but they kept insisting, and it's a small ask to make them happy.

I always get them both their own cake, anyway. It's something my dad always did for Brogan and me. He said that just because we were twins didn't mean we had to share a cake. My chest aches at the thought of my dad. I miss him so much.

"They finally out?" Brogan asks as I take a seat on the opposite end of the couch.

"Yeah, they want their own little cakes like Lilly had today. I think the exact request was, 'We're big girls, but we want little cakes.'" I don't bother to hold in my laughter.

"Those two are something else." Brogan grins. "So, how was it?"

"How was what?"

She gives me a look that tells me she knows I'm full of shit. "The party. Did you get to meet all the guys?"

"I did." I nod, not giving her anything.

"And?"

"And what? You should have come with me if you wanted to meet them so badly." I know she was exhausted, and I don't blame her for not coming, but it helps pull the heat from me to her. At least, that's the hope.

"Are they as gorgeous as everyone claims?"

I should have known my distraction tactic wouldn't work this time. "Everyone?"

"You know, Emerson and Monroe. Keep up, Briar," she teases.

"They're—yes. Yes, they are." Flashes of Forrest filter through my mind. Gorgeous isn't the first word I would think of when it comes to him. Sexy, alluring, kind, sweet, did I say sexy?

"What was that look?" Brogan points at my face.

"What look?"

"The one you just did there. It was all dreamy and—wait. You like one of them?" She sits up straighter and clasps her hands together. "Who? Which one? Tell me all the things, dear sister."

"They're all really nice guys."

"Briar," she groans.

"Fine. Forrest, Emerson's brother, he was really good with the girls. He carried them to the kitchen and was sweet with them. In fact, they all were. Roman was as well when he answered the door, and Forrest and Lachlan helped me carry the girls out to the car when I left."

"Forrest." She reaches for her phone and taps at the screen.

"What are you doing?"

"Going to their website. All the guys have their pictures on there. I checked them out after girls' night, but I can't remember which one is Forrest."

"Creeper much?" I tease.

"You, dear sister, have good taste," she says, staring at the screen. "Honestly, they're all fine as hell."

"If you've already stalked them online, why interrogate me?"

"Because in person is different than behind the lens of a camera." She hands me her phone and I scroll the page that has a picture of each of the five guys.

"Not in this case."

"The next time we're invited, I'm going."

"What if you have to work?" I counter.

"I'll call off."

"No, you won't." I chuckle. "Truly, they were all really nice and welcoming. They spoiled the girls just as much as they did Lilly, well, mostly Forrest, because they stuck to him like glue."

"Sounds like everyone had a good time."

"We did. Now, I'm going to bed. I hope the girls sleep in tomorrow, but that's a dream. I know it's not going to come true."

"I took a thirty-minute nap, but I'm still wide awake. I think I'll read a little more before calling it a night."

"Love you."

"Love you too."

I head off down the hall to my room. The cabin we live in was our grandparents'. We used to spend summers here with our dad. It has four bedrooms and three bathrooms, with a large living area and kitchen. The back porch is covered and gives a beautiful view of the lake on the property. When Brogan and I were little, it looked massive, and we always called it the river. My girls do the same now that we live here. It makes me smile every time, as it brings back memories of my childhood with my dad.

I peek into the bedroom the twins share. I offered them separate rooms, but they wanted to be together, which left the extra bedroom open for an office. It works out perfectly since I mostly work from home, aside from going in for meetings here and there. Those are few and far between. We've settled in nicely here in Ashby. It's our home now, and I wouldn't want to raise my daughters anywhere else.

I can't believe it's been a month already since our last girls' night. When Monroe called to tell me we were meeting again tonight, she also informed me her parents were ready, willing, and waiting for her to call to watch the girls. I still feel guilty, but the smiles on all of their faces as I pulled out of the driveway told me everything I needed to know. Mr. and Mrs. Morrison were thrilled to be spending time with my daughters.

I've been less anxious this time, only checking my phone every twenty minutes or so instead of every five to ten. It helps that Heather has been texting me pictures and updates. I'm so grateful to them, not just for giving me a break, but for the girls too. I know they need more than just me and their aunt in their lives. No matter how scary it is to trust, I need to do more of it, or we're all going to turn into hermits.

"I'm pregnant!" Monroe blurts out.

Everyone at the table cheers and congratulates her. I could tell something has been on her mind all night. She's been smiling like she just hit a billion-dollar jackpot, and she's barely been able to sit still in her seat.

"How far along are you?" I ask her.

"Thirteen weeks." She's glowing with happiness.

"Explains the water," Maggie says, nodding to where a bottle of water sits on the table in front of Monroe. The rest of us have margaritas in front of us.

Everyone looks at me and my bottle. I'm the only other one drinking water while everyone else has a margarita sitting in front of them. "Oh no." I shake my head and hold my hands up in the air. I need to do all the things to let them know I'm not pregnant. "I have two tiny humans to get home to safely."

"I told her I would be the designated driver tonight, but here we are," Brogan says, lifting her margarita to her lips and taking a pull.

"I could have taken you all home," Monroe says.

"Or the guys," Emerson chimes in. "They offered to be DD, but I have preggers over here." She places her hand on Monroe's shoulder.

"That's me." Monroe flashes us a wide smile.

We spend a few minutes talking about pregnancy. Well, Monroe, Emerson, and I do. Maggie and Brogan chime in where they can, but having never been pregnant, it's hard to understand fully until you experience it for yourself.

"So, I have to tell you about this book I just read," Maggie says as she fans her face. "Let me tell you... hot! He's this mafia guy and all he wants to do is knock her up because he needs an heir." She goes on to tell us more about the plot, and I gotta admit, I plan on adding this to my TBR as soon as I get home. I need the name of this book.

"I'm going to need the name of that book," Brogan says, already pulling out her phone to make a note. It's as if she read my mind.

"I'll text it to all of you."

"Our husbands are going to be sending you flowers," Emerson jokes.

"Trust me, they're going to be thanking me for sure." Maggie wags her eyebrows.

Our food comes and we dive in, talking about books, our jobs, kids, pregnancies—everything really. The five of us have really hit it off, and even though this is only our second girls' night, and it's been a month since the last one, it feels like no time has passed at all.

"Oh, before I forget, we're doing cake and ice cream at the house for the girls next weekend. You're all more than welcome to come. I can't believe they're turning four."

"Aw, they're such cuties." Monroe smiles.

"What can we bring?" Emerson asks.

"Nothing. It's just Brogan and me and the girls." I pause, trying to decide whether I should just pull off the Band-Aid and tell them that we really only have the four of us. "Our parents have passed. Our mom, when we were babies, was killed in a car accident, and our dad, we lost him to cancer, a few days after the girls were born." My throat swells with emotion, but I choke it back. I don't talk about this, mostly because up until now, it's just me, my sister, and my twin daughters.

This time of year, close to the anniversary of his death, is always more painful. As days pass, it does get easier to live with the loss of him, but there are days, like the anniversary, that the pain is so real, I could swear it just happened.

"That's... heartbreaking," Emerson says, her own emotion showing, not only on her face but in her tone of voice.

"Can I...." Monroe's voice trails off as she stands and walks around the table. She stands behind Brogan and me and wraps her arms around us in a hug. "I'm so sorry," she whispers.

"Stop hogging them." This comes from Emerson, who moves in to take Monroe's place and hugs us as well.

"I need in on some of that," Maggie says. She pushes back from the table, and her arms replace Emerson's.

"You guys are—thank you," Brogan says, wiping a tear from her eye. She waves her hand between us. "We don't trust easily. Life has... knocked us down, but this little group, it means so much to us. To me."

"Me too," I add, wiping at my tears.

Everyone goes back to their seats, and we continue with our meals. There isn't a single awkward moment after telling them the sad tale or how Brogan and I lost our parents. My heart swells. We fit here, with these ladies, and in this town. I just hope that there are more great things to come for us.

"We'll be there," Monroe says. "Next weekend."

"The girls would love to see you," I tell her.

"What are they into?" Maggie asks.

"Oh, no gifts. Just you." I'm quick to reply.

Maggie looks at Brogan, who is sitting next to me. "You got my number. Fill me in later, will ya?" She winks dramatically, making us all crack up with laughter.

"They're easy, anything really. They have trucks and cars to baby dolls and Barbie dolls. They're happy little girls who will love your company, but they'll love any gift you were to bring too."

"Brogan!" I scold her with a laugh.

She shrugs. "Sorry, not sorry, baby sis."

"Two minutes." I hold up two fingers. "You are two minutes older than me!"

"Two minutes or two seconds. You're still my baby sister." She sticks her tongue out at me.

I open my mouth to sass back at her, but I quickly close it when I see five gorgeous men walking our direction. "Um, ladies." I sit up straighter in my seat and reach for my water. "I do believe girls' night is over." Everyone turns to look at where I can't seem to pull my gaze from.

"Baby girl," Roman says, leaning over his wife to kiss her forehead upside down.

"What are you doing here?" she asks him.

I watch as Legend leans over and places his hand on Monroe's belly as he kisses the corner of her mouth. What would it be like to be loved like that?

"Mom and Dad showed up and wanted some Lilly time, so I texted the guys to see if they wanted to come and grab a beer and a burger," Roman explains.

I know I'm staring at the two couples, so I avert my gaze and my eyes collide with his.

Forrest.

He shoves his hands in his pockets and offers me a grin and a nod. He opens his mouth to speak, but Lachlan beats him to it.

"Ladies." He winks. "Pleasure meeting you here."

"Oh, boy, Lach is laying on the charm, or trying to." Emerson giggles. "I better do introductions before he embarrasses himself further. This is Maggie and Brogan, and you gentlemen remember Briar. Ladies, this is my big brother, Forrest, and this is Lachlan and Maddox. They work at Everlasting Ink with Legend and Roman." She points to her husband and Legend as she says their names.

"The pleasure is all ours," Maddox says with a smirk before his eyes find mine. "Briar, good to see you again."

"You too."

"And me." Lachlan slaps his hand to Maddox's shoulder and winks at me.

I laugh at his antics before letting my eyes settle on Forrest. "Hey, Forrest." I smile, keeping my voice even. His gorgeous green eyes, which are so much like his sister's, hold me captive.

"Briar." He nods.

Is it just me or is his voice husky? Whatever it is, it's sexy and has me shifting in my chair.

"We need a bigger table," Maddox says.

"What?" Emerson and Monroe reply at the same time.

"Nope. No. Not happening."

"This is girls' night," Monroe chimes in.

"I love ladies' night," Lachlan retorts.

"Lachlan!" Emerson scolds. She turns in her chair to look over her shoulder at her husband. "Rome." That's all she says—his name—and he nods, before leaning down to press a gentle, or at least it looks gentle, kiss to her lips.

"We can push that table over," Maggie speaks up. She's looking at Lachlan, Maddox, and Forrest like they are her next meal.

"There's room," Brogan adds.

"Really?" Emerson asks, defeated.

"This won't be our last girls' night," Monroe tells her. "They're here. We might as well let them stay. You know they're just going to be sitting here somewhere watching us, anyway."

"Fine," Emerson grumbles. Roman leans down and whispers something in her ear, making her smile.

The next thing I know, tables are being moved, and chairs are being added. I don't know how it happens, but Forrest ends up sitting next to me, with Brogan on my other side. Lachlan is next to her, and Maddox is next to Maggie. Roman and Legend help their wives stand and pull them onto their laps.

"That's better," Legend says, kissing Monroe's neck.

"Thanks for letting us join you. It would have been boring watching those two stare at their lady loves all night," Lachlan tells us.

"You're just jealous," Roman tells him. "One day you'll get it, and I can't wait to watch it happen."

"Forever isn't for all of us," Lachlan tells him. "Some of us still like variety."

"Oh, we have plenty of variety," Emerson speaks up.

"Em!" Forrest groans. "Just no."

Emerson giggles, while Roman seems to wrap his arms around her a little tighter. "You do want more nieces and nephews, right?" she asks her brother.

"I don't want to hear about the process," he groans. "Besides, hold off and let a guy catch up, huh?"

"Are you in the running?" she asks him.

"No, but one day." He points his finger at her. "One day I will be." He nods as if he's certain it will happen.

To have that kind of confidence. "You want kids?" I blurt the question, despite the answer being obvious.

"Yes." There isn't a single ounce of hesitation in his answer.

"What about you?" I raise my eyes and point my question to Maddox.

He shrugs. "Yeah, one day."

"You're not getting any younger, Mad," Legend reminds him.

"It will happen if and when it's meant to happen."

I lean over Brogan and focus on Lachlan. "And you?"

"I'm sure someday, but not right now."

"Again, not getting any younger," Legend reminds him.

"Bro, you act like we're in our fifties. Since when is early thirties too old to have kids?"

"I'm just saying," Legend replies, "you don't know what you're missing."

"I second that," Roman agrees.

"Fine, what about you?" Lachlan asks me. "More kids?"

"I'd love to have more, but I don't know if that will even happen for me."

He gives me a curious look, but that's all I'm going to say about the matter. Now is not the time to drop more truth bombs on the group.

"And you?" he asks my sister.

"If it never happens for me, I have River and Rayne."

"But do you want them?" Maddox asks.

"Yeah, but I don't know if that will even happen for me." She repeats my answer, and we get curious looks.

"What about you?" Maddox asks Maggie.

"Definitely. As soon as I find a man who's willing to stick around and be there for all of it, I'm in. I've only found losers who want sex and nothing more up to this point."

"Assholes," Maddox mutters.

"What about us?" Emerson asks.

"We already know the four of you are all about reproducing." Lachlan laughs.

"We're good at it," Roman replies cockily. Legend raises his hand for Roman to give him a high-five. They slap hands, and we all laugh.

"Lilly is great," I agree with him.

"So are your girls."

"Thank you. I told the ladies earlier that we're having cake and ice cream for the twins next weekend for their birthday. Nothing big, but Lilly is more than welcome."

"Just Lilly?" Maddox places his hand over his heart. "I'm offended." He juts out his bottom lip just like the twins do when they're pouting, but somehow, he manages to make it look hot.

"You're welcome to come," I tell him.

He nods. "What time? You know what, maybe I should get your number just in case I need directions?"

I feel Forrest stiffen next to me. I smile at Maddox. "All the ladies know how to reach me."

"It's like that, is it?" he asks, crossing his muscled, tattooed arms over his chest.

"Leave her alone," Legend tells him.

Maddox winks at me, and I shake my head. There's a smile on my face I couldn't hide, even if I wanted to. I like these people.

Maybe they can be my people.

FORREST

I WAS FOURTEEN WHEN EMERSON turned four. I was a kid with no money, so spoiling her at that age wasn't possible. Our deadbeat parents didn't even make an attempt with a birthday cake, homemade or otherwise. I did what I could. When I got older, I made sure Emerson had everything she needed. Including celebrating her birthday.

That's why I've been in the toy aisle for far longer than I can admit, trying to decide on the best gift for River and Rayne for their birthday.

At Sunday dinner last week, Monroe mentioned they don't have any family. Apparently, it's just Briar, Brogan, and the twins, and when she and my sister suggested we all go to the twins' fourth birthday party, everyone agreed. I barely know them, so I don't know them. I don't know what they already have or don't have, so this is proving to be more difficult than what I first thought.

Pulling my phone out of my pocket, I call my sister.

"Hello?"

"Hey, what do I get River and Rayne? I've been at the store for an hour and still can't decide on something."

"They're little girls, Forty. They'll love and appreciate anything you get them."

"That's not helpful at all, kid."

"Ugh. I'm a grown woman, a married woman, and a mother. We can drop the kid."

"You're always going to be my kid sister, no matter how old you get, how long you're married, or how many nieces and nephews you give me." I can hear her sigh, and I know I've got her.

"Fine. Let me text Monroe."

"Thank you. What did you get them?"

"They each got a Barbie doll and some clothes."

"Right, Barbie dolls." I walk over to the next aisle and stare at the shelf. That's when I see them. "I think I found what I'm getting them. But what if they already have them?"

"Don't stress. If they have them, Briar can return them and let the girls pick out a gift. It's the thought that counts, big brother."

"Right. Okay, I'm getting them." I pick up a pink and a white Barbie Jeep and toss them into my cart.

"Just make sure you get a gift receipt in case they need to return them."

"Will do. Thanks, Em."

"Anytime." I end the call, sliding my phone back into my pocket.

Looking at the Jeeps in my cart, I'm still not sold. I'm going to give it one more go down the aisles to make sure nothing else stands out to me. I turn to the next aisle, and there's a woman with a little girl who looks close to River and Rayne's age.

"Mommy, I want this!" She points to a camera.

"We'll make sure to add that to your birthday wish list for next month."

"I'll be this many." She holds up her hand, showing five fingers.

"That's right." I hear the mom say before they push their cart down the aisle.

I stop in front of the cameras. There are a few different types. I pick up the one that says it instantly prints the pictures. I smile, because I think the girls would love this. I grab a pink and a purple and toss them into the cart. Then I grab three paper refill kits for each and toss them in as well. Making my way back to the Barbie Jeeps, I pull the two from my cart and place them back on the shelf.

Satisfied I've made a good choice, I push my cart out of the toys. I need to grab a few things for the house. As I pass home goods, the photo albums stick out to me. I reverse and walk down the aisle. I grab two albums, one pink and one purple, which have a spot for a frame in the front. I know exactly what I'm going to put there.

It doesn't take me long to grab the few things I need for home and wheel toward the checkout. Just as I'm getting in line, I remember I'm going to need birthday cards and a gift bag. I feel like I've been in this store all damn day. I trek back to that side of the store and grab what I need, and finally, I'm able to check out.

As soon as I get home, I unload everything and get to work with wrapping gifts. The party isn't until tomorrow, so I have plenty of time.

Monroe has the address, so we all decided to just follow them to Briar and Brogan's place. Lachlan and Maddox met at my house. The three of us are taking my truck, while Roman, Legend, Emerson, Maggie, Monroe, and Lilly are going in Emerson's SUV.

"No shit," Maddox says, as we pull into the driveway. "They live at the old Lewis place."

"I always loved this house. I wonder how they bought it. I've been waiting for it to go on the market for years. I heard they passed, but I know it's never been for sale."

"That's not morbid or anything," Lachlan jokes.

"You know what I mean. I'm sad Mr. and Mrs. Lewis are gone, but this property butts up to Ashby Lake. Perfect for summer boating, fishing, and all that. The house is a cabin I've never seen inside, but it wouldn't matter. It could be remodeled if needed."

"Well, you're about to see inside," I tell him as we file out of my truck, grabbing our gifts. I don't know what anyone else bought the twins, but I'm hopeful they like what I chose.

In a collective group, gift bags in hand, we make our way to the door. Emerson, with Lilly on her hip, and Monroe in front of us, Emerson knocks on the door. Brogan opens it, all smiles, and then gasps.

"Holy wow," she says. "I—come in." She steps back and allows us to enter. "River! Rayne! You have someone here to see you."

Cheers and the pitter-patter of little feet echo through the house. When the girls reach us, they stop and stare.

"Girls, say hello," Brogan coaches them.

"Hi," they say at the same time and wave.

Emerson bends down with Lilly still on her hip. "Happy Birthday. We thought we would come and celebrate you turning four."

"This many." River, I know it's her because her hair is a little darker than her sister's, holds up four fingers.

"That's right," Emerson says.

"Who was at—" Briar stops in her tracks as her eyes take us all in. I imagine it's a sight. Five big guys covered in ink, with three women and a baby, all holding gift bags, standing in the entryway of her house.

"We're here to party." Monroe holds up the two gift bags in her hands.

"Are those for us?" Rayne asks.

"Of course. It's your birthday," Monroe replies.

"Come on in," Brogan says. She motions toward the living area, and we start to move.

It's obvious they were not expecting all of us to show up, even though we were invited. I follow everyone into the living room, and we place the gifts on the fireplace, where there are a few others. The twins are bouncing on their feet. They're so excited.

There's a knock at the door, and Briar and Brogan share a look. "Are you expecting anyone else?" Brogan asks her sister.

"No. I—no. Everyone who was invited is already here." Briar shrugs and moves toward the front door. I stand to follow her, because I know who it is. She opens the door and smiles. "I'm sorry, you must have the wrong house."

The kid looks down at the piece of paper in his hand. "Says delivery for Forrest Huntley."

"That's me." I step up beside Briar and hand the kid his tip. I paid for the food over the phone. "Thanks," I tell him.

"You're welcome. Um, where do you want these?"

"We can unload here. I'll take them." He's just a teenage kid, but I'm not about to invite him into their home.

The kid shoves his tip into his pants pocket, picks up the first insulated bag, and starts unloading pizza boxes. I'm certain I went overboard, but I know that the guys and I can put away some pizza, as can my sister and Monroe. Besides, I wanted to make a splash. I wanted this party to be one the twins will always remember. At least, I hope they will. Since they're only turning four, it's hard to tell. Either way, I hope they talk about it for weeks to come.

"Thank you," I tell the kid once I have all ten pizza boxes in my arms. "Can you point me toward the kitchen?" I ask Briar.

"Sure." Her voice sounds funny, but I can't do much about that with my arms full of pizza boxes. Tilting my head to the side, I follow her to the right, which is the opposite of the living room, and place the pizzas down on the island.

"I did half pepperoni and half cheese. Our gang will eat anything, and I wasn't sure what you all liked, or the girls, so I thought cheese and pepperoni were a safe bet."

Briar stands on the opposite end of the island. Her hands are at her sides, and tears shimmer in her big green eyes. Have I upset her? My gut twists, thinking about how what I hoped was a nice gesture turned into making her upset. I don't think, I just walk around the island and pull her into my arms. To my surprise, she comes willingly.

"I'm sorry," I murmur. "I didn't mean to upset you."

She shakes her head but doesn't speak. She makes no move to pull away, so I hold her a little tighter, letting one hand run up and down her spine to soothe her. I can't help but notice how well she fits in my arms. As if she were made to be here. My heart beats like a drum at a rock concert. She's not mine. I know that, but why does she feel like she could be? I push those thoughts down deep and focus on the task at hand. Soothing her, letting her know I'm here. When she finally pulls away, she wipes at her cheeks and offers me a quivering smile.

"I'm not angry. These are happy tears, which I know sounds insane, but this—" She points to the stack of pizza boxes.

"I know we're a lot, and I assumed you never thought that the guys and I would show up with Emerson and Monroe. I wanted to make sure we weren't an imposition."

"I'll pay you back."

"Nope. This is my gift to the girls for their birthday."

"Forrest."

My name, softly whispered from her lips, is something I could get used to hearing. "I wanted to do this, Briar."

"It's just been us for so long." She's staring at my chest when she voices her confession.

Placing my index finger below her chin, I lift so her eyes meet mine. "Not anymore." Setting these crazy feelings she's stirring inside me aside, I know my sister and her best friend are invested in their friendships with both Briar and Brogan. They're family now, and we take care of our own.

"Now, we have a party to get to." I don't know why I do it, and I wouldn't take it back even if I could. I press my lips to her forehead. Her quick intake of breath tells me I've surprised her, just as much as I've surprised myself.

I have to force myself to drop my hold on her and step back. "Come on, Momma." I grin. "We have two very special little ladies who need to be celebrated." I nod toward the living room. Briar stands tall, wipes her cheeks again, and leads us back into the room.

"Everything okay?" Brogan asks.

"Yeah, this one"—Briar points to me over her shoulder—"ordered pizza."

"Pizza!" River and Rayne cheer. They climb to their feet where they were playing on the floor with Lilly and rush toward me. Their little arms wrap around my legs, and just like with their momma, something inside my chest tightens.

I smile down at them before meeting Briar's gaze. "You ready to eat?"

"We might as well before it gets cold."

I nod, offer each of the twins a hand, and lead them into the kitchen. "You have two choices. Plain cheese or pepperoni."

"Cheese!" they say at the same time.

Fuck, these two are cute as hell.

"Here are some plates." Briar sets a stack of paper plates on the counter. "We're going to just have to spread out." She laughs nervously.

"That's the great thing about pizza. It's basically a finger food, and you don't need a table to sit down and eat," I tell her. "Let's get the girls set up, and the rest of us can fend for ourselves."

"Girls, go get in your seats." I watch as River and Rayne scurry off to the dining area that's part of the kitchen and climb into what I assume are their seats.

"I'm starving," Lachlan says, entering the kitchen.

I look up at Briar and mouth, "I told you so." She gives me a beaming smile in return, and I wish the girls had already opened their gifts so I could have them sneak a picture of their momma for me.

"Pepperoni and cheese," I tell Lachlan, shaking out of my thoughts.

"You're a rock star, Forrest. Don't ever let anyone tell you differently." Lachlan places a few slices of pepperoni on his plate, grabs a napkin and a bottle of water, and heads back toward the living room.

There is a flurry of activity while everyone makes their plates and finds a seat. The dining room table seats six, so we let the ladies and the kiddos take those seats while me and the guys spread out around the living room.

56 | KAYLEE RYAN

"What made you think of ordering pizza?" Roman asks as he takes a seat next to me.

"There are a lot of us. I assumed Briar would never have dreamed that five grown men would take the invite to her four-year-old daughters' birthday party seriously."

"Way to think ahead," Maddox says.

"The contractor wants to meet with us again next week. He's got the revised plans ready for us to take a look at," Legend tells us.

"If we keep making changes, the new building is never going to get built," Lachlan replies.

"Yeah, but it's a lot of money, and this is our dream. We want it to be right," Legend counters. "Besides, he's getting paid for his time. This is his job. We need to make sure we think of every possible scenario or event moving forward to make this the exact space we envision it to be."

"We already have extra rooms in case we ever decide to hire more artists or have guests come in. We have a piercing room, a break room, a waiting room, and a meeting room. What else do we need?" Maddox asks.

"I was thinking about a room for the kids. Maybe a playroom where we can have some toys and a crib or Pack 'N' Play in case we need to have them with us at any time," Roman suggests.

Legend nods. "Mo and I were talking about that last night. It would be nice, even when our wives come to visit, to have a place we know the kids can roam and play freely and be out of harm's way."

"Do you two plan on having more than just Lilly and the one you and Mo have cooking?" Lachlan asks.

"Yeah, and I'm sure all of you will have kids of your own at some point," Legend answers.

"We gotta be wifed-up first," Maddox tells him.

"You better get on that." Roman laughs.

"Trust me, if I could find her, I'd be working toward what you two have." I point to Roman and Legend. I quickly glance toward the kitchen, but I force myself back to my friends and our conversation.

"You never know when she's going to appear. Mo was right in front of me for years." Legend shakes his head. "How I didn't know she was mine all that time, I'll never understand."

"I knew Em was mine, or that I wanted her to be," Roman adds.

We talk more about the new shop and things we think it needs. Legend is going to set up a meeting with the contractor later this week. Once we have a final draft and stop making changes, they can start the build. I'm pumped to see it. Of course, Legend is making this happen for us, but we've all busted our asses to make a name for Everlasting Ink. Having a new state-of-the-art facility is only going to bring in more clients to our sleepy little town of Ashby, Tennessee.

We finish eating and help clean up before Briar asks for everyone to gather around in the living room to watch the girls open their presents. They're giddy with excitement as they sit on the floor with all the gifts in front of them.

There isn't a single person in this house that's not smiling at their enthusiasm. The grins on their faces and the happiness radiating from them is palpable. I'm glad my sister and Monroe orchestrated this. These ladies, all four of them, big and small, deserve more people in their lives who care about them.

Today is their first look at what it means to be a part of the Everlasting Ink family.

I'VE BEEN FIGHTING BACK TEARS since the moment they walked through the door. When I extended the invitation last weekend, and Maddox asked about their invitation, I thought he was kidding. Of course, they're welcome, but honestly, I never dreamed that all five of the guys would show up. I thought the girls would show up with Lilly. We'd have some cake and ice cream, open some presents, and call it a day.

This is so much more than I ever expected, and the smiles on my daughters' faces... it's incredible to see them so happy. They're fascinated with every gift they open. I made sure they got everything on their list. Is it too much? Probably, but Brogan and I are all that they have, and I needed them to feel loved and so damn special on their birthday.

Although, looking around our packed living room, it's not just us anymore.

I don't know what role these people are going to play in our lives, but for today, they've made the twins' fourth birthday one that I know will stand out, one that they will always remember.

"Open mine," Lachlan says. He hands a box wrapped in pink paper to each of the girls. They smile and tear into the packages.

"No way!" Forrest laughs. "I almost bought those. Had them in the cart and everything." He's shaking his head as he watches the girls talk about the new Barbie Jeeps that Lachlan bought them.

"Phew. Dodged a bullet there."

"It's fine," I tell him. "We could have just exchanged them."

"Yeah, but who wants to get two of the same thing?" He looks over at his friends. "We should have coordinated like we did with Lilly. Anyone else buy Barbie Jeeps?" he asks.

"If we did, we wouldn't tell you until the girls opened them," Monroe tells him.

Lachlan winces. "Fair point."

"We are definitely going to coordinate next year," Maddox agrees.

Those tears I've been fighting, they well behind my eyes. I can feel the heat of them threatening to fall. I need a minute to compose myself, but I can't leave while the girls are opening their presents.

"Let's open these babies up," Lachlan says. He moves to the floor to sit in front of the girls to help them break their new Barbie Jeeps out of their packaging.

"Give me one of those," Maddox says, moving to the floor as well, taking the second Jeep and starting to open the box.

"I'll be right back," I murmur. I'm not even sure anyone is paying attention as I stand and move to the kitchen for a breather. As soon as my back is turned on the room, I lose the battle I was fighting. A single hot tear rolls down my cheek. I'm quick to wipe it away as I focus on pulling in a deep breath. Resting my hands on the counter, I bow my head and try to compose myself.

I jolt when I feel a warm hand press to my back. I turn to see Forrest standing next to me, concern written all over his handsome face. "You okay?"

I nod because I'm not sure I can form words right now. I don't know what's happening. Suddenly, there are people in our lives who are good to my daughters. Good to me. I'm thrilled, but at the same time, I don't want to let my heart get used to this. I can't. If life has taught me anything, it's that you can't be too trusting. There has to be an ulterior motive, but for the life of me, I can't figure out what that might be.

"Are you crying?" His voice is deep, gravelly, and sexy, just like the man. "Come here."

Before I know what's happening, this big man with kind eyes covered in ink pulls me into his arms for the second time today. I can't help but wonder if anyone has ever told him he gives great hugs.

"Tell me what's upset you, Briar."

I stand here in the comfort of his arms as I wrangle my emotions. Finally, I step back and peer up at him. "I'm sorry." I wipe my cheeks. "Just an emotional mom." I laugh it off.

"Don't do that. Don't hide from what you're feeling. Whatever it is, it's yours and it's your right to feel it. You can talk to me."

Exhaling a heavy breath, I try to find the words. "They've never had a party like this. It's always just the four of us, and to see the smiles on their faces and to know that complete strangers put them there... it's just a lot to process. I don't know why you all chose to be here, but *you* did that. You and your friends and family made this a special day for them, and I don't know how to thank you." The words tumble out in a rush, and I'm not even sure they make sense.

"You don't have to thank us, Briar. We're here because we want to be. I know we're a lot—" he chuckles "—but I promise you that we mean well. We have pure intentions."

"Grown men who don't know my girls coming to their party is... not at all what I expected."

"You invited us. Besides, we can't pass up a big piece of birthday cake." He winks, and I smile. "We're here because we wanted to be here, Briar. Nothing more. Nothing less." His eyes are kind, and his words seem genuine.

"Thank you for making this day special for them. All of you," I add.

Forrest shrugs. "It's what we do. We show up for family."

It's on the tip of my tongue to argue with him and tell him we're not family, but I let the comment slide.

"Are you ready?" he asks.

"For what?"

"To go back in there and celebrate those two little girls."

He's right. This is their day, and it's more special than I ever could have imagined. "Yes."

Forrest gives me a smile. Walking around the counter, he pulls open the fridge and grabs two bottles of water, handing me one. "What's this for?"

"Our excuse for why we were gone." With that, he twists off the top, takes a long pull, and walks back into the living room, leaving me to stare after him.

With my water bottle in hand, I plaster a smile on my face and walk back into the room.

"Mommy!" the girls cheer excitedly when they see me. "We got Jeeps."

"Whoa!" Legend laughs. "Do they always do that?"

"Yes," Brogan and I answer at the same time, making every adult in the room erupt with laughter. Of course, the kids join in. They have no clue as to why we're laughing, but they don't want to be left out.

"That's some crazy twin vibing." Roman nods.

"I guess we're used to it," I say, taking my spot on the floor next to the girls. However, as soon as Forrest is seated, they both rush to him.

"Look what we gots." They hold up their Jeeps.

"Wow. Nice wheels." The girls place their Jeeps on the floor, and Forrest opens and closes the doors as if checking out the features on a Barbie Jeep is what he's been looking forward to all day.

"Girls, you have a lot more presents to open."

They look at me, and back at Forrest.

"How about I keep your Jeeps safe with me?" he offers. They seem to think about it, then nod, and rush back to me to tear open more presents.

Roman, Emerson, and Lilly got them both lap desks that hold drawing supplies. Not only does it hold the supplies, both desks are filled to the brim with said supplies. The girls love to draw, so that will definitely be used.

"Girls, let's keep moving. You have more to open," I persuade them as they try to dig into the art supplies.

"Mine next," Maddox says, pointing to his two packages. I place one in front of each of them, and they go to town, tearing at the wrappers.

"Shopping!" they say when they see the play cash registers.

"It's supposed to help teach them counting money," Maddox says. "It says four and up."

"It's perfect," I assure him.

"I have to admit, y'all did a great job, not knowing the girls," Brogan tells them.

"We're just that good," Lachlan teases.

"Girls, why don't you open mine next?" Maggie points to two small, wrapped boxes.

I push the boxes in front of the girls, and they get to work.

"Look at that," I say with as much enthusiasm as I can. I know the girls are confused as to what they're holding. "You get to paint rocks, and they glow in the dark! We can put them outside and they'll light up at night."

"Cool!" Rayne says.

"Can we put them in our room?" River asks.

"Of course. We can do both."

"Now?" they ask at the same time.

"Not right now. Later. You still have presents to open and cake to eat."

"More presents?" they ask in awe. That gets a chuckle from the adults.

"Okay, now ours," Monroe says, pointing toward her gifts.

The gifts are barely in front of them and they're tearing into them. "Jewelry!" they exclaim.

"They're bigger pieces," Monroe assures me. "Says four and up, as well."

"It's perfect. They'll love playing with them. Thank you." I turn toward my daughters and watch as they both stand and move toward Forrest.

"Open pwease." They hand the gifts to him.

It's on the tip of my tongue to tell them to wait, but Forrest beats me to it. "I will open them, but you have one more gift from me." He nods to where the two final gift bags are sitting.

"Okay," River says, moving back toward me with Rayne on her heels.

The girls dive into the gift bags, pulling out their gifts. "Whoa," Rayne whispers.

"We can take pictures?" River asks.

Again, I don't get to answer before Forrest does. "You can. It also prints them right away. Before we open them, there is more in the bag. Keep digging," he tells my daughters.

Not needing to be told twice, their little hands dig back into the bags and pull out another small box. "What's this?" Rayne asks.

"That's extra paper for your cameras, so you can take all the pictures you want. There's one more. Keep looking." Forrest nods toward the gift bags. The girls dive back in and pull out what looks like a photo album.

"Those are for you to keep your pictures," he explains. "Bring them here." Dutiful as ever, they rush toward him and hand him their albums. "See this?" He points to the front of each one. "Those are your names. I drew them for you."

"For me?" they say at the same time.

"This twin stuff is a little freaky." Lachlan laughs, while my heart is bursting wide open.

"Yes, for you. Now, what do you want me to open for you first?" he asks them.

They choose the cameras, and he gets right to work opening River's.

"Rayne, bring yours over, and I'll help," Maddox offers.

I don't know how they can already tell them apart. I mean, I know they are not identical, but they've spent very little time around my girls. It warms my heart to know that they've been paying attention.

"I want Forrest to do it." She plops down beside Forrest, the opposite side of her sister, and waits patiently for her turn. Forrest gives her a smile, while my heart trembles inside my chest.

"Maddox is really good at opening boxes," Forrest tells her.

"I want you." Rayne crosses her arms over her chest.

"Rayne, let Mommy help you." I stand, but she's already shaking her head.

"No."

"Forrest will help us, Mommy," River says, defending her sister's decision.

"Okay. Well, I guess I'll go get the cake ready so we can sing 'Happy Birthday.'" With one more quick glance at Forrest with my girls, I move into the kitchen before gathering the candles and the lighter. I bought the number four candles for their little individual cakes.

"You good?" Brogan asks.

"Fine." I don't bother looking up at her as I busy myself with removing the cakes from their boxes.

"Briar."

"What? Grab that other one, will ya?" I nod toward the second small cake on the kitchen island, head toward the table, and set it in front of where the girls sit. They are the exact same cake. I didn't want a fight over one wanting the other. I try to keep them as individual as I can, not making them dress alike, although sometimes they want to. However, in this instance, I didn't want an argument. I'm glad I had the forethought to do that. I would hate for them to argue in front of our guests.

Brogan does as I ask and brings the other cake to the table. "It's nice, all of them showing up."

"I agree. Unexpected but nice. The girls have had an amazing birthday."

"They didn't mean to hurt your feelings," she says, calling me out on my behavior.

My shoulders fall and I know I can't avoid this conversation. "It's not that they hurt my feelings. The girls are excited, and there are new people here for them. It's just that... they're going to get attached to him. To all of them," I amend. "Then what happens? It's you and me who will be left to pick up the pieces to explain to them why their new friends are no longer coming around."

Brogan gives me a sympathetic look, but she knows me and my trust issues. She has trust issues of her own, but they don't run as deeply as mine do.

"At some point, we have to stop letting that night control our lives."

"How? Tell me how, Brogan. I'd love to erase it all, but then I wouldn't have those two tiny humans in there, and they are my entire world."

"One day at a time, little sister. Just as we've done every day since. We take it all one day at a time." She turns to look toward the living room. There's a lot of chatter and excited squeals coming from my daughters. "I think they'll surprise you."

"Nothing surprises me anymore." I'm aware I'm being negative with all of this, but I can't stomach the thought of my girls getting attached and then everyone in that room disappears on them. I know it's just a birthday party, but the worry is there all the same. I was never a worrier until after that night. And when I found out I was pregnant, it only got worse.

"Mommy!" River comes racing into the room. "Say cheese." She holds her camera up, and I smile for her and say, "Cheese," as instructed. She snaps my picture, and I watch as she prints it out and hands it to me.

"That's really cool."

"Now me," Rayne says, running into the room. "Say 'Cheese.'" She points her camera at me, and I repeat the same process. She, too, prints her picture and hands it to me.

"What should we do with these?" I ask them.

"Album!" They turn and race off to the living room to get their albums.

"You should probably make my brother provide monthly refills for those cameras," Emerson jokes as she enters the kitchen. "They're taking all kinds of pictures out there."

"He's done enough. You all have. It was a great gift idea."

Before Emerson can reply, everyone files into the kitchen. Maddox is holding Lilly, while Forrest has both River and Rayne in his arms.

"Girls, what do you tell everyone for your gifts?" I ask them.

"Thank you," they say in unison.

"Now, give Forrest a break and get into your chairs. It's time to sing 'Happy Birthday' and blow out your candles." They do as I ask, and clamber off to their chairs. Legend is the closest to them and helps them climb up. They smile up at him and say thank you, remembering the manners I've worked so hard to instill in them.

Once everyone is gathered around, I light the candles, and we sing to the girls, making sure to say both of their names. Half of us say River first and the other half say Rayne. The girls giggle like it's the funniest thing they've ever heard.

"Make a wish," I tell them. I watch as they close their eyes and make their wishes before blowing out their candles. I don't get a chance to offer them a fork. Instead, they stick their index fingers into the icing just like Lilly did at her party, making everyone laugh.

Moving to the island, I start cutting up the larger cake and placing pieces on paper plates. Emerson jumps in and adds ice cream, while Monroe and Maggie pass them out. The guys are all sitting around the table, making faces and keeping the girls entertained.

It all feels... natural. As if we've known this group for all our lives. My girls act as though this is a normal occurrence when it's not even close. They're soaking up all the attention and that makes me both happy and sad.

"This cake is so good," Maddox says.

"We got it at the bakery in town," Brogan tells him.

"I thought you were going to tell me you made it."

"Nope."

"Good thing, I was about to propose marriage."

"I mean, the cake is good, Mad, but I'm not sure it's that good." Lachlan chuckles.

"If I didn't think old man Carlisle would kick my ass for hitting on his wife, I might still consider it," Maddox says, shoving another bite of cake into his mouth.

"She's in her seventies," Legend tells him, barely containing his laughter.

"This is some good cake." Maddox grins, finishing off his piece.

"Do you want another piece?" I ask him. He hesitates. "We don't need all of this cake for just us. Actually, I'd rather not have any left over at all. You'd be doing me a favor."

"Well, when you put it like that, who am I to turn down the request of a lovely lady?" He smirks.

"Mad," Forrest says. His tone is low, almost a warning.

"I'm just teasing. I'd love another. Thank you, Briar." Maddox smiles before turning toward Forrest. "See, I can behave, *Dad*," he teases.

"Anyone else?" I offer.

"Yes, but I'll help." Lachlan stands with his plate in his hands.

"I can get it. You're a guest."

"That doesn't mean you have to wait on us," Roman tells me. "Trust me, Em and Mo wouldn't let us get away with that. You shouldn't either."

"What he said." Lachlan nods, scooping up another piece of cake for himself and Maddox.

The guys are content to sit with the twins, so Brogan, Monroe, Maggie, Emerson, and I all sit at the kitchen island. This day didn't turn out like I planned, and I can admit—even if just to myself—that it was better. I don't know how I feel about these new people in our lives. Only time will tell.

FORREST

M Y LAST CLIENT OF THE day canceled this morning. When Lyra asked me if I wanted her to try to fill the spot, I told her no. I need to get caught up on a ton of designs for clients in the coming weeks, and it's already three in the afternoon. It will be an early night, so I'll probably see if Roman and Emerson will let me take Lilly for a walk. I'm sure they'll appreciate the alone time. Not that I want to think about my sister and her husband and what they might use that time for. I'm going to pretend it's to get caught up on household chores. Yep, that's what they'll be doing.

Dropping my pencil, I lean back in my chair and stretch my arms above my head. I need to take a quick break and find Roman to tell him I'm stealing his daughter later. I might as well enjoy time with my niece since I'm getting out of here earlier than planned. Standing, I twist and turn, stretching out my back before stepping out of my room.

I make it one step out of the door when a voice I recognize has me turning on my heel and heading for the reception area instead. I'm sure my mind is just playing tricks on me. It's not her, but my feet carry me in that direction, anyway. I haven't been able to get Briar out of my head for weeks. Two specifically, at least since I've been counting. Two weeks ago, her adorable daughters turned four, and I held her in my arms, not once but twice that day.

Twice. I held her twice. Her body molded next to mine perfectly. It's as if she was made to be in my arms. Briar and her lavender scent are all I can seem to think about. I don't know her well. I know she works with Monroe. I know that she's a twin herself, and that her twin daughters are too damn adorable. I've been hoping I would run into her again. I've considered asking Emerson or Monroe for her number, but I've been holding strong by not asking.

Is she really here?

As soon as I step around the corner, I see her. She's standing at the counter, and Lyra is flipping through the schedule. I stop so I can take her in without any interruptions. She's gorgeous, and here. In my shop.

"Do you have a preference on which artist?" Lyra asks her.

"I was told that all of them are great. Whoever is fine," Briar answers.

Yeah, whoever is not fine. If anyone is going to be putting their hands on her, inking her soft, milky skin, it's going to be me.

"Put her with me." In three long strides, I'm standing next to Lyra, smiling at Briar. "Hey, Briar. Good to see you." Her cheeks turn a very light shade of pink. Most probably wouldn't notice, but I do.

"Hi, Forrest." She tucks her long chestnut locks behind her ear.

"You here to get some work done?"

She nods. "Yeah, I don't really have a design, but I have some ideas."

"Do you have some time now? My last client of the day canceled, so I'm free."

"Are you sure? I know I need an appointment."

"And I just gave you one. Come on back." I motion with my head toward my room.

"Thought you were leaving early today?" Lyra smirks.

"Nope." I glare at Lyra, and she covers her mouth with her hand to ward off her laughter.

"I don't want you to stay late for me."

"I was scheduled until eight. I've got plenty of time." Besides, there's nothing waiting for me at home. Sure, I wanted to get Lilly, but I can do that another day. I'm not passing up the chance to spend time with the woman who has consumed my thoughts for the last two weeks.

"Okay." She nods.

"Come on." I step out from behind the counter and wait for her to come next to me. Her lavender scent fills my senses, and I inhale deeply. I didn't know it was possible to miss a smell so much. I'm sure it's the woman, but I barely know her.

"This is me," I say, waving my arm toward my room.

"This is nice. Do you all have your own spaces?" she asks.

"We do. We're actually in the process of building a new facility. It will give us more room to bring on guest artists and a bigger break room. We're also including a playroom for the kids. It's just Lilly right now, but with Legend and Monroe expecting, there will be two, and I'm sure the rest of us will have families one day."

"You want a family, right?" she asks. She quickly slaps her hand over her mouth. "I'm sorry, that was rude of me. It's none of my business."

"There was nothing wrong with your question, Briar. You have nothing to be sorry for. Yes, I do want a family." I know I've mentioned this to her before, but I'm fine with her confirming.

She nods. "So, how do we do this?" she asks. I know she's trying to change the subject. I'm not offended by her question. In fact, I almost asked her if she wanted more kids, but I don't know where the girls' dad is or what her situation is, and I'd hate to embarrass her further. I know she mentioned before that if it never happens for her, she has the girls. And now I can't stop imagining her pregnant. Fuck me, I bet she was glowing and gorgeous.

"Let's talk about your ideas."

"Well, I want something that represents my girls and my dad."

"Something with meaning. This is your first, right?"

"It is." She smiles, and damn, I could stare at her all day.

"So, I get to be your first?" I wink, and she giggles.

"I guess so." Something in her voice changes.

"I'm sorry if I upset you. It sounded bad, but I really was thinking about your ink."

"I know." She shrugs, staring down at her lap. "I've not always been able to choose all my firsts." She lifts her eyes to mine. "I'm glad it's you."

Her words have my heart thundering in my chest. I'm certain if the noise of the shop was gone, she'd be able to hear it. Hell, she still might be able to. "Right. So, any ideas? Is there a direction you're thinking?"

"I have a few ideas."

"Let's hear them." I give her my full attention. Not that she didn't have it already.

"Well, I was thinking something that would be easy to add to or make another of if I have more kids in the future. I mean, I don't know that I ever will, but I would want all my children to be represented."

"That makes sense."

"My dad used to carry a pocket watch that was my grandpa's. He gave it to Dad when we were born, and Dad carried it every single day."

"Do you have a picture of the watch? Or the actual watch?" My mind is already processing design ideas.

"I have it. Not with me, but I have it."

"Perfect. Can you send me a picture of it? You can text it to me, if you still have my number, or bring it by so I can see it."

"Sure, I can do that."

"All right, what else do you have for me?" I ask, making a note of the pocket watch on my tablet.

"I was thinking maybe two pocket watches and have them set to the times that the girls were born. Then maybe have their birth flower around it."

"I can work with that. Any other specifics?"

"No, I'm not much of an artist, so I was hoping you or whoever would be able to take it from there."

"Me. I got you." The words are husky even to my own ears. "I'll need to see that pocket watch because I want it to be authentic to your dad."

"I would love that," she murmurs.

"Next question. Where are you thinking of putting it? Once we have a location, we can talk about size."

"I'm not really sure."

"Do you want it to be hidden? Exposed?"

"I don't really have a preference. I work in medical billing. Most of the time, I work from home, so I don't have to worry about hiding it or anything."

I stand, placing my tablet on the desk. "Well, we could do your shoulder." I lightly run my fingers over her shoulder, and she shudders at the contact. "Your back." I run my hand down her back. "Your hip, your thigh, the possibilities are endless, Briar."

"I want it to be where I can add on to it, should I have more babies."

Do not think about her having your babies. I mentally scold myself. "Right. So, shoulder, back, or thigh are the best options unless you're wanting something smaller."

"No. I mean, I guess I assumed with two pocket watches and the flowers, it would be on the larger side."

"How about this? Once I get a look at the watch, I'll work on a mock-up. Once we have it where you want it, we can place the stencil in a couple of different places so you can have a general idea of how it will look. The idea is that you love this and have no regrets."

Air whooshes from her lungs. "Really? I know that's probably a pain for you, but that would be great, Forrest. It's not that I'm undecided. I'm just not sure. It's hard to visualize, and this is forever."

"It's not a problem. I'll make a few of the stencils, and we'll place them. I won't shave you down until we know for sure where you're going to put them."

"Isn't that extra work for you?"

"That's why Everlasting Ink is the best. We do what's best for our clients. I promise you, it's not an issue." Not to mention I'll get to have my hands on her. Yeah, no hardship at all on my end.

"Thank you, Forrest." She reaches into her purse. "Do I pay a deposit or something?"

I wave her off. "Usually, but you're family, that's not necessary."

"Oh, I don't want special treatment."

"Too bad." I laugh. "You're getting it, anyway." I give her a look that tells her not to argue, and she nods. "Just let me know when I can get a look at that watch."

"I'm going home now. I can send you a picture if you want."

"You know, I'm heading out too. I could follow you home and take my own pictures. To make sure I have the details right." I'm basically inviting myself into her space again, but she's leaving and I'm not ready for her to go. I need more time with her, even if it's just a few minutes to take pictures of the pocket watch.

"Don't go out of your way."

"I've got nothing and no one waiting at home for me. I've got lots of ideas brewing already."

She gives me a beautiful, radiant smile that lights up her entire being. "I'm so excited."

All I can do is return her smile. She's taken not only my breath, but my ability to form words.

She stands from the chair. "I guess I'll see you soon?"

I swallow hard, getting my emotions under control. "Absolutely. I just need to clean up here, and I'll be right behind you."

"Thank you, Forrest. I can't wait to see what you come up with." She shocks me when she steps forward and wraps her arms around me. I don't hesitate to hold her close. She pulls away far too quickly, and my arms feel bare without her in them.

I don't understand this weird pull she has over me, but I plan to dive a little deeper and find out. I've never spent this much time thinking about a woman. I clear my throat before replying,

"You're welcome, Briar. We'll keep working until it's exactly what you want it to be."

"That's... perfect."

You're perfect.

"I'll see you soon, Briar."

She waves and walks out of my office. I jump to my feet and make one last check that I've got myself set up for my first client tomorrow. It takes no time at all, and I leave the sketches I was working on where they are. No way I can focus on them now that I have Briar's ideas brewing in my mind.

I'm turning out the light and stepping into the hallway when Roman does the same a few doors down. "Heading home?" he asks.

"Yeah, well, I have to stop at Briar's first, but yes."

"Briar?"

I nod. "She came in to make an appointment and I was at the desk." Not exactly true, but close enough. "I had my last client cancel, so I sat down and talked to her about what she wanted."

"Something for the girls?" he asks.

"Yeah." I don't give him all the details, because that's Briar's story to tell. "She has a picture I need, so I'm going to swing by her place on my way home and take a look so I can start the sketch."

"You stopping by ours for dinner?" he asks.

"Nah, I think I'll head home and get started on this. You know how it is when there is a design in your mind."

He grins. "We have the best fucking job ever." He claps a hand on my shoulder. "You know you're always welcome." With that, he heads down the hall, and I follow him. We wave to Lyra and make our way outside.

My truck is barely in Park before I climb out and walk toward the front door. I knock and shove my hands into my pockets to avoid reaching for Briar when she opens the door. Then again, it could be Brogan who answers. Either way, this is the stance I've taken.

The door opens, and Briar smiles. "Hey, come on in."

I step into the house and smile when I hear the girls playing. "Enjoying their new toys?"

"They are." Briar smiles. "They've taken a picture of everything they can think of. You did good with those cameras. It was a great idea."

"Maybe you have future photographers on your hands."

"At this rate, you might be right."

"Mommy, who are you—Forrest!" Rayne says excitedly. She comes barreling toward me, wrapping her tiny arms around my legs.

"Forrest?" River joins us in the hallway. "Are you here to see us?" she asks, with awe in her voice.

I kneel and open my arms. They both move in for a hug. "Of course I'm here to see you. Have you been taking a lot of pictures?" I ask them, even though I already know the answer.

"So many," they reply at the same time.

"Come on, we'll show you." River grabs my hand.

I stand and offer Rayne my other hand and allow them to lead me into the living room.

"I'm sorry," Briar says, following us.

"I'm not. Show me these pictures." The girls race to grab their albums and climb up on the couch, one on either side of me. They hand me their albums, and I open one on each thigh and take turns flipping the pages, trying to give them both equal amounts of my attention.

"Wow. These are great, ladies."

"We know," they say, making me laugh.

"Girls, manners," Briar reminds them.

"Thank you," they chorus.

"I'll go grab the watch," Briar says.

"We're fine here, Momma. Do what you need to do." I keep flipping through the girls' pictures. Some I'm not exactly sure what I'm looking at, but there are several from their birthday party, and of their mom and their aunt. "I'm proud of you. You're doing an amazing job. Both of you," I praise them, closing the albums.

"We're real good at pictures," Rayne tells me.

"I can see that."

"Hey, Forrest, guess what?" River asks.

"What?"

"We're having sketti for dinner!"

"No way. I love spaghetti."

"Can you eat with us?" Rayne asks. "Mommy makes the best. Don't tell Aunt Brogan we don't want to hurt her feewings."

I laugh. "Your secret is safe with me."

"Here it is," Briar says, walking back into the room.

"Mommy, can Forrest eat sketti with us?" Rayne asks.

"Of course he can. Forrest, would you like to stay for dinner? It's just us. Brogan had a hair appointment in town."

"I don't want to impose."

"Pwease?" River asks.

"Oh, pwetty pwease?" Rayne asks.

These girls. So fucking cute. My eyes find Briar. "Are you sure?"

"Absolutely."

"I'd love to try your momma's spaghetti," I tell the twins. They cheer and bounce off the couch, tugging on each of my hands, and leading me toward the kitchen. "I guess it's time to eat?" I ask through my laughter.

"Yes!" the twins reply.

"Girls, go wash your hands."

"Forrest, you have to wash too." River changes direction and pulls me down the hallway.

I laugh and follow them. I watch as they step up on their stools at the double bathroom vanity and wash their hands.

"Now you," Rayne says.

"Yes, ma'am." I make quick work of washing my hands and drying them. "Let's eat," I tell them. They start giggling as if I'm the funniest person in the world and race down the hall to the kitchen with me hot on their heels.

"Take your seats," Briar tells them.

"What can I do to help?" I ask Briar.

"I've got it."

"I'm sure you do, but I can help. Come on, put me to work."

She smiles. "Thank you. Grab yourself something to drink, and I already have sippy cups for the girls on the island."

"What about you? What are you drinking?"

"If you don't mind, you can grab me a bottle of water."

"On it." I snag two bottles of water from the refrigerator before scooping up the girls' cups and placing them in front of them. "Where does Mommy sit?" I ask them.

"There." They point to the head of the table. I drop one of the water bottles there.

"You sit there." River points to the seat directly next to Briar.

"Aunt Brogan sits there." Rayne points to the opposite end of the table.

I set my water bottle down and move to help Briar. "Are those for the girls?" I ask. They are smaller plates.

"Yes."

"I'll take them." I grab them from her hands before she can object and deliver them to the twins. Briar follows me and places a plate for both of us on the table.

"I just need to get the garlic bread and the napkins." She looks around the table, making sure she has everything.

"Sit. I'll get it." She tries to argue, but I'm already on the move. I collect the basket of garlic bread and the stack of napkins from the island and place them in the center of the table.

As I sit with these three ladies, I can't help but wonder what it would be like if this was my life. If I had a wife and two daughters to come home to each night.

What would it be like if they were my family?

BRIAR 8

"THAT WAS DELICIOUS," FORREST SAYS, dropping his napkin to the table. His eyes are locked on mine. "Thank you, Briar."

"You're welcome." I smile, hoping to hide the effect of his deep voice saying my name does to me. Who am I kidding? It's more than just him saying my name. It's the man. I think back to his office earlier when I hugged him. I don't know why I did it. I don't make it a habit to hug men I don't know. Hell, any man, not since I lost my dad.

"I ate mine. All gone," Rayne tells him.

"Me too," River adds.

"I can see that. You ladies did a great job," Forrest compliments them.

I watch my daughters preen under his praise, proud as peacocks to have his attention. They're all smiles and nods, being on their best behavior cleaning their plates. This is their favorite meal, but there was no encouragement needed on my end for them to finish their dinners tonight.

"Will you play with us?" Rayne asks.

It's on the tip of my tongue to tell them Forrest has things he needs to do at home, but he beats me to a reply.

"You bet. Let me help your momma clean up, and then we can play." He stands and picks up our plates before he heads toward the sink.

"Forrest, you're a guest. You don't have to do that." I scramble to pick up cups and water bottles and rush after him.

"That's not how this works, Briar. You cooked. I can clean up. It's the least that I can do." He places the plates in the sink and begins rinsing them off.

"The dishwasher," I mumble.

"That I can do." He smiles as he continues washing up from dinner.

"You know, you don't have to stay and play with them. I know that's probably not high on your list of things you want to do on a Thursday night."

He stops rinsing and turns to look at me. "You'd be wrong, Briar. Your daughters are a breath of fresh air, and all I have waiting for me at home is silence. If you don't mind, I'd like to keep my word and stay."

"Yes. Of course," I squeak. I don't know what his motive is, but I'm going to remain on guard. The last thing I need is for my daughters to get attached to him, only for him to disappear from their lives. I know I can't project my trust issues on them, but they're four-year-old little girls. They don't know who to depend on. That's my job as their mother.

I don't give my trust freely, but my gut tells me we can believe him. I just don't know how long he'll be willing to spend this kind of time with my daughters. They're far too young to have their hearts broken.

"What about the leftovers?" he asks, placing the last dish into the dishwasher.

"Oh, I'll take care of that."

"Briar." His tone is a playful warning.

"Forrest," I parrot. I smile up at him. "Go on in and play with the twins. I'll be right behind you."

He studies me for several long heartbeats, until he leans in and places a kiss on the top of my head. He doesn't say a word. Not one syllable is muttered as he saunters off to the living room. I can hear the girls talking at once and his deep chuckle, but it sounds as if I'm in a tunnel.

He kissed me.

Me.

I mean, not really, but a kiss to the top of my head counts. It's been—never. Never has a man made me feel like this. Like my heart is going to pound right out of my chest. I realize I'm holding on to the counter and shake my head. That man has literally made my knees go weak.

This can't happen.

He's getting too close.

Pulling myself out of my Forrest trance, I rush to get the leftovers put away so I can join them just as I said I would. I'm certain he won't stay long, and then I can tear apart every second of my day from the time I stepped into Everlasting Ink earlier this evening.

When I walk into the living room, I'm not sure what I expected to find. What I do know is that I didn't expect to find Forrest with his back against the couch while he sits on the floor and lets my daughters put bows in his hair.

He looks up when he hears me and grins. "What do you think, Momma? Looks good, right?" he asks.

"We're making Forrest pretty, Mommy," Rayne tells me.

"I can see that." What I don't say is that he was just fine without the pink and purple bows. I also don't tell them the word they're looking for is sexy. That would be inappropriate to teach my four-year-old daughters.

"He's our patient," River explains.

"Sweetheart, patients are for doctors. If you're doing his hair, he would be your client or your customer."

"Do you want to be that, Forty?" River asks him.

"Forty?" I question.

"That's what Emerson used to call me. She still does sometimes."

"We get to call him Forty cause hims our friend," Rayne says proudly.

"He," I correct her.

"We making you beautiful, Forty," River says.

"Nails next," Rayne tells him.

"Girls, I don't think Forrest wants you to paint his nails. You can paint Mommy's nails."

"It's fine," Forrest tells me. "Let them have their fun. What color are you ladies thinking?" he asks the girls. He holds his hands out for them to inspect.

"Let's go get the polish, sissy," Rayne tells her sister. They climb off the couch and rush down the hall to their room.

"I'm so sorry. You can leave and I'll tell them something came up," I tell Forrest.

"What?" He looks horrified at the thought. "I'm not leaving. They're looking forward to this. I could never disappoint them like that."

Something happens inside me. Something I can't explain. My belly twists, and my heart, it feels like it's melting at his words and confession. "They've never been around men," I confess. My voice is gravelly as I let my admission slip free. "They like you."

"I like them. They're great girls, Briar. You've done an incredible job with them."

That melting sensation intensifies, and I feel it everywhere. What is this man doing to me?

Forrest is watching me. His gaze is intense, and I can't help but smile at him. Here is this man who is tall with broad shoulders and covered in tattoos sitting on my living room floor letting my four-year-old daughters do whatever they want to him, and from the looks of it, he wants to be here.

How is that possible?

I need to ask him... to protect not only their heart but mine if the way it's raging against my rib cage is any indication. However, before I can form the words, the girls are racing back into the room. Forrest holds his arms out, spreading his fingers out for the girls.

"What did you decide on?" he asks them.

"I got purple sparkles." River holds up the bottle of sparkling purple fingernail polish to show him.

"Excellent choice." He smiles at her. I can see her stand a little taller at his approval. "What about you, Rayne?"

"I got pink sparkles. See." She shoves the bottle close to his face, and he chuckles.

"Perfect. Razzle dazzle me, ladies." He's relaxed as the girls each move a hand to the hardwood floor and flip to their bellies to paint his nails. When they struggle to open the bottles, he helps them with ease, handing them back and placing his palms flat against the floor.

"Forrest." He turns his head to look at me as I ask, "Are you sure?"

"Absolutely." The smile he gives me is genuine.

Curling up in the chair, I listen as my daughters talk to him, and he engages in their conversation. The three of them are lost in their own little world. I wish I could record this moment because my girls, they're smiling and happy, and the tattooed sex god in my home is the one to thank for that.

I hear the front door open, and I know it's Brogan coming home. "Hey," she says cautiously.

"Hi, Aunt Brogan!" the girls call loudly.

"Hey, girls. Whatcha doing there?"

"Oh, we're making Forty beautiful," River explains.

"Razzle"—Forrest nods to River—"and Dazzle"—and nods toward Rayne—"are doing their thing. Good to see you, Brogan," Forrest greets her.

"We're not razzle dazzle." Rayne giggles. "I'm Rayne." She points to her chest, almost tipping the bottle of nail polish over.

"I'm River, silly," River adds.

"Well, you're calling me Forty, just like my sister does. It's only right I have a nickname for the two of you."

"I'm Razzle." River points to her chest.

"That's right." Forrest grins at her.

"And I'm Dazzle." Rayne nods as if she accepts the new nickname.

"What about Mommy?" River asks.

"She's momma. She'll always be your momma."

"But she's not *your* momma," River points out.

"No, but being your momma is her most important job ever, so the name fits."

The girls nod, seeming to accept that answer.

"What about Aunt Brogan?"

"She's always going to be Aunt Brogan. She's equally as important as your momma, so Aunt Brogan sticks."

"So, you just have names for us?" Rayne asks with awe in her voice.

"My niece, Lilly. Do you remember Lilly?"

"She's a baby," the girls answer at the same time.

"That's right. She's my Lilly Bug."

"So just babies and girls, not mommies or aunts. Right, Forty?" River asks, always inquisitive.

"That's right."

"I left a plate for you in the microwave," I tell Brogan.

Brogan nods before motioning for me to follow her. "Girls, are you okay for a few minutes while I go talk to Aunt Brogan?"

"We have our Forty," Rayne tells me.

Just like that, my twin girls have become possessive of the sexy man, and I don't know how I feel about that, but there is nothing I can do at the moment. Besides, I need to talk to my sister. After standing from the chair, I make my way to the kitchen, knowing my sister is going to have questions.

"Spaghetti and meatballs," I say when I enter the kitchen.

"I didn't know we were having company."

"I didn't either. Not really. I mean, I knew he was stopping by, but I didn't expect him to stay for dinner, and that"—I point behind me toward the living room—"I did not expect that."

"What is *that* exactly?"

I sigh, knowing she won't let up until I tell her. "I went to Everlasting Ink to get on the books for my tattoo. Forrest was there. He had a cancellation and took me back to his room to discuss what I wanted. He wanted to see Dad's pocket watch and said he could stop by on his way home to take a few pictures and look at it."

"When you told me you stopped to get on the books before I left for my hair appointment, you left that out." She's grinning, so I know she's not pissed at me for not telling her.

"Yeah, I was going to tell you when you got home. Anyway, he shows up and the girls think he's here for them and invite him for dinner. He said if it was okay with me, he would stay, and I couldn't say no. So we had dinner."

"And?"

"And he helped with the girls and helped clean up. They asked him to stay and play, and I gave him an out, but he didn't take it."

"What do you mean, you gave him an out? Details, Briar. I need details." The microwave beeps and she pulls her plate out, sits at the island, and digs into her dinner.

"I just told them that I'm sure he had more important things to do."

"What did he say?" She's eating, but her eyes are glued to mine.

"Something about nothing waiting at home for him but an empty house or something like that." I know exactly what he said and could recite it word for word, but I'm not going to. Paraphrasing is all she needs. His words are mine, and I groan inwardly at my possession of a conversation. It must be something in the air.

"And he just let the girls put bows in his hair and paint his nails?"

"He did. I tried to give him an out for the nails too. I told him he could go while the girls were in their room picking out colors and he looked horrified at the mere thought of disappointing them. He said as much too."

Brogan grins. "I like him."

"He's a nice guy. However, I don't want the girls getting attached to him."

Brogan sets her fork down on the corner of her plate and wipes her mouth. "That night was different for you than it was for me. I know that. However, I want you to be happy, Briar. You can't keep living pushing everyone away."

"I'm not," I counter. "We've had two girls' nights. The ladies are great."

She rolls her eyes. "You know exactly what I mean. They're not all bad."

"They're not all good either."

She stares at me for so long that I shift my stance under her gaze.

"You like him. I know you do. He wouldn't have been invited into our home with the girls if you didn't. He wouldn't be in the living room alone with the girls if you didn't."

"He's Emerson's brother." I shrug.

"Stop it. Just stop, Briar. At least think about it. Don't push him away. You can keep giving him choices. Let him decide if he wants to be around you and the girls."

"Maybe he's trying to get to you."

She laughs. Not just a "ha ha, you're funny" laugh. No, this one of those "tosses her head back, eyes closed, body shaking" kind of laughs.

"What's so funny?"

"That man is not here for me. I walked through the door, and he barely glanced at me when he said hello."

"That's because he was giving his attention to the girls."

"Sure, we'll go with that."

"I need to get back in there." I point over my shoulder.

"Sure. I'm going to finish up, and then I'll make myself scarce."

"No. This is your home." I don't want her to feel as though she's not welcome here because we have a guest.

"I know that," she says gently, realizing she's hit a nerve with me. "I'll say hello, and I have a book I've been dying to start. Tonight sounds like the perfect night to do that."

For the—hell, I've lost count how many times this man has taken me by surprise tonight. What I do know is I didn't expect to find him sitting on the couch with my girls on either side of him, reading them a story. I stop and stare as I listen to him change his voice to fit the book. The girls are enthralled and not moving a muscle as he reads to them. I stand here, lost in the sight before me.

"Briar," Brogan whispers. She rests her head on my shoulder, wrapping her arms around me. "That's—I think my ovaries just exploded."

I nod. I can't admit... okay, I *won't* admit that I feel as though mine did too. I've never met a man like Forrest. Not that there have been a lot of men in my life. Not since the night I got pregnant. I've been too busy being a single mom, grieving the loss of my father, and just living one day at a time.

When Forrest closes the book, Brogan steps away from me, and I move into the room. "Girls, it's time for bed," I tell them.

"Forrest, can you tuck us in?" River asks.

"If it's okay with your momma, I'd love to."

"Please, Mommy?" the girls beg.

I glance at Forrest, and he gives me a subtle nod. "Okay, go get in your jammies and brush your teeth."

"I'll help," Brogan says. "Forrest, it was good to see you."

"You too," he replies, and this time I see it. He barely glances at her. His eyes are all for me. Heat coats my cheeks. I'm not used to having a man's attention. Not like this. One look has me feeling as though I could combust.

"They're great," he says, breaking the ice.

"Thank you. I'm sorry for that." I point to his hair and to his nails.

He shrugs. "Their smiles were worth it."

"Are you always this... charming?" I ask him.

A slow, sexy grin pulls at the corner of his mouth. "You think I'm charming?"

I wave him off, hoping like hell I appear to be unaffected. "You know what I mean."

"I'm just me, Briar. I'm a man who hasn't been able to stop thinking about you since the twins' birthday party. I heard your voice today, and I knew it was you. I had to see you. Then tonight—this—it was perfect."

I scoff. "Spending your evening with my four-year-old daughters doing your hair in bows and painting your nails was perfect?" I'm being a bitch for no reason, but I can't seem to help myself. His confession softened my heart, and I can feel the bricks around it starting to crack. I'm not ready for that.

"Yes. Great food, and even better company."

"What do you want, Forrest?"

"I want to get to know you. I've never had a woman consume my thoughts like this. Tell me you feel this?"

"I'm a single mom."

"I know that."

"What happens when they get attached to you and you decide you don't want to be around anymore? I know heartbreak is inevitable, but I'd like for them to live a little longer without it."

He stands from his seat on the couch. It takes him a few strides of those long-ass legs of his to be standing in front of me. He bends his knees so we are eye to eye. "I'm not here to hurt you or them. I'm here because I want to be. I feel a connection to you, and I can't stop thinking about you. Let me show you."

"I—I don't know how. I don't know if I can."

"Baby steps," he assures me. "We'll take baby steps and when you know, when you're ready, you tell me."

"Forty!" the twins yell down the hall. "We're ready!" they call out.

A smile breaks out across his face. "Hold that thought." He stands, and this time when he leans in, he presses his lips to my forehead. He saunters off down the hallway as if he's been here a thousand times. It takes a few seconds, but my legs finally start to work, and I follow after him.

"Did you ladies brush your teeth like your momma asked?" he asks them.

I stand in the doorway watching.

"Yes."

"Perfect." He walks over to River's bed. He leans down and tucks the blanket around her body, making her look like a tiny human burrito. "Night, Razzle." He moves and repeats the same process with Rayne. "Night, Dazzle."

"Night, Forty," they say together.

He stands and walks toward me. I go in and kiss the girls goodnight before meeting him in the hallway. Forrest places his hand on the small of my back and leads me back toward the living room.

"I won't push you, Briar. But this"—he waves his free hand between us—"whatever it is, we deserve to see if it can be more."

"This is... out of left field."

"Not really. I would have worn my sister or Monroe down for your number, eventually. You coming into the shop today was meant to be."

I open my mouth to speak, but the words won't come. My brain is too busy trying to process what's happening. He wants me.

"Sleep on it. I left my card that has my cell phone number on the coffee table." With his hand still locked with mine, he leads us to the front door. "Goodnight." His lips press to my cheek, and then he's gone. I stand in the doorway watching as he leaves until I can no longer see his taillights.

It's not until I'm in the house, sitting on the couch, trying to wrap my head around today's turn of events that I realize I didn't show him the pocket watch. Picking up his business card, I contemplate texting him pictures but ultimately decide not to. Maybe I can have Brogan stop by the shop and let him take his pictures? Then again, maybe having Forrest do my tattoo isn't the best idea.

My head is a mess, and nothing needs to be decided tonight. I lock up the house, turn off the lights, and head to my room. I contemplate knocking on Brogan's door, but I don't even know what I would say. I need to process before I talk about it.

FIVE DAYS. THAT'S HOW LONG it's been since I had dinner at Briar's place with her and the girls. Five days with no calls, no text messages, no drop-ins at the shop. Nothing. Absolutely nothing from her in five days.

Five days of the guys giving me shit for having pink and purple sparkly painted fingernails. It's been a good conversation piece with clients. I finally broke down last night and went over to my sister's and used some of her remover to take it off. I felt guilty for doing it. That's crazy, right? It's just the thought of hurting River and Rayne's feelings guts me.

What's worse, I was supposed to be stopping by Briar's to look at her dad's pocket watch that night, but all I could see was her and her daughters. As soon as I stepped through the door, all thoughts of the watch were pushed to the back of my mind. When I pulled away that night, I realized I had forgotten, but I didn't want to go back in after already saying goodbye. I thought it would be another excuse to see her.

It's been five long days.

I assumed she would reach out. I left her my number, but she hasn't. I've been kicking myself in the ass because I didn't get her number. That means, today, it's time to take drastic measures.

Glancing at the time on my phone, I see it's just after seven. If the girls have the same routine as the night I was there, they will be in bed soon. Decision made, I hit Emerson's contact and place the phone to my ear.

"What's up, big brother?" she answers.

"Just holding down the couch," I tell her. "I have a favor."

"Sure."

Just like that, she's agreeing, but she also doesn't know what I'm asking for. "I need Briar's number."

"Briar?"

"Yes. She came to the shop, and we talked about her tattoo, but I forgot to get her number, and I have some questions about her piece."

"You forgot to get her number? Did she not fill out an intake form?"

"Nope."

"That's... unusual," she replies.

I know I'm busted. She's going to reach out to Lyra and Drake, the two shop employees who work the desk and find out why. Emerson trained them, after all. "It's not a big deal, but I need to call her and give her an update."

"Well, I love you, Forty, but I can't just give out her number without asking her. Let me text her."

"Fine. Call me back."

"No need. I put you on speaker and sent the message. She just read it. Oh, she's replying. And... she says it's fine. I'll text it to you."

"Thanks, kid."

"Married and a mom," she says, reminding me.

"Love you, kid."

She chuckles at my refusal to call her by her name. She will always be my kid sister.

"Love you, too, Forty."

The call ends, and I immediately open her text message and save Briar's contact. Instead of a normal call, I hit video call. It's been five long fucking days since I've laid eyes on her. She's consumed my thoughts, and I just need to see her. Besides, maybe the twins will be up and I can say goodnight to them.

The call connects, and her face appears on the screen. She's sitting down, and the girls are on either side of her. I smile. "Hey, ladies."

"Forty!" The girls wiggle with excitement and try to get closer to the phone.

"Razzle, Dazzle, are you being good for your momma?"

"We're reading a story," River tells me.

"And then we have to go to bed," Rayne adds.

"Sleep is important," I tell them.

"That's what Mommy says," Rayne says solemnly.

"Girls, go potty and get in bed. I'll be there soon to tuck you in."

"Bye, Forty. Wait." River grabs the phone and holds it so close to her face that I can barely distinguish her features. "When are you coming to see us again?"

"Soon." It's a promise I intend to keep. "I'll talk to your mom, and we'll make plans."

"Okay."

"Goodnight, Forty," they chorus.

"I'll be right there," Briar calls after them. She watches them walk away before her gaze comes back to the phone.

"Hey, Momma." I grin at her.

Her eyes soften. "Hey, Forrest."

"I was so busy enjoying the company of the Pearce ladies last week, I forgot to take a few pictures of your dad's pocket watch."

"Yeah, we kind of got sidetracked."

"No regrets." My reply is instant. I need her to know that hanging out with her and her daughters was the highlight of my week.

"Do you want me to send you a few pictures?" she asks, biting down on her bottom lip.

"I think seeing it in person would be better." It's a lie. A picture is fine, but I want to see her, and not through this damn phone.

"Oh, okay. When are you at the shop? I can drop by and show it to you."

"You know, I'm actually off tomorrow. Why don't you come over around six and I can repay you for the dinner you fed me last week? Brogan is welcome too," I add. Sure, that's not much of a date, but I'll take Briar anyway that I can get her.

"That's not necessary, Forrest."

"I know it's not, but I want to. Nothing fancy. I'll toss some burgers and hot dogs on the grill. Do the girls still like hot dogs?" I remember when Emerson was little she would change her likes by the day.

"They do, but you don't have to go to any trouble."

"It's no trouble, Briar. I'll text you my address."

"Sure. Okay. Six tomorrow."

"It's a date."

Her eyes widen, and I have to bite down on the inside of my cheek to hide my smirk.

"I better go tuck them in."

"Give them a kiss from me," I tell her. Her eyes widen again, as if she can't believe I said that. Was it too much? Hell, I don't know. I'm out of my depth here, but I know that if I was there, I'd be helping tuck them into bed, and a kiss to the cheek or forehead would be a given.

"Night, Forrest."

"Night, Briar."

She waves and ends the call.

Tossing my phone on the couch, I close my eyes and imagine the three of them here in my space. Thinking about them here brings a smile to my face. This quiet house will be full of life for one night.

Today was my day off. I've cleaned all day. Not that my house was nasty, but Briar and the girls are coming over and I need—want to make a good impression. It's just after four, and I'm full of excited energy. I've been really good. I've only texted her once to send her my address. The only reply I got was a thank-you. I can't take it anymore. Grabbing my phone from the coffee table, I fire off a text.

Me: *I have chips, and I was going to make some mac and cheese for the girls. My internet search tells me that it's a hit with kids.*

Briar: *Actually, the girls are going to stay here with Brogan.*

I stare at her message, unsure of how to take it. Does she not want me around her daughters?

Me: *I'll miss them. What about you? Mac and cheese?*

Briar: *You don't have to feed me dinner, Forrest.*

Me: *I'm feeding you, Briar.*

I can imagine her biting down on her bottom lip.

Briar: *Burger and chips are fine. Nothing fancy is necessary.*

Me: *How about steak?*

Briar: *Nothing fancy. Burgers are fine.*

Me: *Do you eat steak?*

Briar: *I do.*

Me: *How do you like it cooked?*

Briar: *Well done.*

Me: *Well, since it's just going to be us, I'll mix up the menu a little. See you at six.*

Briar: *Okay.*

One single word. I can't get a read on her. I don't know if she's dreading seeing me or if she's excited. Is she trying to downplay her excitement? Fuck, why does this have to be so damn complicated?

I contemplate calling Roman or Legend but decide against it. I've got this. This went from seeing her and her daughters, and maybe her sister, to just the two of us. Quickly, I stand from the couch, grab my keys, and tap my back pocket, making sure I have my wallet before heading out the door.

Briar just changed my plans for the night, and I'm more than okay with that. A quick trip to the store and a new plan falls into place.

By the time six o'clock rolls around, I have a vase of flowers sitting on the kitchen island for her. Steaks are soaking in marinade, baked potatoes are already on the grill, and the salad is mixed in the fridge. I have wine, beer, sweet tea, bottled water, and a few kinds of pop to offer her to drink. I even have juice boxes and a new gallon of milk that I'd already bought for the girls, and spill-proof cups. I'll need them eventually for Lilly, and Legend and Monroe's new baby, anyway.

When I hear her car pull into the driveway, I rush toward the door and pause. Pulling in a deep breath, I slowly exhale before opening it. Should I let her knock? Probably. However, she's here, and it's been six days since I've seen her in the flesh. When all I've been thinking about is her, having chill or whatever you want to call it isn't necessary.

I smile widely as she approaches the front porch. "Briar."

"Hey, Forrest." She waves and smiles shyly.

She steps up onto the porch, and I lean in and kiss her cheek. "Come on in. The potatoes are already on the grill. I need to get the steaks going."

"I hope you didn't go through a lot of trouble. Anything is fine."

She's wrong. This is our first date. She might not know that yet, but that's what this is, and anything isn't fine. I need to show her I want to see what this is between us. I need to understand why I can't stop thinking about her.

"No trouble. Come on in. What would you like to drink?" I ramble off my options.

"You drink a lot of juice boxes, do you?" she teases.

"I bought those for the girls when I thought they would be here with you."

"Forrest." Her tone is soft, and her eyes sparkle. "You didn't need to do that."

"I want to. So, what will it be?"

"Just water for now. What can I do to help?"

"Nothing. I'm all set." I hand her a bottle of water. "Let me toss these steaks on the grill, and I'll be right in."

"I can come and keep you company."

"You sure? It's hot as hell out there."

"I won't melt." She chuckles.

"Come on, then, Momma. Let's get these on and we can chat while they're cooking. Wait, I have salad too. Do you want that now or later?"

"Later is fine."

I nod, letting her know I heard her. With the steaks in one hand, I open the door with the other, and motion for her to step out onto the deck.

"Need this?" she asks, holding up the second bottle of water I placed on the island.

"Yes. Thanks."

She grabs my bottle of water and follows me out onto the deck. I check on the potatoes that are almost done and place the steaks on the grill before taking a seat across from her at the patio table. "How was your day?"

"Good. Uneventful. There's not much excitement with medical coding."

"Do you enjoy it?"

"I do. It was the right choice for me at the time. I was young and had the twins to take care of. Choosing a career that allowed me to work from home made sense. I was lucky enough to find a position from home when we lived in Nashville and when we moved to Ashby."

"So you're from Nashville?"

"Born and raised. What about you?"

"Ashby native. I've lived here all my life."

"It's a nice town. I'm glad I decided to move here to raise the girls."

"And Brogan decided to tag along?" I'm trying to learn more about her without prying too much.

"Yeah. We lost our mom when we were young. Just before our second birthday. Car accident."

"Damn," I mutter. "That's tough. I'm sorry for your loss."

She smiles and shrugs. "We didn't know her. We don't remember her. We have pictures. Our dad, he was incredible. He made sure we had everything we needed. We never felt like we were missing the love of a parent. Of course, we missed having a mom, but he talked about her constantly, and her memory was kept alive."

"I noticed you said was."

"Yeah, we lost him too." She clears her throat. "He was in the hospital at the same time I was delivering the twins. He was fighting stage four pancreatic cancer. We lost him a few days later." Her eyes well with tears, but she blinks a few times, pushing them away.

"Briar." I don't know what to say to that. I know that there is nothing I can say that would make her feel any better. Now the reasoning behind her tattoo being for her father as well makes even more sense. "Bring it in, Momma." I stand, move to her side of the table, and wrap her in a hug where she sits. She half laughs, half sobs, and I hold her a little tighter. Eventually, I have to pull away. I wipe her tears with my thumb before forcing myself to take my seat.

"My parents are assholes," I blurt out my confession. "They're alcoholics who never should have been able to have kids. There are ten years between Emerson and me. I did the best I could. When I was old enough and moved out, I took her every weekend and every other time my parents would allow it. Honestly, they didn't care. They were only worried about the welfare check that came their way until she turned eighteen."

"That's tough."

"As soon as I could, I bought this place." I point to the house. "I wanted her to have a safe place. A true home. The day she turned eighteen, I moved her in with me and paid her way through college."

"And she's married to Roman, who works with you," she says, as she tries to keep everyone straight.

I laugh. "Yeah, one of my best friends. He's good to her, and they're happy. That's all I want for her. For both of them."

"So, you were fine with it?" She raises an eyebrow, and her tone tells me she's surprised that I would be.

"Not at first, but I'd have to be blind to not see the love between the two of them."

She's quiet, and I feel exposed. I wanted her to know about my life, but I also hate to talk about it. Standing, I turn the steaks before returning to my seat. I want to ask her more. I want to ask about the girls' dad. I want to know... everything. However, I need to pace myself.

"I have a lot of ideas for your tattoo," I tell her.

Her entire body seems to relax at the subject change. "Yeah?"

"I guess you inspire me." I wink. She laughs, and I love the sound and the way her face lights up.

"I don't know about that. Speaking of tattoos." She reaches into her small purse that's still hanging across her body, pulls out the pocket watch, and hands it to me.

I take it and inspect it, my mind already going crazy with ideas and details for the tattoo design. "Do you mind if I take some pictures?" I ask her.

"Of course not."

After digging my phone out of my pocket, I zoom in and take several pictures from different angles before handing it back to her. "Thank you."

"I should be the one thanking you. I feel like you're putting a lot of work into this."

"I would love to tell you that you're special. Well, you are special, but this is what we do. We make sure every client is in love with their design before we ever start. We've made a name for ourselves, not just from our talent with a tattoo gun, but the artistry as well."

"I'll admit I did some internet research after Emerson and Monroe told me your shop was the best. Not that I didn't trust them, but this is permanent."

"Exactly. We want it to be everything you could have ever dreamed it would be before we even start to lay the ink."

"Do all of your clients get a steak dinner?" she asks curiously.

I smile. "Nope. You're the first client I've ever invited to my home."

"For dinner."

"For our first date."

Her lips part, but she quickly recovers. "Who said this was a date?"

"Well, I invited you over. We're having dinner, good conversation, and I bought you flowers."

"What?"

I've managed to surprise her. "Those." I point to the house and the bouquet on the kitchen island. "I was so excited to see you. I didn't give them to you when you first got here. You scrambled my brain, Briar."

"You bought me flowers?"

"That's first date appropriate, right? We could call this our second date, but the last one wasn't planned." I've shocked her, so I give her time to process the news. I stand and check on dinner. It's ready. "Time to eat." I turn off the grill.

"Let me help." She hops up from her chair and pulls open the patio door. "What can I do?"

"Plates are in the cabinet to the right of the sink. Grab us two and start making yours. I'm going to get the salad. I have ranch and French."

"Ranch, please."

I smile because ranch is also my favorite. Emerson eats both, which is why I have both. We work together, making plates and our salads before sitting down together at the table. The conversation flows easily. The more time I spend with her, the more I crave time with her.

"This was great," she says, wiping her mouth. "I can't eat another bite."

"Well, I guess you'll just have to take some dessert home with you."

"No room," she groans.

I stand with a chuckle and clear our plates. She stands to help, but I wave her off. "Oh no, that's not how this works," she says, trying to imitate me. "You cooked. I clean."

I smile. "Fine, I'll rinse, and you can load the dishwasher."

"Deal."

We work in comfortable silence. When the kitchen is cleaned, I offer her dessert again, which is just a pack of chocolate chip cookies I picked up at the store earlier, but she declines.

"I should be getting home. I want to be there to put the girls to bed."

"Sure. Let me grab your flowers and the cookies."

"Oh, we don't need those."

"Tell the girls I bought them for them, and the flowers are for you." I move to the kitchen and grab both, meeting her at the door. She opens the door for me and closes it behind us as we walk toward her car.

"Thank you, Forrest. For dinner, the flowers, cookies, and my tattoo. I'm really excited to see what you come up with, and... I'm glad it was you I got scheduled with."

I don't tell her that whoever she was scheduled with, I would have made damn sure her name showed up on my schedule instead. It sounds insane even to me, so I keep that information to myself.

"You're welcome, and me too."

She straps the flowers into the passenger seat and sets the cookies next to them. She closes the door and smiles at me.

Unable to help myself, I lace her fingers with mine and walk with her to the driver's side of her car. "When can we do this again?"

She stares up at me. "I'm a single mom."

"I know. Razzle and Dazzle are great." I wink at her, and she chuckles.

"This is my first date since the girls were born. If that's what we're calling it."

Something possessive washes over me that it's been years since another man has had her attention like I did tonight. "Understood."

"What do you understand, Forrest?"

Keeping one hand laced with hers, I place the other against her cheek. "I understand that this is something new not only for you but for your girls. I understand that there are three hearts involved. Wait, four, because mine should be included in this as well." I pause to collect my thoughts as she stares into my eyes. "I understand that we're going to need to take baby steps. I understand that those girls are your first priority, and I'll handle that however you want. I'll follow your lead. I understand that I really like you, Briar. The more time we spend together, the more that feeling grows. I've never felt this—whatever it is. I think we owe it to ourselves to see what we could be together."

"I don't want their hearts to be broken."

"I promise you, no matter what happens, I will be in their lives. I'm an adult, and it might kill me to not have you, but I will never turn my back on those girls. If this doesn't work out, I'll still be there for them, and for you."

"You're saying all the right things."

"But?"

"I'm going to need for you to show me, Forrest. My trust was broken and now, I don't give it freely."

"Done."

"Just like that? What if it's weeks, months, or even years? I haven't dated for so long. I don't know...." Her voice trails off.

"You tell me when you're ready. I'll be here. I'll follow your lead with the girls. I just want to spend time with you. I would be honored if you would give me the chance to show you I'm a man of my word."

Indecision is written all over her face.

"Take some time. Think about it. Can I call you? Text you while you're thinking?"

She nods. "I'd like that."

Leaning down, I press a soft kiss to her lips. Just a peck, but it lights a fire inside me. "Drive safe, Momma. Kiss the girls for me."

"Bye, Forrest." She opens her door and slides into the driver's seat. I step back and watch her as she pulls out of my driveway. I stand here until I can no longer see her before heading into the house.

I laid it all out on the line tonight. I know she's scared, but she doesn't have to be. I want her, and I know she's a single mom. Those girls are a part of her, just one of many parts that I can't wait to explore.

BRIAR 10

WHEN I TOLD FORREST HE could text and call me, I didn't think it would be something he'd do every single day. That was Wednesday. It's now Saturday morning and I'm staring at the same text I've woken up to the last three days.

> **Forrest:** Morning, beautiful.

In the sanctuary of my bedroom, I don't hide my smile at seeing his message. Forrest is unlike anyone I've ever met. He's kind, funny, and direct. He doesn't hide away from discussing how he's feeling. My heart flutters when I think about him. That's been a lot lately, more so since dinner at his place earlier this week.

I desperately want to trust in him and his intentions. I know there are smooth-talking men. I fell for one once, and it ended in pain and a night that changed the course of my life.

> **Me:** Good morning.

The pitter-patter of feet on the hardwood floor has me throwing off the covers and climbing out of bed. The girls will need breakfast, and then we need to go grocery shopping. We're all getting together tonight at Emerson's house for girls' night.

The kids will be there. Emerson wanted the twins to come and have a play date with Lilly, and all the other ladies are coming so we can have a "big girls' and little girls'" day. Those are Emerson's words, not mine.

I'm a little worried about hanging out with all of them tonight. I don't know what Forrest has told them—if anything—and he's going to be right next door. I'm out of my element here. Not only that, but here's this man who is older than me and has his life together. He says he's interested, but I have two little girls to think about. I can't just dive headfirst into whatever this is and hope for the best.

Forrest says he knows there are four hearts involved, and I'll admit that was sweet. His words relaxed me and endeared me to him even more, but they're words. I know words can be empty. It's actions and time that speak volumes. Time to make sure it's not an act. Time to get to know him and for him to know me. There is still so much he doesn't know, and there is this huge fear that when he finds out, he'll change his mind.

"Mommy!" the girls sing when I reach the living room. They're sitting on the couch with their blankets and Rayne has the remote in her hand. At four, they are smarter than most adults. The TV is on and their favorite cartoon is playing.

"Good morning." I smile as I take a seat next to them on the couch. "What do you want for breakfast?"

"Pancakes." Their reply is instant.

"Pancakes it is." I kiss their cheeks and then head toward the kitchen to make breakfast.

"Mommy, can we hold the baby?" Rayne asks.

My eyes find Emerson's and she nods. "Sure, but you have to sit on the couch." The girls scramble to the couch, sit side by side, and pat their laps.

"Who's first?" Emerson asks.

"We can hold her together," River tells her.

"Right. I should have thought of that." Emerson smiles. She places Lilly in their laps and bends to make sure she doesn't fall.

"Hi, Lilly," River says.

"We're your friends," Rayne says.

"My heart," Monroe says. "How in the he—heck do you stand the cuteness?" she asks me.

"We used to be the cuteness." Brogan chuckles. "I guess we're just used to it."

"Mommy, we want a baby," River tells me.

"Oh, you do, do you?" I ask, smiling at my daughters.

"Yep," they answer proudly.

"Monroe is going to have a baby. Then you'll have one for each of you," I tell them. I'm not ashamed that I'm directing their interest from me to Monroe.

"Another baby?" Their eyes are wide.

"I'm going to need your help. You girls are so good with Lilly. I'll need help with this baby too," Monroe tells them.

"We're good helpers," Rayne tells her.

"Real good," River adds.

We're all laughing when the front door opens.

"Was there a party I wasn't invited to?" a male voice asks. It's a voice I recognize all too well, one that I hear in my sleep these days.

"Forty!" the girls cheer.

Forrest walks into the room, and his eyes immediately find mine. He doesn't stop until he's standing in front of the couch. He crouches down and smiles at my girls. "Razzle, Dazzle, I didn't know you were going to be here."

"We're having girls' night," River explains.

"And we're helping with the baby," Rayne adds.

"I can see that." He smiles at them as he offers Lilly his finger, which she holds onto and turns his smile on me. "Hey, Momma."

"Hi."

Emerson lifts Lilly from the twins' laps and stands. "I thought you were at the shop with Rome tonight?" Emerson asks.

"I was. I finished the piece I was working on. We just had some shading to wrap it up. Rome is almost finished, and he'll be on his way home."

"Well, y'all need to go to your place," Emerson tells him.

"Or mine," Monroe offers. "Legend is there."

"I actually came to take Lilly to my place," he tells his sister.

"Lills, you want to go hang out with Uncle Forrest?" she asks her daughter. Forrest stands and reaches for Lilly. She leans into him as he pulls her into his arms.

"Of course she does," Forrest answers, placing a kiss to her cheek. Lilly rests her head on his shoulder, and he snuggles her close.

"Mommy, we want to go with Forty too," Rayne says.

"Can we, Mommy? Please?" Rayne asks.

They're bouncing on the balls of their feet, anxious for my answer. "Girls—" I start, but Forrest interrupts me.

"If your mommy says it's okay, it's fine with me," Forrest tells them. All three turn to look at me.

"Three is a lot to handle," I tell him.

"Pfft, we've got this. Razzle and Dazzle will be my big helpers with Lilly bug."

"Yeah, we're helpers," the girls announce proudly.

"Girls, Forrest has worked all day. He needs to rest."

"Mommy, he said we could. Right, Forrest?" River asks.

"You girls are always welcome, but we have to listen to your mom."

"Please?" Their lips jut out and I know tears are about to flow.

"Girls, let's go get a snack," Brogan suggests.

"We don't want a snack," Rayne says.

Forrest nods for me to follow him into the hallway. I stand, aware that all eyes are on us. He hands Lilly off to Emerson, and with his hand on the small of my back, leads me away from all the eyes and ears.

In the hallway, he moves us so that I'm standing with my back against the wall, and steps in close. "Hi." His voice is husky.

"Hi."

He tucks my hair behind my ear. "Tell me what you're thinking?"

How am I supposed to think with him this close to me? Touching me? I take a deep breath and gather my thoughts. "I'm thinking you don't want to spend the rest of your Saturday night watching my daughters."

"You'd think wrong. I'd love for them to come and help me with Lilly. You and your girls are welcome at my place anytime, Briar."

"How old are you?" I blurt.

"I'm thirty-two."

"I'm a twenty-two-year-old single mom." He's ten years older than me. Surely, he wants his own family, not a ready-made one. I can hear Brogan's voice in my head telling me I have to stop looking for and thinking the worst of everyone because of my past. I need to keep looking forward.

"You're a twenty-two-year-old beautiful, single mom with two adorable daughters who I happen to adore as much as I do their mother."

"Sweet words."

"I promise you they will be safe with me, Briar. I'd never let anything happen to them." His gaze is penetrating as he wills me to believe him.

"Trust is hard for me."

"I know. Baby steps. I'll be right next door. You can come and check on them or text me anytime you want. Let me take them with Lilly, and you ladies can have some adult time. Ask them about me. Sure, it's my sister and her best friend, but they won't bullshit you."

"I would never do that to you."

"I know, which is why I'm telling you to."

"I don't know if I'm ready for this."

"For what? Me watching the girls?"

"*You*, Forrest. I don't know if I'm ready for you. For this... invisible string that seems to keep me tethered to you even when you're not around. I just don't know."

"I'm not rushing you. You know where I stand. Regardless, I made a promise that I would always be there for the girls, and this will give you a small breather. Every parent needs a break now and then."

I process his words. I'm being unreasonable, but I don't know how to get past it. I want more than anything to not fear every man's intentions, but I'm scarred. Damaged goods, if you will.

"Come here." He stands back to his full height and tugs me into his arms, and I go willingly. He embraces me so tightly, it's hard to understand why I'm pushing back with him. "You can trust me, Briar. I'll prove it to you."

"Okay." The words slip from my lips, and I know I need to take this step. I want this with him. I want to be free to have relationships, and being in his arms, it feels right. I've never been hugged like this by anyone other than Brogan and our dad, and Forrest. He gives the best hugs.

"Yeah?" He releases his hold on me, but not completely, as he keeps an arm around my waist.

"Yes. Don't complain when I send you a million texts."

"No complaints here." He bends his head and kisses my lips softly. "Thank you. Come on. Let's go tell the girls." He reaches for my hand, but I pull away.

"One day you'll let me show the world you're my choice," he whispers before walking ahead of me into the living room. "Razzle, Dazzle, Lilly, it's time to party."

The twins cheer.

By the time I join them, he already has Lilly back in his arms, who is content to rest her head against his shoulder. The girls are holding hands, with River's hand in his. "Come, give me a hug," I tell the twins. They look reluctant to let go of Forrest— worried that I might change my mind.

"Go tell your mom goodbye before we go," he urges them. They walk toward me, and I crouch down and open my arms for them.

"Love you. Please be good for Forrest."

"We'll be so good," Rayne tells me.

"And help with Lilly," River adds.

"Okay. I'll be over to get you in a little while." With a hug and a kiss from each, they race back to Forrest's side, taking the same formation, holding hands, and River's hand in his.

"Take care of my babies," I tell him.

"Always, Momma." He winks and leads the girls out of the house with Lilly on his hip.

I watch them leave before turning back to the room. I find four pairs of eyes watching me intently.

"Damn." Maggie waves her hand in front of her face. "Was it just me or were there some major sparks flying?"

"He's like my brother, but even I'm a little turned on with how he called you momma with the wink," Monroe says.

"You've been holding out on me," Brogan says, crossing her arms over her chest.

"My brother wants you," Emerson adds.

"He's just being nice."

"Is that why your face is all flushed?" Maggie teases.

My answer is to cover my face with my hands. "I don't know," I confess.

"He's a good guy," Monroe offers. "They all are. They're sexy, tattooed teddy bears."

"Don't let your husband hear you say that," Emerson teases her.

Monroe waves her off. "I'd say the same thing to him."

Emerson sits on the couch and pats the cushion next to her. "Come sit."

I want to run and hide, but I know that's not an option, so I take the cushion next to her. "He's my brother, but you're my friend. This is a safe place, Briar. You can tell us, and there will be no judgment, and nothing will get back to the guys. Especially Forrest."

"He says he wants to date me," I blurt, feeling my face heat even more. I'm sure I'm as red as a tomato. I'm a twenty-two-year-old single mom who has no dating experience. I'm acting like a teenager.

Emerson nods. "Then he means it."

"I'm... a mess, Emerson. I have no dating experience past a few dates in high school. I'm a single mom of twins. What could he possibly see?"

"He sees a beautiful woman with adorable daughters," Maggie says.

"Briar, Forrest isn't the kind of man to take advantage of a situation." Monroe eyes me carefully. "He's a man of his word. I've known him my entire life. He's one of my husband's best friends and my best friend's older brother. He's one of the good ones."

"It's just hard for me to trust," I tell them.

"Briar." Brogan says my name, and I feel a lecture coming on. I turn to face her, knowing I can't avoid my twin. "He's been to the house. He let the girls put his hair in bows and paint his nails. He invited you and the twins and even extended the invitation to me to his house for dinner. He just offered to take your daughters for a couple of hours so you could get a break. Let all of that sink in, sister. How many times has he tried to sleep with you with the interactions the two of you have had?"

"None. Well, I mean, he hugged me, and he's kissed me. Just quick... a couple of times."

"Aw, my big brother has a crush," Emerson coos.

"I don't know that I'm ready for casual or serious. I have to think about the girls," I tell my friends and my sister.

"Forrest has the patience of a saint." Monroe laughs. "He put up with us when we were younger." She points to Emerson. "He was nineteen when he moved out. We were nine. I can still remember when he came to my house and sat down with my parents. He told them that he was Emerson's big brother, and...." Her voice trails off.

"Our parents suck." Emerson picks up where Monroe left off. "Forrest moved out and would get me as much as my parents allowed. The minute I turned eighteen, he moved me in with him. Before that, he would let me spend the weekends and breaks from school with him; sometimes, even during school. It's not like my parents cared. If his schedule allowed, I was with him. He went to Monroe's parents and told them all of that. He told them that Monroe was my best friend, and he'd very much like for them to allow Monroe to come and stay with me sometimes when I was with him. At nineteen, he had more maturity than our mom and dad put together."

"What we're trying to tell you is that it's not an act. It's who he is," Monroe jumps back in.

"I'm scared," I admit.

Brogan takes the seat next to me and wraps me in a hug. "We can't let the past define us, Briar. You light up when he's around, and so do the girls. Take this at your pace. But promise me you'll keep an open mind. Let him show you."

I nod. "Fine, can we move the heat off me? What about you?" I ask my sister. "Your dating history matches mine." I give her a pointed look. Our stories differ, yet they're similar. She's been there with me every step of the way since that night, and I know calling her out is a shitty thing to do.

"If and when there is a man that comes into my life who proves he's worth my time, I'll hold on to him with all I've got," Brogan announces. She didn't hesitate with her reply.

"And you?" Monroe asks Maggie.

"What they said." She grins. "It's so damn hard to find the good ones. Emerson and Monroe, well, and now, Briar." She wags her eyebrows. "You're the lucky ones to have found good men."

She's calling Forrest mine, and I don't know what to do with that. What would that look like? Being his. Him being mine. It's a dream to find a man to love all three of us. Sure, I'm scared and trusting is hard for me, but I'm still me, and finding the love of a man who will love me and my daughters with all he's got, even I can dream about that.

Thankfully, the conversation changes to Monroe's baby shower, which somehow leads to Brogan telling them that our birthday is next weekend.

"We have to celebrate," Monroe tells us.

"My place or yours?" Emerson asks her.

"We'll figure it out and let you all know. Bring a side dish. We'll handle the meat and the birthday cake," Monroe replies.

"What?" I laugh. "No, you don't have to do this."

"We want to. That's what friends are for." Maggie shrugs.

I part my lips to argue, and Emerson shakes her head. "Nope. It's happening. We celebrate all the small things to all the large things. Birthdays are a part of that. Next Saturday night, you four better be there. Monroe and I will get all the details worked out and let everyone know the time and location."

Brogan lifts her lips, pulling up into a grin.

"Thank you," I concede.

The rest of the night, we talk and laugh and enjoy each other's company. I only text Forrest a few times, and each time he sends a picture back of the girls. They're having the time of their lives, and it makes me happy to know he's doing that for them.

"I better go get the girls."

"I'll walk with you to get Lilly," Emerson tells me. "Roman is over there with them."

"You should have told us. We've overstayed our welcome."

"No, you most certainly did not. He's got our little girl, his best friend, and your girls to keep him company. He's fine. He knew I was having girls' night here tonight."

I follow her out the front door as she leads the way to Forrest's house next door. She doesn't knock as she pushes open the door and steps inside. The house is quiet, and I start to worry until I bump into Emerson, where she's standing just outside of the living room. Moving to stand beside her, my heart melts at the sight before me.

Roman is asleep in the chair with Lilly on his chest. Forrest is on the couch with a twin on either side. He has his arms wrapped around them, holding them close, as if he's afraid to let them go.

"Oh my God," I whisper.

Emerson reaches over and grabs my hand. "This. This is why you trust him," she murmurs. "He'll love them with all he has. He'll love you with that same intensity."

"It's a little soon to talk about love," I mumble.

"Just let it happen, Briar. I don't know what's in your past—and if you ever want to tell me, I'm here for you—but I can tell you it doesn't matter. Trust me. Forrest and I are the last people to judge someone for their past or where they came from." With that, she drops my hand and steps into the room. She moves to Roman and runs her hands through his hair. His eyes pop open, but they soften when they land on his wife.

"Baby girl," he rumbles as he slides his palm behind her neck and kisses her.

I move to the couch and sit next to River, who is sitting to the left of Forrest. The urge to take a picture to remember this moment is strong, but I hold back.

"We'll see you at ours. You need help carrying them over?" Emerson asks.

"No. I'll be fine."

"You sure?" Roman asks.

"I got it," a deep, gruff voice replies.

I whip my head around to see Forrest's eyes on me.

"Hey, Momma." He smiles. After lifting his hand, he palms my cheek. "How was your night?"

"Good. Yours?"

"Perfect. This house is too big, too empty. It was nice to have it full again."

"Thank you for watching them."

"Thank you for letting me." He manages to stand and not wake the girls. He lifts his index finger to his lips, telling me to be quiet as he does. Once he's on his feet and it's obvious the girls are not going to wake up, he offers me his hand and I take it, allowing him to help me stand. I follow him to the kitchen.

"What are we—" I'm cut off when Forrest spins, grips my hips, and lifts me to sit on the kitchen island.

His hands cradle my cheeks, and he moves in close. My legs open for him without question, allowing him to be close. So close I'm not sure where he ends and I begin. "If you don't want me to kiss you, tell me now."

I do. I do want him to kiss me. But— "I might be bad at it."

Forrest shakes his head. "Impossible."

"The last time I was kissed, really kissed, I was eighteen, and I didn't exactly have a lot of experience."

"Good."

"Good?"

"I get to show you. I get to be the one to make you realize that you're not bad at it. Just me. You're only going to be kissing me."

"Just you, huh?" I ask. I try to hide my smile, but it's no use.

"Are you ready?" he asks.

I hesitate, then nod. My hands are shaking, and I'm glad I'm sitting because I'm sure my knees would have buckled by now.

Forrest leans in and presses his lips to mine. He slides his large, calloused hand behind the base of my neck and holds me close. His other hand wraps around me and pulls me into his chest. I feel his hard length and I gasp. He takes that as his opening to slide his tongue past my lips. I don't know what I'm doing, but I meet him stroke for stroke, hoping I'm not making a fool of myself. He's got years of experience on me, and me, well, I've got a few fumbling events that led up to that night.

Shaking out of my thoughts, I can't think about that. Not right now. This is my moment. My time with him. And even though I don't know if this is going to be more than this, I'm savoring every second.

When he pulls away, we're both breathing heavily. He rests his forehead against mine. "I don't want you to go."

"I need to get the girls home and in bed. Brogan is next door."

"Fine. Let's get the girls in the car." He gives me one more peck on the lips before lifting me from the counter and leading me to the living room.

The girls are sound asleep. He takes Rayne and I take River, and we walk them to my car and get them strapped in. "I need to go get Brogan and say goodbye to the girls."

"I'll wait here with them." He snags an arm around my waist and kisses me again before I force myself to pull away and make my way back into the house.

"Thank you for having us," I tell Emerson. "Forrest is at the car with the girls, so we need to go."

"This was fun," Brogan says, standing and hugging Maggie, Monroe, and Emerson. I do the same, and with a final wave, we're out the door.

"Brogan, good to see you."

"You, too, Forrest." My sister climbs into the passenger seat and shuts the door.

"Call me when you get home."

"It's late."

"Fine. At least text me and let me know you made it home, okay."

"I can do that."

"Thank you. Night, beautiful."

"Night, Forrest."

One more kiss and I'm climbing behind the wheel and pulling out of the driveway.

Brogan reaches over and places her hand on my arm. "Baby steps, sister, but I have a good feeling about that man."

"Yeah," I tell her. All my fears aside, I do too. I just hope neither of us are wrong.

FORREST 11

"NEXT WEEKEND, WE'RE HAVING A party," Emerson announces. We're at her place having Sunday dinner.

"Not that I don't love a good party," Lachlan comments, "but what's the occasion?"

"It's Briar and Brogan's birthday."

"What?" I sit up straighter in my chair. "It's her birthday?"

"*Their* birthday, yes," my sister corrects me.

"Why didn't I know that?" I scowl.

Emerson laughs. "Why does it matter? She's my friend."

"Mine too," Monroe adds.

"She's my—" Fuck me, I don't know what she is, but I should have known it was her birthday. Why didn't she tell me? We're trying this, right? Whatever this is? Dammit. I should have told her that whatever this back and forth is, it's exclusive. Would she have told me then?

Son of a bitch.

"My place," I tell my sister.

"What?"

"The party. It's at my place."

"I have a house to host a birthday party for my friends."

"Emerson." My voice carries a warning that I never, ever use on my little sister.

Emerson tilts her head to the side to study me. "She's a single mom."

"I fucking know that," I grit out.

"I don't know what, but she's been through something."

"I know that too."

"What are your intentions with my friend, Forrest Huntley?"

I watch as my sister places her hands on her hips, ready to go to battle for Briar, and even though it should piss me off that she's doubting me and my intentions, it doesn't. It makes me smile that she's in Briar's corner. Something tells me my girl, her daughters, and her sister haven't had many people in their corner lately, if at all. I know very little, but I know she lost her mom, and then her dad. I know the girls' dad isn't in the picture. She hasn't flat-out told me that, but my gut tells me that I'm right.

She needs Emerson, Monroe, and Maggie too. I want her to have a tribe to stand beside her. I just want her to let me be a part of that as well. I want to stand with her in whatever she faces, past, present, or future.

"I want her."

"She's not a plaything!" Emerson stomps her foot. Her hands are still braced on her hips.

I'm aware that our family is watching us, and I'm certain every person in this room, well, aside from baby Lilly, is wondering what my intentions are.

"Let me finish, kid," I scold. I think about Briar, and how I have this need inside me to be near her. Not just her, but the girls too. When I say I want her, it's not just in my bed. I want her in this house. I want her girls here as well. I want all three of them to be mine. I've never had this feeling before. I've never wanted someone to be mine. We have a long way to go, and she has trust issues, but I want to be the man who tears through them. I want to be the man who tears down the walls around her heart and helps her build them back, but with love, not fear, or hate, or whatever else it is that caused those walls to be erected so damn high.

"Wow," Emerson breathes.

I shake out of my thoughts. "What?"

"Um, Forrest, bud, you were thinking out loud," Maddox tells me.

I just stare at him while I process what he's saying, then I shrug. "Saves me from repeating my thoughts."

"Forrest?" Roman says my name, pulling my attention. I turn to one of my best friends, who is now my brother-in-law.

I stare him in the eye as I prepare to answer his silent question. "I understand. I get it now. I'm not there—not where you were, but I get it."

"Hell yes, welcome to the club, brother," Legend says.

"What am I missing?" Maddox asks.

"Right? Share with the class," Lachlan chimes in.

"One day...." Roman grins and places a kiss on Lilly's cheek before doing the same to my sister—his wife.

Yeah, I finally fucking get it.

Finally, after a week of planning, the day is finally here. Briar and Brogan's birthday. I didn't ask Emerson what she said when she told Briar the party would be at my house. I've also talked to Briar every day this week, and neither one of us mentioned it. In fact, I didn't even let on that I knew it was her birthday today.

I know why she didn't tell me. She didn't think I would care. She's wrong, so very wrong. I care more than I thought I ever could or would outside my sister and niece. That's something I've admitted to myself this week as well. The more I get to know Briar, the more I crave her. With each new detail of today's party, those feelings were cemented more than ever.

I take one final look around the house before guests start to arrive. Emerson and Monroe came over earlier to help me decorate. I waited until they were gone to bring out the things I bought. The twins needed a place to sit outside, so I got them a picnic table just like Lilly's. The three of them will have lots of fun sitting at their own table. I can imagine the smile on River's and Rayne's faces, knowing they have their own table at Forty's house. Lilly is still too little to understand, but she's used to me and the rest of the guys spoiling her. This is new for the twins, and I want to be the one to start the trend.

Once I ordered the picnic table, I realized that they would need their own chairs as well. I went ahead and ordered three, so that Lilly would also have one. They're small plastic Adirondack chairs, just like the ones we have around the firepit, and cute as hell. I can't wait until they see them.

That led to them needing items for the pool. I don't even know if they know how to swim, so I bought some arm swimmies, goggles, and way too many other toys. I even got this little inner tube that has a canopy over it for Lilly. I went overboard, but that's okay. I know my niece will spend a lot of time here, and so will the twins if I have anything to say about it.

I hear the front door open, and I move to the living room to find Maddox and Lachlan standing and taking in the decorations.

"Damn, Mo and Em went all out," Lachlan says.

"Hey, I helped." I pretend to be offended.

"Good job, buddy," Maddox says, patting my shoulder.

"Fuck off." I laugh.

"What else needs to be done?" Lachlan asks.

"Nothing. We're all set. Just waiting for everyone to get here."

"What are we eating?" Maddox asks, rubbing his stomach.

"Steak and chicken breasts. I have some burgers I can toss on the grill if anyone wants one, and hot dogs for the girls. There's pasta salad, potato salad, chips, and baked beans in the Crock-Pot."

"Damn, you went all out."

"Cake," Lachlan says. "Did you get the girl a cake?"

"Yes, I got a cake. I also have cookies that say *Happy Birthday, Briar and Brogan* and *Welcome to 23* on them."

"Who talked you into those?" Maddox laughs. "Emerson or Monroe?"

"Neither. I thought the girls might like the cookies better than cake."

"You've got this girl-dad thing down, Huntley," Maddox teases.

Girl dad.

I know that River and Rayne come with Briar. They're a package deal, and an adorable one at that, but it hasn't really hit me until this moment that if this goes where I hope it does, I'll be a girl dad. I smile at the thought.

"We lost him," Maddox jokes.

"I can kill that," I tell them.

"Kill what?" Legend asks as he and Monroe step into the house. I didn't even hear the door open.

"Girl-dad life," Lachlan explains.

"Bro, you've got this in the bag." Legend nods.

"I agree. I should know... you practically raised Emerson and me."

"Baby, that sounds creepy as fuck. Forrest and I are the same age."

"Cradle robber." Maddox coughs into his hand.

"Stop." Monroe laughs. "It's ten years, Legend. Not twenty. Besides, Roman and Emerson have the same age gap."

"Don't remind me," I groan.

"Um, Forrest, you do realize that you're thirty-two, right?" Monroe asks.

"I know how old I am, Mo."

"And you know that your girl turns twenty-three today. I know this is hard, but let me help you. Thirty-two minus twenty-three is nine. As soon as it's your birthday, it'll be ten years."

"Ha ha, smartass. I know how old she is, and how many years there are between us." I just don't give a fuck.

Monroe's phone pings, and she pulls it out of her back pocket. "It's Emerson. Briar, Brogan, and the girls just got to her place.

She's walking them over. She wants us all to yell 'happy birthday' when they walk in."

Maddox rubs his hands together. "Let's do this." We form a line so that they'll see us as soon as they walk in.

"Wait." I turn and grab the bag of party favors and start tossing them out. Noise makers and hats are a must, right?

"They're turning twenty-three, not three." Monroe chuckles.

"Shut it. We're doing it right. They haven't celebrated with anyone but each other for four years." Legend gives me the stink eye for telling his wife to shut it, but I just smile and toss him a party hat. Monroe might as well be my little sister, and I'm not going to treat her otherwise just because my best friend married her.

The door opens, and my heart rate kicks up into a higher rhythm.

She's here.

Emerson leads them into the house, and as soon as Briar and Brogan enter, we call out "Happy Birthday."

Briar's mouth falls open. She takes in the room and all of us standing here with crazy hats and noisemakers. The twins are standing still with awe in their eyes. Roman slips out from behind them and grabs a hat for Lilly, placing it on her head.

My feet are moving before I know what I'm doing. I lean down and press a kiss to Briar's cheek. "Happy Birthday, beautiful." Tears shimmer in her eyes, but the smile she's giving me tells me they're happy tears. At least, I hope they are. And because her daughters are watching, I do the same to Brogan. "Happy Birthday." I move back to Briar, needing to be next to her.

"Forty, I didn't know we'd see you," Rayne tells me.

"Yeah, we didn't know," River agrees.

I crouch down so that I'm at their level. "I'm glad you're here." I'm taken off guard when they both wrap their arms around my neck. Something shifts inside me as Maddox's words play through my mind.

Girl dad.

"Did you bring your swimsuits?" I ask them.

"We did. Do we get to swim?" River asks.

"Do you know how to swim?" I ask her. I glance up at Briar and she nods.

"Yes!" the girls cheer.

"Well, all right then. Let's go outside and get this party started."

"Do we get a hat too?" Rayne asks.

"Of course you do, Dazzle."

"Dazzle?" Emerson asks.

"That's my name. My sister is Razzle. And he's Forty." Rayne points to my chest.

"Well, Razzle and Dazzle, let's get our swim on." Lachlan winks at them and they look to me, not their mom. Me. They look to *me* for permission.

"It's okay. You can go. I'll be right behind you."

"Hey, I want a twin." Maddox pretends to pout.

"I'm a twin." River points to her chest.

"Razzle, you want to be my swim buddy today?" Maddox asks her.

"Yes!"

"Dazzle, that leaves you and me." Lachlan holds his hand up for a high-five, and Rayne slaps her tiny hand against his.

"Don't let them out of your sight, and in the water you're with them," I tell my friends.

Maddox nods his approval. "Yeah, you got this in the bag, Huntley."

"I'll go with them," Brogan says, following out the patio door.

Glancing around the room, I see it's just the two of us. "Come here." Snaking an arm around Briar's waist, I pull her into my chest and hug her. "Happy Birthday."

She sighs and settles into my embrace, her arms wrapping around my waist. I hold her for a few minutes, relishing the feel of her in my arms.

"You said that," she finally speaks up.

"I know, but I didn't get to do this." Leaning back, I tilt her chin and press my lips to hers. The kiss is PG but does nothing to quell my desire for her. I nip at her bottom lip, forcing myself to pull away before I won't be able to.

"I can't believe you did all of this. Forrest, it's too much." Her lips are swollen and shining from our kiss.

"Nonsense. Come on. Let's go check on the girls."

Releasing her, I lace her fingers with mine.

"They don't know," she says, and she doesn't need to explain. I know she's talking about her daughters.

I nod. "Okay. You let me know when you're ready." Dropping her hand, I lead us outside.

"Mommy!" River and Rayne call out. "Look!" They're sitting in their chairs I bought them. Roman is next to them, keeping a close eye on them.

"Wow," Briar responds. "Those are cool."

"They're for girls," Rayne tells us.

Briar looks up at me. "You don't need to spoil them."

"What makes you think it was me?" I ask, placing a hand against my chest as if I'm offended.

"Right." She laughs. "Those chairs have you written all over them, Uncle Forty," she teases.

Before I can tell her I'm not her uncle, Monroe and Emerson pull her away with Brogan to greet Maggie.

I've smiled so much today, my face hurts. It's been incredible to have everyone here while getting to spend the day with Briar and the girls, even if I do have to share them. It's made it even better.

"Time for gifts!" Monroe announces.

I'm sitting on a lounge chair with River and Rayne. I have one on each side, and they're sleep soundly. The sun and swimming wore them out. Briar and Brogan both offered to take them in to lay them down, but I refused. We're sitting under an umbrella, keeping the sun off them, and I'm just enjoying the moment.

Briar and Brogan smile and blush as they open each gift. Maddox and Lachlan got them both gift cards to a boutique in town, claiming they didn't know what to get them. Maggie got them tumblers with their names on them that all five of the ladies gush over.

Monroe and Legend got them each a bath set. With lotions, and salts and all that stuff that I only know about because of my little sister and her best friend.

Emerson got them both some kind of wallet that they all also gushed over. It's a woman thing, and I'm okay with that. As long as she's happy, that's all that matters.

"Last one." Emerson hands them my gifts. An envelope for each one.

I watch as they open them and grin.

"Spa Day." Brogan holds up her envelope and waves it in the air. "Thanks, Forrest."

"You're welcome." My eyes find Briar. "That comes with a day of childcare. You let me know when you ladies are going, and I'll make sure I'm off to watch the girls."

"Forrest," Briar breathes.

"Don't worry, Briar. We'll make sure he's supervised," Lachlan jokes.

Everyone laughs, including Briar and me, but her eyes that are locked on mine tell a different story. She's happy, and she's surprised that I would offer to keep the girls. That's fine too. She'll understand eventually. When she's ready to open up her heart and let me finish tearing down those walls of hers, it will all make sense to her. In the meantime, I'm going to keep showing up. I'm going to show her that my words are what's in my heart with my actions.

"Cake!" Lachlan calls out, making us laugh.

"We're on it," Maggie says, as she and Monroe head into the house to get the cake.

Briar comes over to me. "Thank you, Forrest. Not just for the gift, but for today."

"You're welcome, beautiful."

She offers me a shy smile.

"I have another gift for you. Grab the bag behind the lounger."

"You've done enough."

"Humor me."

"Fine." She stands and finds the small gift bag behind the lounger, which I left before everyone arrived. "What's this?"

"Open it."

She reaches into the bag and pulls out an envelope. Tearing it open, she tugs out the small stack of cards. "What are these?"

"Mom coupon cards."

"What?"

"I found coupon cards online that were blank, and well, I filled one out for mom things." I nod and she starts sifting through them.

"Dinner, date night, babysitting, laundry, housecleaning, car wash," she reads off some of the cards.

"Those are all things I'll do for you. You just have to hand me a coupon and consider it done."

She keeps flipping through the cards. When she stops, she looks up at me with tears in her eyes. "Forrest, this is too much."

"No, baby, it's not too much." I place my hand over hers, careful not to wake the girls. "I know it's been you and Brogan taking care of the girls all on your own, but that's not the case anymore. I want to be there for all of you. Girls' night, bring them to me. I'll come to you, whatever works, but I want to do this. I enjoy spending time with them. You've raised two incredible tiny humans, Briar."

"Are you real?" she mumbles. She's shaking her head as if she can't believe the words I'm saying. How could I not want to spend time with the twins? Not only are they a piece of her, those little girls already own two-thirds of my heart.

"Very," I assure her.

"Cake!" Maggie calls out.

"Go on. It's time for you to blow out your candles. Don't forget to make a wish."

"A wish."

"Make it a good one."

"I can't think of a single thing I could wish for that I don't have in this moment." My chest expands and tightens at the same time. I want to make all her wishes come true.

"If you don't want me to kiss you in front of our friends and family, you better get moving."

"Forty, who are you kissing?" Rayne asks sleepily.

I chuckle as Briar's eyes widen as she stands and scurries away. "No one, sweet girl." *Your momma.* "Did you have a good nap?"

"I want cake," River says, waking up.

"Yes," Rayne answers. "Can we swim?"

"After we eat some of Mommy and Aunt Brogan's birthday cake."

That perks them up. They sit up and rub at their eyes.

"Okay." They climb off the lounger and move toward the table where everyone has gathered around. Lachlan and Maddox see them, and each lift a girl into their arms so they can see what's going on. We sing "Happy Birthday," and then dive in to some cake and ice cream.

The rest of the day is much of the same. Good friends, good food, and lots of memories.

BRIAR 12

A T TEN MINUTES UNTIL FIVE, I pull up outside Everlasting
Ink. Forrest nailed my design on the first go. When I saw it,
I cried because it was everything I hoped it would be. He texted
me last night and told me he could get me in today. It's Saturday
night, but he assures me working late isn't an issue.

I know that they usually don't work late on Saturdays unless
it's a long-term client. Forrest is doing this for me. He knew I'd
need a sitter for the girls, and he's making the time to make this
easier on me and my sister. I argued at first, telling him I could
come in any evening after work, but he was insistent that tonight
was perfect. How he knew that Brogan wasn't working today is
beyond me, but I'm grateful and excited to be here.

I might also be a tiny bit excited to see him. We text every day
and more often than not, he calls me. However, I haven't seen
him since last weekend at my birthday party, which was held at
his house.

So, here I am. I'm nervous because this is my first tattoo, but
it can't be worse than giving birth to twins, right? That's what I
keep telling myself. Reaching over to the passenger seat, I grab

my purse, drop my phone inside, pick up my keys, my tumbler of water, and climb out of the car.

When I enter the shop, I notice it's quiet, which I didn't expect. I thought there would be at least a few straggling customers still here. Forrest is sitting behind the counter and offers me a welcoming smile.

"There she is."

I don't know what I expected, but it's not for him to come rushing around the counter and wrapping me in a hug. He lifts me in the air, holding me tightly.

"I missed you," he murmurs.

His words have my heart fluttering and my belly doing flips. When you look at Forrest, you see the ink, the hair, those mesmerizing eyes. The combination makes you think bad boy. You're wrong. Forrest Huntley is nothing but a giant, tatted-up teddy bear, and he makes it impossible for me not to feel... something—everything where he is concerned.

He places me back on my feet, and it's on the tip of my tongue to tell him that I missed him, too, but I can't seem to form the words. "Are you sure this is okay? I hate that you're using your Saturday night for me."

"Briar, if we weren't here, we would be doing something with the girls. My Saturday night was always going to be for you."

His words make me dizzy, but in a good way. He's so open about wanting to spend time with me. It's refreshing and confusing all at the same time. However, I can admit—even if just to myself—that I don't hate it. I also don't hate how he seems to always be thinking about my daughters and how they'll fit into any situation.

"Thank you."

"Let me lock the door. You can go on back to my room. It's just the two of us here for the rest of the night."

"Oh." I suspected, but I wasn't sure, and to hear him say it makes me nervous. Not because I'm afraid of being alone with him. It's quite the opposite. I think if I let myself, it might be something I could and would crave.

I move on down the hall, turning into his room or office. I'm not really sure what I should be calling it, but I'm here, where we initially went over my idea for my tattoo. I spy a bag of food on the desk in the corner as he walks in the room. "Did I interrupt your dinner?"

"Nope. We're having dinner together. I thought we could eat before we start. I don't need you passing out on me." He gives me a grin that my body instantly responds to.

"You bought me dinner?"

"I did. Just BLTs and fries from the place around the corner. There are drinks in the break room. Water. There are some sodas too; I'm not sure what. You're welcome to take a look."

I hold up my tumbler. "I have water. I assumed this would be a long session, and I wanted to be prepared."

"It's pretty big. We'll probably have to break it up, but that's fine. Gives me more time to see you." He moves toward the desk and pulls out a rolling chair, offering it to me. I take it, and he gets to work passing out our dinner.

"Thank you, Forrest. I was really nervous, but you've managed to help calm my fears by just being you."

"I was hoping having dinner together first might help relax you a little." He unwraps his sandwich and takes a bite. He holds up his index finger while he chews and quickly swallows. "I printed several stencils so we can apply them in different places unless you've made a decision on where you want your ink."

"I'm still undecided. I was hoping you could help with that. Where do you think it would look best?" I pop a french fry into my mouth, although I should have waited because I almost choke when he runs his heated gaze over my body. I cough and reach for my water.

He clears his throat. "We can try a few places. We won't start until you're thrilled with the location," he assures me.

"Thank you." I pop another fry into my mouth.

"What did you and the girls do today?" he asks.

"I did some cleaning and laundry. We took a walk around the river. The girls have decided they want to try fishing."

"Yeah?" His eyes light up. "Is that something y'all do often?"

"No. Never with the girls. Brogan and I used to go a lot with Dad. We would come to stay with my grandparents, and then after they passed away, Dad kept their house, which is now the house we live in, and we would still come and spend a couple weeks in the summer and lots of weekends. That's actually how my girls got their names. Dad always took us to the river and said that the fish would bite the best in the rain. I don't know... but with my name being Briar, it just kind of fit, and it's after a memory I'll always cherish with my dad and sister."

He stares at me for several seconds, a small smile pulling at his lips. He nods and wipes his mouth on his napkin.

"What? What's that look?" I point at his face.

"It was meant to be," he replies with a smirk.

"Yeah, I mean, I guess so." I'm not sure where he's going with this, but I don't want to be rude.

"Briar, River, and Rayne." He lists off our names. "And Forrest." He points to his chest. "We match. I don't know why I didn't think of that before now, but we're meant to be."

I can't help but return his smile. "Just names." That's what I say, but my heart thunders as if it knows he's right.

"I'm just saying, if we have more kids, we could name them Hunter, Sage, Willow, Clay. The possibilities are endless."

"M-More kids?" I croak.

"Yeah, you want more, right?"

I nod. I start to explain to him that I don't know that I'll trust enough again to get to that point, but he already knows that. So, a nod is all he's going to get as I take a huge bite of my sandwich to keep from having to reply.

"Me too." He winks.

"That's kind of soon, right?" I ask him.

"Nah. That's what dating is for. To get to know someone and see if your life's goals align. We need to have these conversations."

"We were just seeing how it goes."

"We are. Exclusively," he adds. "I will never give you anything but one-hundred-percent of who I am. I'll never lie to you, and I'll never hide from you. That's me, and the truth, even if it's not what you want to hear."

I let his words sink in. "You remind me of him, you know. Of my dad." I whisper the confession. My palms are sweating. I don't do this. I don't open up, but Forrest makes it so damn easy to talk to him. Being around him and with the way he's always including my daughters, endears me even more to him. I don't know if this is a long game he's playing, but something in my gut tells me that's not the case. I was just lucky enough to find one of the good ones. I was lucky enough to find a man like my father.

"I wish I could have met him," he tells me.

"Yeah." I offer a soft smile. "Me too."

"So," he says, once we've both finished eating. "We talked about your shoulder, your thigh, and your back. We could do your arm, but it would be a half-sleeve. We could do your ribs, but that's pretty tender."

"What do you suggest?"

"Honestly, I think the arm is out. This is a pretty big piece, and I feel like the other locations would be better than your arm."

"Okay. Can we see what they look like? Is that too much work for you?"

"Not at all. I encourage it. That's why I made extra stencils. I have stencil remover we can use to get rid of them."

"That sounds like a lot of work. Maybe I should just pick a spot?"

"How about this? Let's narrow it down to your top two locations. You might love one of them more and we'll be all set, but I'm prepared to try all of them."

"Okay. I think shoulder and thigh are my top two."

"Great. Go ahead and take off your shirt and remove your bra strap from your shoulder. We might need to remove it all the way."

Shit. Why didn't I think about that part? I've never been naked in front of a man, at least not any times that I can remember. Taking a deep breath, I give myself an internal pep talk. I can do this. With shaking hands, I lift my T-shirt over my head and hold it against my chest before pulling my bra strap over my right shoulder.

"I should go ahead and shave these areas in case this is where you decide to get the tattoo."

"Sure," I croak.

His large hand lands on my bare shoulder. "I've got you, B. There is no one here but us, and I locked not only the front door but mine too. It's just you and me."

I nod, because there's a lump of nerves in the back of my throat preventing me from speaking. Closing my eyes, I focus on breathing evenly while he shaves my shoulder and applies the stencil.

"I need to unhook your bra. Are you okay with that?"

I nod, but nothing happens. "Yes," I say, finally finding my words. He unhooks my bra, and I press my T-shirt a little tighter against my chest.

"Hold on a second." He moves around the room and comes back with a dark gray plush blanket. "I'm going to turn around. Wrap this around you, and I'll lower the back to where I need it. Maybe that will make you feel more comfortable. It gets washed after every use. I keep it because sometimes during long sessions it gets cold in here and some clients find it comforting."

"Thank you, Forrest."

"I'm turning around. You tell me when you're ready." I watch as he turns his back to me and faces the opposite side of the room. Quickly, I remove my bra and wrap the blanket around me. I shove my bra into my T-shirt and place it on the desk.

"Okay."

Forrest turns slowly, and his eyes trail over me. "Mirror," he croaks. "Come to the mirror." He motions toward the full-length mirror on the wall. "Hold this one." He hands me a mirror to hold and positions me so that I can see the tattoo stencil. Gently, he moves the blanket so that I can see the full thing.

"What do you think?"

"I think you're fucking gorgeous," he breathes.

Lowering the mirror, I meet his gaze. "I meant about the placement."

"That too. It doesn't matter where you put this piece on your body, Briar. It's going to be incredible. I'll make sure of it."

His confidence eases my fears and helps to boost my excitement. "Let's check on the thigh."

He nods for me to move back to the table in the center of the room. "You'll need to lower your shorts unless you want it to be closer to your knee."

"I think higher," I admit.

He swallows hard. "I'll turn around."

He does so, and I try to hold on to the blanket to keep myself covered while taking off my shorts, but I lose my balance. I yell as I catch myself on the table and the blanket drops to the floor. Forrest turns in a flash, his eyes full of worry until he takes in the scene before him.

I rush to grab the blanket, but I'm standing on it, and I'm flustered. My shorts are unzipped, hanging open, my bare breasts are on display, and Forrest, he's staring at me like I'm his next meal.

He holds my gaze as he steps toward me. Dropping to his knees, he gently lifts one leg then the other, rescuing the blanket. He places the blanket on the table while he peers up at me. No words are exchanged as he grabs the hem of my shorts and pulls them over my thighs.

My heart is racing.

My knees are weak.

My head is spinning.

I want to run, to remove myself from the situation, but I hold steady. I know this man. He's never given me any reason to think he would hurt me or take advantage of me. However, we're here alone. Locked in this room. I start to panic when I feel his lips press to my quivering belly.

"Breathe, baby," he says, keeping his voice soft. "It's just me."

138 | KAYLEE RYAN

I nod. I don't bother to hide the panic. I know he can see it written all over my face. I open my mouth to explain, but the words won't come out.

"You're beautiful, Briar. Every fucking inch of you."

"Stretch marks," I mumble.

He smiles. It's soft and endearing, and my muscles relax from that simple act alone. "Those marks brought you two very adorable little girls. They're a part of you and your journey to becoming a mom. They're sexy because they're a part of you, Briar."

His palms fall to my ankles on each leg, and he slowly trails them up. When he reaches my thighs, he presses a tender kiss to each, before doing the same to my belly. Climbing to his feet, his eyes stay on mine as his hands roam over my ribs. When he reaches my breasts, I suck in a sharp breath as he tests their weight in the palms of his hands.

"Should I stop?"

I shake my head because I'm not capable of words. What I can do is feel. His hands are rough yet soft at the same time. His touch is tender, yet it lights a fire inside me that I've never felt before. Heat pools between my thighs, and I wonder if he knows. Can he see what he's doing to me? Does he know that my body craves him, when my mind still tells me to be cautious?

His thumbs brush over my nipples, and I can't stop the moan that falls from my lips. My face heats with embarrassment, but not enough for me to ask him to stop. Not even when he leans in close, and his hot breath fans over my breasts. His eyes never leave mine.

"Are you good?"

I nod.

"Do you want me to stop?"

I shake my head.

"Words, baby. I need to hear them."

"N-No."

He watches me, looking for what I'm not sure, but he must find it, because he closes the last little bit of distance, and runs his tongue over one nipple then the next. My hands move to his shoulders. I don't know if I want to push him away or pull him closer.

"Forrest." I breathe his name like a soft caress.

"What do you need?"

"I—I don't know."

He takes another taste of one nipple, then the next before his lips trail over my collarbone and up my neck. He slides one hand behind my neck, the other around my waist, and pulls me in close. My chest rises and falls as if I've just run a marathon. My knees are wobbly at best. My hands are clammy, my heart feels like it might explode, and my panties are ruined.

I'm on sensory overload.

He leans in, and I close my eyes, waiting for his lips to touch mine. They never come. Instead, he rests his forehead against mine. That's when I focus on him. His breathing is also labored, and his grip on both my neck and my waist is tight, as if he's afraid I might disappear.

"You're beautiful, Briar. The most beautiful and sexy woman I've ever laid eyes on. Thank you for trusting me and for giving me this moment with you." He pulls away, pressing his lips to my forehead.

Reaching around me, he grabs the blanket and wraps it around me. I grip it tightly, not wanting it to fall again. Not that it matters at this point. He's seen all of me already. Well, all but what my black lace panties are hiding. He grips my hips, and he lifts me to the table. He moves the blanket out of the way and gets to work shaving my thigh before applying the stencil. My heart is pounding, and I'm sure he can hear it. I expel a heavy breath as he stands from his stool to get out of the way, and I watch as he adjusts himself.

He's hard.

For me.

"Let's take a look." His voice is gravelly. He again lifts me from the table and guides me to stand before the full-length mirror. "What do you think?"

I have to swallow a few times and clear my throat to find my voice. "I like them both."

He smiles. "Me too, baby. Your shoulder is easier to hide. We could move this up to your hip." His hand reaches under the blanket and gently traces my hips.

"I think the shoulder is my favorite. It will feel more appropriate to show the girls."

"Good thinking, Momma." He smiles. "Let me get this one washed off and we can get started."

With his hand on the small of my back, he leads me back to the table and again lifts me to sit. I don't argue that I'm capable of doing it on my own. The way he touches me, it makes me feel cherished. Wanted. That's not a feeling I've ever felt. Not outside my family.

Forrest gets to work cleaning the stencil from my thigh and then starts setting up for my tattoo. I should probably get dressed, at least back into my shorts, but I don't make a move to do so.

"Do you want your shorts before we get started?"

"I—No. I'm okay," I reply softly.

"This is a big piece. We'll start with the outline and see how you're feeling and then move on to the shading. It might take us a few sessions."

"I'm fine with that." I'm quick to agree. I mean, look how this one is turning out. I'd be a fool to pass up more time with him.

"Lie on your belly."

I do as he says, thankful for the blanket as a barrier against the leather of the table.

"Do you want some music?"

"No, I'm okay."

"If you change your mind or need a break, let me know."

"I will. Thank you, Forrest."

He's got his gloves on and the tattoo gun in his hand from his spot on his stool. I'm lying on my belly as he leans in and presses a soft kiss to my lips. "My pleasure, baby."

FORREST 13

*G*ET YOURSELF TOGETHER, HUNTLEY, I mentally scold myself.

My cock is hard as steel, and that's not where my attention needs to be. It also doesn't need to be on the softness of her skin, how her breasts were made for the palms of my hands, or how sweet she tastes. And I really don't need to be thinking about the mewling sound that was almost like a moan that fell from those pretty lips as I tasted her pert nipples on my tongue.

Oh, and she's fucking naked, minus a pair of tiny black panties that are doing nothing, regardless of their dark color, to hide her desire.

Basically, I'm fucked.

I need to block it all out so that I don't fuck up her tattoo. This is important. They're all important, but giving my girl her first ink, that's special.

If Roman could hear my thoughts, he'd never let me live it down.

"Are you ready?" My voice is thick and raspy as I try to tamp down my desire for the beauty lying on my table.

"I think so."

"Once we're through the outline, we can stop if you want to."

"Okay." She offers me one of her sweet smiles, and I just can't fucking help myself. I lean in and give her one more peck on the lips. Her eyes are bright when I pull away from her. She looks a little dazed but also happy. I make a vow to see that look in her eyes every damn day from here on out.

It's time to focus.

I ink a few lines and give her a break. "You doing okay?" Her body is tense. I'm hoping that I can get her talking and relax her a little.

"I am. It's not as bad as I anticipated it would be."

"Some places are worse than others." I get back to work. "Tell me something," I say to keep her mind and mine occupied. I need to think about something other than devouring her as soon as we're done here. I know she's not ready for that.

Fuck me, today was unexpected and is most definitely going down as one of my favorite days with her. I know there will be many more, but today, she opened up to me. I can feel her bricks starting to crumble one by one.

"Like what?"

"I don't know anything. I'll start. Green."

"Green, what?"

"My favorite color is green. Like the color of your eyes."

"Forrest Huntley, are you hitting on me while I'm lying on your tattoo table?" she teases. Her shoulders ease just a little.

Fuck me, I love getting to see this open and playful side of her. "Nope. Just stating facts. Okay, here's another one. Lasagna."

"Let me guess, that's your favorite food?"

"Ding ding ding."

She laughs. "I'm a pasta fan myself. Well, carbs in general, really. Bread, pasta, all the carbs. My ass hates me for it."

"Briar!" I scold. "Don't talk about my ass like that."

"I said my ass."

"Exactly!" I say as if I'm exasperated, and a small giggle fills the room. "Moving on. Fall is my favorite time of year."

"Me too. We used to spend a lot of time at the cabin. Well, our house now in the fall. Brogan and I liked to see the leaves change, and of course, Dad was always fishing. We'd have a fire and roast marshmallows."

"Yeah? I'm always up for a good fire and some marshmallow roasting. We should plan that with the girls this fall."

"That's several months away."

"I know. I need you to pencil me in now, so you don't have an excuse to not bonfire and marshmallow with me."

Another small laugh fills the air. "I'll see what I can do. My social calendar is incredibly busy."

"Hence the advanced notice," I remind her. "Favorite holiday?"

"It used to be Thanksgiving because I love all things fall, but after the twins were born, that switched to Christmas. I guess it's a tie, really. I love watching their eyes on Christmas morning."

"I can't wait to see that." The reply slips out before I can think better of it. Not that I would have filtered it. I told her she was going to get all of me, and that I would never hold back.

"That's even further away," she finally replies.

"With that busy social calendar of yours, I need to start early. Pencil me in for that too, will ya?"

"I don't know if I'll be able to remember all of these dates," she teases.

"Don't worry, beautiful, I'll remind you." I smile even though she can't see me. I love being here with her. I love that her first ink is from me, and I love even more that her shoulders are completely relaxed as we get to know one another. I want to know everything.

"My turn to start. Morning person or night owl?"

"I can do both honestly. If I have to choose, I'm going to go with a night owl. Who doesn't like to sleep in? What about you?"

"Morning. However, that could be because I have two tiny humans who go to bed early and are up bright and early the next day. I don't really have a choice in the matter."

"Well, we can fix that. You and the girls can come spend the night or the weekend at my place, and we'll let you sleep in."

"I don't think we're at the sleepover stage. Especially not with my daughters."

"Sure, we are. I have a big, empty house just waiting for all of you."

"Forrest." I'm not sure if her tone is more warning or disbelief.

"Briar," I mock. She sighs, and I smile. "Bucket list item."

"I don't really know."

"Come on. There has to be something."

"You don't want to hear it."

"I can assure you, I do. Come on, this is a safe space. We're getting to know each other better. Tell me."

She's quiet. The only sound in the room is the hum of the tattoo gun. I'm giving her time to process, to decide whether she wants to give me another piece of her. Just when I'm about to tell her we can skip this one because she's obviously uncomfortable, she speaks.

"I want to fall in love."

My heart stops.

It starts again and thunders so hard against my rib cage, I'm shocked I don't have a cracked rib. Can she hear the roaring beat above the sound of my tattoo gun? What do I say to that? That I'm all in? That's what I want to say, but is that the right thing? I don't want to scare her off. Tonight, this time with her has been nothing short of incredible and I don't want to ruin any of it.

"Me too," I finally answer. "Maybe we can work on marking that off our lists together."

Her quick inhale of breath is the only reply I get. I've shocked her. I stay quiet, giving her time to get lost in her thoughts.

As I trace the lines of the stencil, I get excited again about her tattoo. I love the design and the concept, along with the meaning behind it. I'm honored that she trusted me with this. Not that I gave her much choice. I pretty much hijacked her as a client the day I heard her voice at the counter. Either way, she's here, on my table, and it's my work that is going to be a part of her for the rest of her life.

"Greatest accomplishment?" she asks, her voice soft.

"Let's see, I have two actually. So it's a toss-up."

"Give me both."

"First is this place. Everlasting Ink was a dream the guys and I had, and we busted our asses to not only open our shop, but to excel at the artistry. We've made a name for ourselves, and we have people from all over visiting our little town to have a piece done by one of us. It took a lot of hard work and dedication, but we pulled it off."

"You should be proud of that. This place is incredible."

"Thanks." Hearing her say that has pride filling my chest.

"And the second?"

"Emerson. I love my little sister, and I'm so proud of the woman she is. She didn't have it easy, and I did what I could, and to see her thriving, not falling to the life our parents lived, that's—it gets me in my feels every damn time I think about it. She's married to a man who worships her. She has a great job, good friends, and an adorable little girl. I'm so fucking proud of her, and I'm damn proud that I was able to be her pillar of support and guide her away from how we grew up."

"You're a great big brother."

"She makes it easy. What about you? What's your greatest accomplishment?"

"My daughters. How we started was— It doesn't matter. They will forever be not only my greatest accomplishment, but my greatest gift in this life."

I want to ask her what she was going to say. I want her to know that she can lean on me, that I'm here for anything. Everything. However, I don't want to push her. She's opened up a lot to me tonight, and we've moved past the idea that we're just friends. She let me touch her, feel her soft skin, and taste her. She's letting me put my mark on her in the most permanent way. Sure, it's her design idea, but it's me that will forever be a part of her. Tonight has been more than I could have hoped for, and I don't want to ruin that.

"Do you need a break?" I ask her.

"How much longer?"

"We have about another hour or so of the outline. Longer if we keep going."

"Can you finish? If we were to keep going, is that too much for you?"

"Nah, I'm used to it, and I was off today, so I'm fresh. What about you? Do you think you can handle it?" Part of me wants her to say no so that I have an excuse to get her here, back on my table alone again, but I'll follow her lead.

"Let's keep going on the outline and reassess. Is that okay?"

"Yeah, baby. That's more than okay. You sure you don't need a break? Need a drink?"

"I'm good."

"Let me know if anything changes," I tell her and get back to work.

"You're all set," I say, wiping the tattoo clean. "You want to take a look?"

"It's done?"

"Yep. You were a fucking rock star for your first time."

Something flashes in her eyes, but it's gone before I can figure out what it means.

"Take your time sitting up. I'll help you." Tearing off my gloves, I move to the opposite side of the table and offer her my hand. I hold the other out in case she gets lightheaded. She sits up and blinks a few times. I grab the blanket and hand it to her so that she can cover herself up.

"I want to see."

"Are you good? Not lightheaded?"

"I feel fine." She smiles, and damn, I could stare at this woman all damn day.

"Let's do it." I place my hands on her hips and lift her off the table, placing her on her feet.

She grips the blanket and takes small steps until she's standing in front of the full-length mirror. She turns her back to the mirror, and I give her the handheld one so she can take a look. She stares into the small mirror, and her eyes fill with tears.

"Forrest." Her watery gaze lands on me. "You're incredible. It's everything I hoped that it would be. It's better than the drawing you showed me. I—thank you. I love it so much." She steps forward, places the mirror on the table, and lifts her arms. The blanket falls to the floor, pooling around her feet, and her arms wrap around my waist.

I return her embrace, mindful of her tattoo, and hold her closely. "I'm glad you like it."

She leans back just enough to peer up at me. "Love it, Forrest. I love it."

Keeping one arm locked tightly around her waist, holding her closely, I lift the other to push her hair back out of her eyes. "I'm glad."

Her eyes soften, and she licks her lips.

"If you don't want me to kiss you, now is your chance to tell me."

She's quiet as a mouse.

I cradle her cheek as I position her to accept my kiss. I lean in close, my breath fanning across her lips. There's not even an inch between her lips and mine. "Last chance."

Still, she says nothing, yet her silence speaks volumes.

Closing the last remaining distance, I kiss her.

Once. Twice. Three times.

On the third pass, she opens for me, and I'm never one to pass up an opportunity. I slide my tongue against hers, and she moans. Her hands dig into the back of my shirt. She meets me stroke for stroke, but it's not enough.

I need more of her. I need all of her.

Dropping my hands, I bend, never breaking our kiss, and grip the backs of her thighs. "Legs around my waist, baby," I rasp before I dive back in for another taste of her lips. She squeals as I lift her, but she does as she's told and wraps those sexy legs of hers around my waist.

My cock feels like a titanium rod pressing against my zipper. I rock her against me, and she moans. It's a deep, raspy sound from somewhere inside her. Breaking the kiss, she buries her face in my neck and holds on tight as I rub her panty-covered pussy over my crotch.

"Forrest," she murmurs.

"Do you want me to stop?"

"N—No."

Thank fuck.

Turning, I walk toward the guest chair, the one that's not on wheels, because I don't need either one of us tumbling to the floor, and sit with her on my lap. Her head is still buried in my neck, and I can feel the rapid rise and fall of her chest with each breath, not to mention that it's fanning across my neck.

"Briar?"

"I don't know what to do," she whispers in my ear.

Her confession has my mind racing. What does she mean? Does she mean she doesn't know how to handle me? Does she not know what to do sitting on my lap? She's a mom, so I know sex isn't new for her. My wheels are spinning, but I reel it in and focus on the woman in my arms.

"Tell me what you need."

"I—I don't know." Her fingers dig deeper into my shoulders as she holds on tight.

"Do you trust me, Briar?" I know that's a loaded question where she's concerned. "I promise I'll stop as soon as you say the word. Besides, the first time I'm inside you, it's going to be in a big comfy bed where I can enjoy you and take my time. Not here in my office."

"I—I think so."

Well, fuck. Looks like I got some more work to do. "You control this. You control me." My voice cracks because fuck me, the thought of hurting her kills me. "How about this? I'm going to drop my hands to my sides, and I'm going to tell you what to do. You'll have all the control. We can even tie my hands behind my back if that makes you feel better."

Slowly, she lifts her head, and her big green eyes find mine. "You'd be okay with that?"

I swallow hard. "Yes."

"I think… arms at your sides. It's not that I don't want you to touch me."

I cradle her cheeks again. "I know, baby. I know there's a piece of you that you're keeping from me, and that's okay. Do you know why?" She shakes her head. "Because I'm still here. I'm still going to be here when you finally trust me enough to tell me. In the meantime, I need you to be open and honest with me and tell me what you need. I'm right here, Briar, and, baby, I'm all yours."

Those big green eyes of hers stare into my soul. When she finally speaks, she breaks me open, and it's painfully obvious that I'm hers. I'm all in.

"My heart and my trust were broken. I used to think that there was no putting them back together. However, I'm starting to think you might be the man to fix them both."

I want to touch her. I want to pull her into my arms and never let her go, but my hands remain fisted where they hang at my sides. "I am that man, Briar. I'm yours. I'm all in, baby. We take this at whatever pace you need for us to go for you to feel safe. I want your heart and your trust. I promise you, with everything that I am, that they're both safe with me. I'll help mend them back together, but I'm keeping them."

Her eyes shimmer with tears. "I want to try."

I don't know what she wants to try, but whatever it is, I'm here for it. "My hands are at my sides. You have my word. I won't move."

She nods. Her cheeks are an adorable shade of red, but that doesn't stop my brave girl from rocking her hips. Her pussy rolls over my hard cock in my jeans and her eyes widen.

"Take what you need."

"I don't know what I need," she replies quietly.

"Me, Briar. I'm all that you need. There is nothing you can do that will change that. You're safe with me. Always."

She rocks again as she bites down on her bottom lip. "Is this okay?"

I smile at her. "My gorgeous girl is grinding on my cock, and her tits are in my face. Yeah, this is more than okay."

She smiles and rocks again. This time, she doesn't stop. Her movement grows faster as she finds her rhythm. She moans and closes her eyes, tilting her head back. I want to demand that she keep her eyes on me, but this is her show. I'm merely a spectator, and I'm doing my damnedest to memorize every moment. Every sound she makes. Every curve of her body. Every spark racing through my veins as she slides her body over mine.

Her breathing picks up, and her movements become jerky. I want more than anything to grip her hips and help her find her release, but I'm keeping my promise. Her fingers that are resting on my shoulders dig deep. I'm certain even through the thin material of my T-shirt there will be evidence of her hands on me.

I watch as she starts to shake. She doesn't stop grinding until the last of her orgasm has raced through her body. Slowly, she blinks her eyes open.

"Can I touch you?" I blurt.

She nods, and I don't waste a single fucking second. Wrapping my arms around her, I pull her into a hug. I just need to hold her. I need my hands on her, and I need to come. But that's going to have to wait. This is her time.

"I'm sorry."

"What?" I ease back and lift her chin so that her eyes are on me. "Don't tell me you're sorry. Not when I just experienced the hottest fucking moment of my life with you. You're not allowed to apologize for that."

"You don't have to say that."

"I don't say what I don't mean, Briar. You're here in my arms, riding my cock. That's a memory I will never forget."

"But you didn't—"

"This was all you, baby. All you. I got a hell of a lot more out of that than you think I did. I got memories of you that will last a lifetime. That's all I need."

She nods and bites down on her bottom lip.

"What's going on in that pretty head of yours?"

"You kept your promise."

"This one and every single promise in our future," I assure her.

She rests her head on my shoulder, and I relax into the chair and enjoy holding her. She's not trying to run from me, and that's a huge fucking win. We lie in silence for I don't know how long, but I do know it's not long enough.

"It's pretty late. I should get going."

"Let's get your tattoo wrapped. I'll go over aftercare, and we can get you dressed."

She nods and climbs off my lap. I miss the feel of her in my arms instantly. I quickly cover her tattoo, go over aftercare, and we gather our things.

"I'm going to follow you home," I tell her.

"What? No, it's late. You don't have to do that."

"I'm doing it because it's late. It's not a problem. I won't be able to sleep unless I know you made it home safely."

"I never imagined I'd meet a man like you, Forrest Huntley."

"Funny, I always knew I'd find you."

"How?"

"Because I was waiting for you. I was waiting for the woman who'd turn my world upside down. I was waiting for the woman who would make my heart race. The one who would consume my thoughts and feed my soul. That's you." I kiss the tip of her nose.

She smiles shyly as she climbs into her car. "Thank you for everything. Oh, I didn't pay you."

I laugh. "Right. If you think for a single second, I'm letting my girl pay for ink, you've lost your mind." Leaning in, I kiss her softly. "I'll be right behind you."

"Okay."

I close the door and rush to my truck, pulling open the door to climb inside. I flash my lights, letting her know I'm ready, and follow her home. The drive is quick, and I flash my lights again as she pulls into her driveway. I stop in the middle of the road. There is no traffic this time of night, and I watch as she climbs out of her car, waves, and makes her way to the front door, disappearing inside.

I drive to my place with a smile on my face and an aching cock. As soon as I'm inside, I don't bother with the lights; I head straight to the shower to handle business. I come, embarrassingly fast, and within ten minutes, I'm in bed. I didn't expect this turn of events, but I'm fucking stoked all the same.

BRIAR 14

G UESS WHAT?" MY SISTER ASKS as she comes bouncing into the living room.

"What?" I ask as my phone vibrates in my hand. I glance down, because I already know it's Forrest. Since my tattoo two weeks ago, we've been texting and talking on the phone nonstop. He's come over for dinner a few times, and I've taken the girls to his place to swim and for dinner as well. He's been pushing for me, the girls, and Brogan to join them for their weekly Sunday dinners, but I've been holding off. That seems serious, and even though this thing between us feels serious, I don't know if we're there yet.

"Is that your boyfriend?" Brogan teases.

"He's not—it's Forrest." Is he my boyfriend? We haven't labeled this. Just that we're not seeing other people and he's letting me go at my pace.

"He is."

"We've never labeled whatever it is that we're doing," I tell her.

"You might not have, but your boy has." She reaches for her phone and taps the screen before handing it to me. "This was what I was going to tell you, but I'll let you read it for yourself."

Taking her phone, I see it's a text message thread with Forrest. Scrolling to the top, I read through the messages.

Forrest: *Hey. How does Saturday sound for your spa day with Briar?*

Brogan: *Does my sister know you're planning our spa day?*

Forrest: *Nope.*

Brogan: *Nice. We can do Saturday. I'm off work. We'll need to find a sitter for the girls.*

Forrest: *I'll keep the girls.*

Brogan: *Cashing in on the mom coupon book? Great idea, by the way.*

Forrest: *Nah, this is just me volunteering to watch my girlfriend's kids, who happen to be cool as hell, so that she can have a spa day with her sister.*

Brogan: *Girlfriend?*

Forrest: *My girl. Girlfriend. Mine. However you want to spin it.*

Brogan: *I wouldn't be a good big sister if I didn't ask what your intentions are with my sister.*

Forrest: *End game.*

Brogan: *Can't say I was expecting you to say that.*

Forrest: *I have nothing to hide.*

Brogan: *Does Briar know? That she's your end game?*

Forrest: *I hope so. If not, she will. I'm giving her time. She's mine. The rest will come in time.*

Brogan: *Don't hurt them, Forrest.*

Forrest: *Never.*

Forrest: *Saturday?*

Brogan: *That sounds good. I'll tell Briar tonight. Are you sure you're good to keep the girls?*

Forrest: Razzle and Dazzle are my buds. We'll be just fine.
I'll be at your place at nine. You need to be at the
spa at ten.

Brogan: Okay. I'm sure you'll be hearing from my sister.

Forrest: Looking forward to it.

I'm still trying to process what I just read when I hand Brogan her phone. He called me his girlfriend. I guess that makes sense. We've just never said it out loud. Not that I'm upset about it. It's just weird thinking that I have a boyfriend after all this time, after everything that's happened.

A boyfriend that doesn't know all the details of my past. I need to tell him soon. Before the girls and I get any more attached. I'm truly broken, and a man like Forrest, he deserves better.

"He scheduled our spa day?"

Brogan laughs. "Skipping over the 'she's mine' part, are we?"

"We said that we wouldn't see other people while we figure this out."

"I like him."

"Yeah," I agree. "I do too. He doesn't know, Brogan."

"Maybe you should tell him. Your past doesn't define you."

"No, but what if he looks at me and the girls differently?"

"Then he's not worth your time. But I don't think that's going to happen. He seems genuine, and we've spent enough time around the group that we can say that with certainty."

"He is. They are, but this is different. I'm broken. The girls—"

"You're not broken, and those girls are special angels. They're your daughters. That's what matters. You are a package deal, and I feel like I can say with confidence that Forrest wants the entire package. He's not a halfway kind of guy, Briar."

"How do you know?"

"I work with his sister. We talk a lot, and just the things she says about him, and the rest of the guys. They're a good group. They're genuine."

"It feels that way to me, too, but what if I'm wrong?" That's the real problem here. I was so trusting before, and I was wrong.

"Trust yourself, little sister." She winks.

My phone rings, and I can't help but smile when I see Forrest's name on the screen. "It's him."

"I know. Your smile tells all. I'll go round the girls up for dinner." Brogan walks away as I put the phone to my ear.

"Hey."

"How was your day, baby?"

Why do I melt into a puddle when he calls me baby? I never thought I would like that, but from Forrest, it's sweet and sexy at the same time. "Good. I just had an interesting conversation with my sister just now."

"Really? About what?"

"Our spa day."

"Are you excited?"

"I am. Are you sure you want to keep the girls all day? They can be a handful."

"I'm more than sure. I'll be there early. I'm bringing snacks. I have the entire day planned."

"Really?" I ask, feeling the weight of worry lifting from my shoulders.

"Yep. And I don't want you to rush home. Go shopping, grab dinner or a movie. Whatever you want to do, kid-free. Before you say anything, I know that you love your daughters, but every parent deserves a break. As for me, I'm looking forward to spending the day and evening with the girls. We're going to be at your place, so you don't have to worry. You can call and check on us as much as you want. I'll send lots of pictures to ease your mind. I want this day for you. For you and Brogan. You're both raising those girls on your own, and I just want to be a part of it. I want to be someone you can lean on."

I don't know what to say to that. If he were here, I'd wrap him in a hug, but over the phone, the best I could do is say, "Thank you, Forrest."

"Anytime, baby. I need to go. I want to get the yard mowed before it gets dark."

"Paying someone to mow for us is the best decision I've ever made." I laugh.

"Stop paying whoever it is. I'll take care of it for you."

"No. I can't let you do that."

"I can mow my girlfriend's grass," he grumbles.

"And I can pay the teenager down the road to do it too."

"Fine," he gripes. "I'll call you later."

"Have fun."

His laughter is all I hear as the call ends.

It's a big deal to let him keep my daughters for that long, and I do trust that he will take care of them. If I'm being honest, somehow over the last couple of months, I've come to trust him. I know I need to give him that trust and tell him about my past. That's the only way I'll know if he's here to stay. I need to do it soon because my girls are already attached to him. Okay, fine, I am too. I've let him into our lives. He slipped between the cracks. And now, the girls and I are too far gone for him, too used to him being in our lives.

My heart didn't even see him coming.

When there's a knock at the door, ten minutes until eight, I smile, knowing it's Forrest. The girls are on the couch, having just finished breakfast and watching their favorite cartoon. I smile as I make my way to the door and pull it open.

"Hey, baby." He leans in and kisses me softly.

"Aw, Forty!" I hear a female voice.

Glancing over his shoulder, I see Emerson with her head sticking out of the passenger side window of Monroe's Tahoe. "Did you have them drop you off?" I ask, but then I see his truck in the driveway.

"Nope. Rome heard me making the appointment for the day and told me to add another for Emerson. Then Legend found out and called back and added a spot for Monroe too. Then the girls found out and decided Maggie should be involved, so it's a girls' day at the spa."

"Really?" I ask as excitement bubbles up inside me. I was already looking forward to today, but having the rest of the ladies there makes it even better.

"Yep. I told them they had to wait in the car. I didn't want the girls to get all worked up before you left."

"I haven't told them you're watching them today. I knew I'd never hear the end of it."

He grins. "Today's going to be fun."

"Come on in. We might as well tell them now, so we can head out." He follows me into the house. "Girls." I step up behind the couch with Forrest next to me. "You have someone here to see you," I tell them.

That gets their attention. They tear their eyes from the cartoon.

"Forrest!" they call out his name.

He laughs, a deep throaty laugh. "Hey, girls. I thought we could spend the day together while your mom and Aunt Brogan have an adult girls' day."

"Yay!" they cheer.

"Best behavior." I point at them using my most stern mom voice. Their little heads bob, giving me their agreement.

Brogan walks out, slinging her purse over her shoulder. "Ready?" she asks.

"I am."

"Girls, I'm going to walk your mom out. Stay put, I'll be right back."

"Okay, Forty," they tell him at the same time. "Bye, Mommy. Bye, Aunt Brogan," they chorus.

I don't have an ounce of panic at leaving him with my daughters today. It's clear to see he adores them just as much as they do him. They're comfortable with him, they trust him, and that means everything. I give them both a kiss on top of their heads over the couch and follow Brogan out the door, with Forrest right behind us.

"What's going on?" Brogan asks when she sees Monroe's Tahoe in the driveway. I quickly explain what's going on, and she grins before heading toward our friends, leaving me alone with Forrest on the front porch.

"Thank you for this."

His eyes soften. "Anytime, baby. Have a great day. Don't rush back. I've got this."

I have the sudden urge to kiss him, so that's what I do. I stand on my toes and press my lips to his. He wraps his arms around me and holds me tightly. "That's a first," he whispers, stealing another kiss.

"What?" I have to tilt my head back to look at him.

"You kissed me first." He grins like a schoolboy who was just told he won dodgeball captain in gym class.

"Is that okay?" I don't know why I ask. His smile tells me exactly how okay he thought my kiss was.

"More than okay. Feel free to kiss me anytime you want. I'm yours after all."

"Mine." I lean in and kiss him again. My heart flutters at the contact. I don't think I'll ever tire of kissing him.

"Yeah, you are." He gives me one more tight squeeze before releasing me. "You better go before I keep you in my arms all damn day."

I don't know how he does it, but he makes me feel wanted. Special. Treasured. Most of all, he makes me feel happy. "I'll see you soon."

"See you soon, baby." He kisses my forehead and disappears back into the house.

When I reach the SUV, my sister and our friends yell out, "Get it, girl," making us all fall into a fit of laughter.

"Stop." My face heats, but I'm not mad. Just embarrassed. This is all new for me.

Emerson turns in her seat. "I'm happy for both of you. My brother needs a good woman in his life."

"You can bet your ass those girls of yours will be spoiled rotten when we get back," Monroe says from the driver's seat.

"Oh, you know it," Maggie says. She's sitting in the third-row seat. Well, sitting is a stretch. She's lying down, with her arm covering her eyes.

"Are you feeling okay?" I ask Maggie.

"I'm fine. I picked up a half shift at the hospital last night. I didn't get home until 3:00 a.m. I'm just tired."

"Well, I'm glad you're coming with us, tired and all," Brogan tells her.

"I wasn't missing this," Maggie tells my sister.

"Right? When Legend told me about it, I was pumped. They have a momma massage package. I'm all over that." Monroe chuckles.

"How are you feeling?" Maggie asks her.

"Great. I'm twenty-two weeks, so over the halfway mark."

"Wait. Do you know what you're having?" Brogan asks her.

"We do. We found out last week."

"Don't even try. She won't tell me," Emerson grumbles.

"I told you. This week is our week to host Sunday dinner. We're going to tell everyone together." Monroe laughs. "It's tomorrow. You can hold out."

"You've known since last Friday, Mo. That's over a week. Eight days of withholding important information."

Monroe's laughing so hard, her shoulders shake. "You'll be fine."

"Well, you'll have to let us know," Maggie says. "I need to start shopping."

"Oh, you're invited. All three of you are. The girls too," Monroe says, finding my eyes in the rearview mirror quickly. "I want all my people there when we announce what we're having."

"Oh, we don't want to intrude."

Emerson turns in her seat and gives me a look that I'm sure will scare the hell out of Lilly when she's older. "I know for a fact my brother has been inviting you the last two weeks."

"He has," I tell her. "But it's a family thing."

"You're his girlfriend. That means something. He's not taking this relationship lightly," Emerson tells me. She sighs. "I'm sorry. I don't mean to get crazy." She rolls her eyes playfully. "He really likes you, Briar. A lot. He wants you there. We all do."

"It's so early."

"It's been months," Maggie speaks up. "The two of you have been dancing around this for months. I'd say it's time."

"I happen to agree," Brogan says. "And if you don't want the girls to go, I'll stay at home with them."

"What?" Emerson says, turning around to face us as much as her seat belt will allow her to. I wasn't expecting the shocked look on her face. "No. The girls are coming. All four of you. Five, Maggie, this is for you too. We want you all there. That's how this works. Those girls are a part of you, Briar. They're coming."

The car is silent. It's Monroe that breaks the silence. "What she said."

Maggie cracks up laughing, and soon we're all joining her.

"We'll be there," I tell Emerson. I bite down on my cheek to hide my smile. Forrest has been asking me the last two weeks to come with him. Speaking of Forrest... my phone pings with a message.

> **Forrest:** How did I do, Momma?

It's a picture of the girls' hair in pigtails. "Oh my," I say, covering my mouth with my hand.

"What?" Brogan asks.

"Look." I turn my phone so that she can see.

"A for effort." She chuckles.

"Let me see." I show Maggie, and she cackles.

Monroe turns into the parking lot for the spa. "I feel left out."

"Here." I pass my phone to her, and she and Emerson look at the picture.

"I think those girls could talk him into anything," Emerson says, handing me my phone just as it pings again.

I can't hold in my laughter when I see Forrest smiling at the camera and his hair in two short pigtails on top. Brogan takes my phone from my hand, and it gets passed around again.

"He's too much." I shake my head as I type out a reply.

> **Me:** I hope my spa day staff is more qualified than yours.

> **Forrest:**   *Hey, my girls are rock stars.*
>
> **Me:**   *Yes, they are.*

I shove my phone into my purse and climb out of the SUV, following our group inside to enjoy our spa day.

FORREST 15

"**N**OW THAT WE'VE HAD OUR spa day, I thought we could go fishing," I tell the girls. Our spa day consisted of them doing my hair and painting my nails, and I did the same for them. We all looked like a four-year-old handled the situation. I need to step up my game of doing their hair. Briar wouldn't let them out of the house looking like this. Lucky for them, it's just the three of us today. I'm rocking my pigtails and my blue and green sparkle nails.

"Fishing?" River wrinkles up her nose. "We don't know how to fish, Forty."

"How do you do it?" Rayne asks.

"Lucky for you, I was thinking ahead. I bought you fishing poles."

"You did?" They gasp at the same time.

I smile at their reaction. I love that they are so in tune with each other. I've not spent a ton of time around Briar and Brogan without a big crowd, but I can imagine they are the same way.

"I sure did," I answer. "But before we go, we have to go over some rules."

"We'll be good, Forty," Rayne assures me.

"I know, sweetheart, but these rules are to keep you safe."

River gasps. "Is fishing scary?"

"Not at all. Fishing is fun, but it can be dangerous if you get too close to the water."

"We swim," Rayne says.

"You do, but a big body of water is deeper than a pool. It's important that you stay with me, and don't wander off or get too close to the edge."

"We can do that, right, sissy?" River says.

"We can do that." Rayne nods in agreement.

"Thank you. Now, I've got a cooler in my truck all packed up and our poles. Do you have some old play shoes?" I ask them.

"We gots flip-flops," River says.

"I better ask your momma." Grabbing my phone, I fire off a text to Briar. I hate to bother her, but I'd rather be safe than sorry.

> **Me:** Hey, babe. Can I take the girls fishing at the river in flip-flops, or do they have old play shoes?

Her reply is immediate.

> **Briar:** Flip-flops are fine. They do have play shoes. They're at the bottom of the closet next to the front door.
>
> **Me:** Thank you.
>
> **Briar:** They don't have poles.
>
> **Me:** They do now. I bought them for them last night.
>
> **Briar:** Don't spoil them, Forrest.
>
> **Me:** Okay, I'll most definitely spoil them. Enjoy your day, baby.

Shoving my phone into my pocket, I smile at the girls. "Okay, ladies, your momma said flip-flops are fine. Go use the potty and we'll go."

"I don't gots to potty," River tells me.

"Well, can you try for me? I'm going to go too. There's not a bathroom down by the river."

"I'll try for you," Rayne says.

"Me too." They take off, racing down the hall. My phone vibrates and I know it's Briar. Unable to resist a message from my girl, I dig my phone back out of my pocket to see what she has to say.

> **Briar:** What am I going to do with you?

"I can think of a few things," I mumble as I type out my reply.

> **Me:** Keep me.
>
> **Briar:** Tempting.
>
> **Me:** I'm already yours, so you don't have a choice. I just wanted you to think you did.

She replies with a string of laughing emoji. I can see her smiling face and her sparkling green eyes in my mind. I hope she's enjoying herself as much as I am. I truly enjoy spending time with the girls. I'm honored that she trusted me with them. I know what that took for her.

"Ready!" Rayne and River say as they come racing back into the room.

"Okay, I'm going to go use the potty. Wait here for me." I take off down the hall and make a quick bathroom break. There is water all over the bathroom sink, and a small puddle on the floor. I chuckle as I grab the towel to mop up the mess. At least they washed their hands.

I find the girls standing next to the door, bouncing on the balls of their feet with excitement. "Oh, I'll need to lock the door. Let me text your mom."

> **Me:** Do you have a spare key so I can lock the house while we're down by the river?
>
> **Briar:** My keys are on the hook by the front door.
>
> **Me:** Thanks, babe.

Grabbing her keys, recognizing her keychain with a picture of the girls as babies, I shove them into my pocket and lead the girls out to my truck.

Briar:	There's a wagon in the garage if you want to take that.
Me:	Nah, I think we'll be fine.
Briar:	It comes in handy.
Me:	I got this, Momma.
Briar:	Have fun!

"Let's do this." I grab the fishing poles and toss the cooler strap over my shoulder. The small tackle box I brought just for this, their small chairs in a bag I bought with the poles, along with a larger one for me, and the small bag of snacks I picked up for the excursion. Thankfully, I didn't bring my pole. I figured I'd have my hands full helping the girls.

"That's much stuff," Rayne says, eyeing me warily.

I'm loaded down, so I don't have a free hand to hold theirs. Looks like Briar was right, and the wagon is a good idea. "You know what? Let's take the wagon. Mommy said it was in the garage."

Placing everything on the driveway, I walk hand in hand with the girls back into the house and to the garage to get the wagon. Once we have it outside and the house is locked up again, I load up the wagon, and we're ready for our adventure.

"Girls, hold hands, and one of you hold mine." They do as they're told, linking hands as Rayne slides her tiny hand in mine. "Let's do this."

I might have misjudged the girls liking fishing. It's been an hour, and they've already lost interest. They're sitting on their lawn chairs with their heads tilted back, looking up at the clouds.

"You ready to head back to the house?" I ask them.

"I'm tired," River whines.

"Me too," Rayne agrees.

"Okay. Let's get loaded up and we can head back and take a nap."

"I don't like naps." River crosses her arms over her chest and juts out her bottom lip. It's cute as hell, but of course, I keep that to myself.

"Okay, we'll just relax then." I make quick work of packing up the wagon, grateful Briar suggested it when Rayne drops a bomb on me.

"I want to ride."

"Dazzle, the wagon is full."

"Mommy lets us ride." Her lip juts out to match her sister's, and her eyes grow wet with tears.

"Right." Mommy lets them. I take a few seconds to assess the situation. I can't make them walk back to the house. Sure, it's not that far, but they're little. Quickly, I unpack the wagon. "Hop in," I tell them.

Their frowns are turned upside down as they scramble from their chairs to climb into the wagon. "I'm going to need your help. Do you think you can help me?"

"With what?" River asks cautiously, as if she thinks I'm going to make her get back out of her cushy spot in the wagon.

"I can't pull the wagon and carry all of our stuff. Can you be my big helpers and hold some of it for me?" I ask them.

"I like to help," Rayne replies.

"Me too," River agrees.

They're missing their usual enthusiasm, so I know they're tired. I didn't think about them needing a nap. We've had a pretty exciting day so far. Rookie mistake on my part. I'll get better at this. I hand River the tackle box while Rayne holds the bag of snacks. That leaves me with all three chairs and the cooler. "Do we have room for these?" I ask, nodding to their small chairs.

"I can hold more." Rayne speaks up.

"Oh, me too," River says, not one to be outdone by her sister.

I add their chairs to the wagon, sling my chair and the cooler over my shoulder, hold their poles in one hand, and begin the short trek back to the house with the wagon held in the other. It's not far, maybe seven hundred feet or so. By the time we reach the house, their eyes are drooping. I have a feeling if I get them on the couch, or in their beds and it's nice and quiet, they'll both be down for the count.

Twenty minutes later, the wagon is unloaded. The supplies are back in my truck, and the girls are on the couch with a cartoon, eyes drooping, just as I suspected. I sit down on the couch, and they crawl over to me. I have one on each side, and within minutes, they're asleep. I snap a quick picture to send to Briar and close my eyes. Sleep when they sleep, right? That's what Roman and Emerson preached when Lilly was a baby. I figure that still fits if they're four. Either way, I'm too comfy to move, and I don't want to wake them, so a nap for the three of us is just what the doctor ordered.

"Ladies, you made me proud. You ate all of your dinner." I praise the girls when I toss their paper plates in the trash. When I asked them what they wanted for dinner, they said pizza. Thirty minutes later, we had a hot delivery on the doorstep.

"It was yummy." River smiles. She looks adorable. They both do with sauce smeared all over their faces.

"What now?" Rayne asks.

They've kept me hopping all day. Our nap lasted all of twenty minutes before the girls were wide awake and ready to party. I gave them horsey rides around the living room. My knees are thankful for the nice plush carpet in that room. Then we played with their Barbies, which consisted of me pushing their Barbie Jeeps around, making car noises, and the girls giggling like they were at a comedy show. After Barbies, they decided my hair needed to be done again, so it was back to the salon I went.

"Once we clean up, I have a plan." I rub my hands together to show them my excitement, and they take the bait.

"What is it?" Rayne asks.

"I can't tell you until you're cleaned up and in your jammies." It's a little after seven, and they're usually in bed by eight. I'm exhausted, so they have to be. I have an all-new respect for Briar doing this on her own. I know she's had Brogan, but Briar's their mom, and my girl deserves props.

"Okay!" they cheer and race off down the hall. I wipe down the table before joining them in the bathroom. I help them wash their faces and brush their teeth before we move across the hall to their bedroom. Once they have jammies picked out, I help them change. I know they don't need it, but they asked for it, and who am I to refuse them?

"Now, this is very important. Are you ready?" I ask them. They nod, their little bodies vibrating with excitement. "I need you to grab your pillows from your beds. Do you know where mommy keeps the extra blankets?"

"We gots lots of those," River tells me.

"In the hallway." Rayne points toward the hallway.

"Perfect. Take your pillows to the couch and wait for me."

"Okay!" they chorus as they rush to grab their pillows and take off down the hall toward the living room.

In the hallway, I open the closet door and sure enough, there are lots of blankets. I grab an armful, and head to the living room. River and Rayne are standing in front of the couch in their jammies, holding their pillows.

I drop the blankets in a pile on the floor. "Have you ever built a fort?" I ask them.

"A fort?" Rayne tilts her head to the side.

"What's a fort?" River asks.

"We move the furniture around and build a fort, kind of like a tent with blankets," I explain.

"Can we help?" River asks.

"You bet. First, I'll need you to hop up on the couch." They do as I say. "Hold on," I tell them as I move the couch a few feet forward. The girls are laughing as I do. "Stay there while I move the rest." I get busy moving the coffee table, and the love seat and two chairs. I get them in a nice three-sided square.

"Now what?" Rayne questions.

"Now, we drape the blankets over them and place pillows and anything we can find that won't break to hold them up." The girls climb off the couch and the three of us get to work. It takes some time, but thirty minutes later, we have a pretty damn nice blanket fort in the living room.

"Now what do we do, Forty?" River asks.

"Now, we enjoy our fort." Dropping to my knees, I crawl into the fort and settle on the pad of blankets and pillows. The girls giggle and follow me in. "Let's snuggle and read a book." I reach for the small stack of books I got from their room and the flashlight I found in the hall closet when I was grabbing more blankets. The twins curl up next to me and, by the glow of the flashlight, I read them a story. They're both out cold before I get to the last page.

Turning off the flashlight and tossing it to the side with the book, I snuggle them close and close my eyes. I'm not going to sleep, just rest. Running after two tiny humans and keeping them occupied is harder than I thought it would be. Regardless, I wouldn't change a single thing about today. I've enjoyed my time with them.

My eyelids pop open, feeling like someone is watching me. Once my eyes are focused, I see Briar kneeling at the opening of our fort, with a soft smile on her face.

"Hey," she whispers.

Before I greet her, I carefully move the girls off my chest and crawl out of the fort. As soon as I'm on my feet, I wrap my arm around her waist and pull her into a kiss. "Hey, baby. Did you have a good day?"

"We did. Looks like you did as well."

"They're great kids, Briar."

"Fancy building skills you got there," Brogan whispers, her tone light and teasing.

"Thank you. I had two adorable little assistants."

Brogan chuckles. "I'm calling it a night. See you in the morning." She waves over her shoulder as she disappears down the hall.

"I should carry them to bed," I say, looking back at the fort where the girls are sleeping.

"They're fine for now. Are you in a hurry to get home?"

"Am I in a hurry to leave my girls? Nope. What are you thinking?" I pull her a little closer because I can never seem to get her close enough.

"Let's sit outside. It's a nice night. Not too hot."

"Lead the way, baby." I release her, only to lace her fingers with mine. She leads us outside to the back patio. The lights are off, but the moonlight gives off a nice glow.

Briar releases my hand and takes a seat on one of the loungers. Something is off, but I don't know what it is. She seems to be stressed. Was it something I did with the girls today? Did my sister or one of the other ladies upset her? My mind is racing. Whatever it is, she's giving off vibes that she doesn't want me to squeeze into the lounger either. Instead, I drag another close to her and take a seat.

I don't speak, letting her collect her thoughts. I don't want to push her, but she invited me out here, so that tells me she wants to talk. She's just not ready.

Tilting my head back, I stare up at the night sky. It's a full moon, and the stars are shining brightly. It's the perfect night for a bonfire, and a few years ago, that's exactly how me and the guys would have spent this night. However, as with everything, life changes. Roman and Legend each have a wife and a family. Well, Legend has one on the way. We're still close, but we're not all we have anymore.

"I don't know who their dad is."

Briar's voice is raspy as she drops that truth bomb in my lap. What do I say to that? What does she mean, she doesn't know who their dad is?

"Let me get through this. Please."

"Okay," I croak. My voice is gravelly as my mind races, and I try to understand what she just said.

"It was the summer after graduation. Brogan and I got invited to a party. It was a college party. We were excited to be invited. We were eating at a restaurant in downtown Nashville when a group of guys came in. Their table was next to ours. They flirted. We flirted back. They invited us to the party, and we accepted."

I can already tell I don't like where this is going.

"We didn't tell our dad where we were going. Just that we were hanging out with friends. We showed up at the party and didn't know anyone there. That didn't stop us, though. We had each other. We grabbed drinks from the keg. We watched the pour, and I even insisted on looking inside the cup before they poured. The guy was annoyed with me, but he let me do it. I don't know how it happened, Forrest. We were so careful."

Her voice cracks on a sob, and it's killing me not to pull her into my arms and comfort her, but she asked me to let her get through this, so I sit here with my heart tearing to shreds as I listen to her story. Not just her story, but her truth.

"I don't remember any of it. Nothing. I woke up the next morning with a pounding headache, my pants around my ankles, and an ache between my thighs. There was blood on the sheets."

My hands ball into fists.

"They took that from me. My first time. My innocence. Brogan, she woke up alone. Her clothes were intact and no sign of—that. Of rape. Not like me."

Motherfucker.

She sucks in a ragged breath, trying to get a handle on her emotions. "I didn't know what to do. I got dressed. My movements were sluggish. I found Brogan in the living room screaming the place down, demanding to know where I was. As soon as she saw me, we bolted. I didn't tell her until we got home. I didn't tell anyone other than Brogan. I just wanted to forget it ever happened. I couldn't remember it, so I pretended as if it had never happened."

"Briar—" I try, but she shakes her head, holding her hand up to stop me.

"Brogan stuck by my side. We stopped going out with friends and spent a lot of time at home. When it was time for me to get my period, and it never came, I knew. In my gut, I knew. My sister, she went and bought one of every brand of pregnancy test, and I took them all. They were all positive."

She's breathing hard, tears coating her cheeks. I know because I'm staring at this beautiful woman in the glow of the moonlight as she tears open old wounds to let me into her life, and I hope like hell into her heart.

"I was so scared. Brogan, she was my rock, the only solid piece of my crumbling foundation. She was with me when I told our dad. I was so worried that he was going to be disappointed in me. He was angry on my behalf, but it was too late. Any evidence was long gone, and I had no way of knowing who... violated me that night. My dad he... he was the best dad. He told me it was my choice. The three of us went to my first OB appointment, where the doctor listened to my story and reviewed my options. At the time, I thought it was one baby."

Her breath shudders, but she keeps pushing through while my fists are so tight, I fear my skin might break open.

"I took two weeks to think about it. I read everything I could about each option, but at the end of the day, the baby was a part of me. The only option I could consider was keeping it."

She smiles, but it's a sad smile that doesn't reach her eyes. "When I found out it was twins, I was stunned but didn't have time to dwell. Two days later, my dad was diagnosed with stage four pancreatic cancer."

My chest is tight. My heart is cracked wide open for this woman. My woman. I'm trying to tamp down my anger for her benefit. Now is not the time to be raging mad. I know that. I'm trying, but I'm so fucking angry that this happened to her. She's been dealt a tough hand, one I never could have imagined. I knew she had a past, something she was keeping close to her chest, but I never imagined that it was this.

"I know this changes things. I know it's a lot, but I have one favor to ask of you."

"Anything," I force the reply past my lips.

"Don't—Don't hold it against them. They love you, Forrest."

"What the fuck?"

"Thank you for listening. Please... can you keep this between us?"

"Briar." She doesn't look at me. "Baby, look at me."

"I can't," she cries. "It's too painful. Just go."

Go? How in the fuck am I supposed to leave after that? Does she really expect me to walk away?

Yeah, no. That's not how this is going to work.

BRIAR 16

MY HEART IS SHREDDED. THERE isn't a single piece that's
still intact. When I saw Forrest snuggled up with the girls
in their fort in the middle of my living room, I knew my time was
up. I had to tell him. The girls are attached. I'm attached. I
couldn't let us keep falling for this man, knowing he's missing a
huge piece of who we are as a family. My girls and me, and even
my sister.

"Go?" Forrest grits out.

I can feel his heavy gaze, but I can't make eye contact with
him. It's too much. Losing him is too much. I knew better, but
it's not all my fault. He slipped into our lives, and into our hearts
like a thief in the night, and here we are.

Our hearts are invested.

"Please don't make this harder than it already is," I plead
through my tears.

I hear him rustling and my heart stutters in my chest. This is
it. This is the moment when he walks away. In a way, this is just
as soul-crushing as that night all those years ago. He's not a
nameless, faceless memory.

He's our Forrest.

Our Forty.

He's in our hearts, and the pain is already unbearable.

I startle when he slides his arms beneath me, lifting me from the lounger. He takes my place with me nestled on his lap. There's a lump in my throat that makes it almost impossible to swallow back the sob that's threatening to break free.

"You had your turn, baby. Now it's mine. I need you to listen."

I nod because words fail me. I don't know what he's about to say, but being in his arms, it feels right, as if this is where I've always belonged. This very well could be the last time I feel his strong arms wrapped around me. So, while this is torture, I'm soaking up every second of time with him.

"I'm not going anywhere. Do you hear me, Briar? I'm right here. You're safe in my arms, and that's where you belong. That's where I need you." His breathing is labored, and his voice is stern.

"I wish you could see it," he continues. "I wish you could see you how I see you." He pauses and presses his lips to the top of my head. "Every day, Briar, you are the first thing I think about when I wake up. Not just you, but the girls too. I can't tell you how many times during the day I want to call you to tell you something. From a song on the radio to something I think the girls would love."

He stops again, and I notice his breathing is calmer. He seems to be settling down, and oddly enough, it's calming me too. His words race through my mind, and I don't have time to really decipher them when he starts talking again.

"At night, my house is quiet and lonely. I find myself wishing you and the girls were there with me."

I lift my head to look at him. He wipes at my tears with his thumbs. "Really?" I ask. I'm having a hard time processing all the emotions of the evening.

"Really. Baby, I hate what you went through. I hate what was stolen from you. It hurts my heart that you think I'd walk away because of it."

"I'm broken, Forrest. I've had sex once in my life, and I don't remember it. That one night that I can't remember gave me two of the greatest gifts in this world. I have a lot of emotional baggage."

"I have broad shoulders. I want you to lean on me, and use my strength. I want to help you find yourself again. I want to help you build your confidence and learn that trusting is okay. I want to make you smile and see your eyes light up, and those girls, they're mine too.

"And don't get me started on you thinking I would treat them differently or think differently of those little angels because of circumstances beyond your control or theirs. They are your daughters. They are a part of you. I'm very aware that there are three hearts I'm fighting for."

"Are you? Fighting for them, I mean, for us?" I bite down on my bottom lip. Hope soars inside my chest. I'm almost afraid to think about what that means for us. For me and my daughters. Forrest wants to be a part of our lives, and I know without the shadow of a doubt, we want him to be a part of it.

"You're damn right, I'm fighting for my girls."

His words hit me square in the chest, and I can't hold my tears. A sob escapes, and Forrest pulls me back to his chest. He rubs his hands gently up and down my spine until I get myself under control.

"I don't know when I'll be ready," I confess to his chest.

"That's fine. We have forever."

Forever.

How can one word make me feel giddy? It's easy to picture Forrest as a permanent part of our lives. I want that. I know this is a me issue. I've never really dealt with what happened to me, and then Dad passed right after the twins were born. I think it's time I talk to someone. Honestly, it might be good for Brogan to as well.

It's time to move forward.

"I want this with you, Forrest."

"Good. I'm not going anywhere."

"Can we try something?"

"What's that, baby?"

"Do you maybe want to stay here? Tonight, I mean. It's getting late, and the girls will be up early, but I'm not ready to be away from you." My confession is a huge step for me, one I never could have seen myself taking before I met the man who's holding me as if I'm the most precious thing in his life.

We both know what my request means. Forrest has my trust. He's had it for a long time. It's the next step of me moving forward, and he's not the only one who's thought about what could be. I've lain awake staring at shadows on the ceilings, wondering how it would feel to fall asleep next to him, wrapped in his arms. He's not some nameless, faceless frat boy.

He's ours.

"What about the girls?"

"They adore you."

"What are we going to tell them? I can be up early and sneak out."

"No. I don't want that. I want you here with us, Forrest." I think about his question. "We'll tell them that you're my boyfriend and that we're all going to be spending a lot more time together."

"Yeah?" His eyes brighten in the moonlight.

"Baby steps."

He lifts my hand and places it over his heart. "There is so much I want to say, but I know it's not the time. When you're ready, you let me know. Until then, just know that this is where the three of you are. That's what you mean to me."

My eyes widen because I'm pretty sure he's saying that he loves us, or is this just my lonely heart reading too much into his words?

"Okay."

"Come on, baby. Let's go to bed." I stand and offer him my hand. He takes it, allowing me to help him stand. Hand in hand, we step back into the house. Forrest locks the door behind us as I go to peek in on the girls. "They're out," I whisper.

"Let's let them sleep here tonight."

"Yeah. I'll turn the light on over the stove in case they wake up."

He waits for me to handle the lights and follows me to my room. My hands are shaking and my stomach rolls with a little excitement and a little fear of having a man in my room.

"We're just sleeping, Briar, and if you've changed your mind, I can head home."

"No. I'm just nervous."

"Go get changed for bed, baby. I'll be right here."

Nodding, I grab what I need and disappear into the en suite bathroom. When I emerge a few minutes later, he's shirtless, still in his shorts, lying on top of the covers.

"You tell me how this is going to go, Briar. Under the covers? Me on top of them? Lights on? Whatever you want this moment to be is how it's going to play out. You have all the control here, baby."

"I apologize now if I wake up freaking out. I've never done this."

"Understood. I'll be here regardless until you tell me to leave."

"Under the covers." Turning out the light, I walk to the other side of the bed and slide beneath the cover. Forrest does the same. Anxiety rolls through me. I take a few minutes to dissect how I'm feeling. I'm tired of running and avoiding life. After a few minutes, I know the cause of my anxiety. It's not because I'm scared. It's because I'm nervous.

"Tell me what you need, Briar."

"Will you hold me?"

"All night long," he promises.

I feel the bed dip, and then his arms are around me. He kisses my shoulder. "Tomorrow, you're coming to Sunday dinner. You and the girls. Brogan too," he adds.

"Okay." I don't tell him that I already promised Emerson I would be there.

"Thank you. Night, baby."

"Night."

I assumed it would take me hours to fall asleep with him next to me, being my first time and all that, but his arms around me have the opposite effect. The Forrest effect, I guess, because I feel safe, relaxed, and cherished. Sleep claims me quickly.

"Mommy." I hear a little voice.

"Mommy, Forrest is sleeping in your bed," another little voice announces.

My eyes pop open to see the girls standing beside the bed. Their eyes are wide and curious. "Good morning."

"Did Forty have a sleepover?" River asks.

"He did."

"Hims could have slept with us." Rayne pouts.

"I did sleep with you," Forrest says. He leans over me and bops each of the girls on the nose with his index finger. "We fell asleep in our fort. When your mommy got home, I didn't want her to be lonely, so I came to bed with her."

River tilts her head to the side. "Aunt Brogan was probably lonely too. We should find her a friend to have a sleepover with."

Forrest huffs out a laugh.

"Girls, why don't you go to the living room, and we'll be right there to make breakfast?"

"Forrest too?" Rayne asks shyly.

"Yeah, sweetheart. I'm staying."

"Yay!" the girls cheer as they rush out of my bedroom and down the hall toward the kitchen.

"Morning, baby."

"Hi." I feel embarrassed, but I don't know why.

"How did you sleep?"

"Better than I have in a long time."

"Me too. We should do this more often. I like waking up to my girls."

"You don't have to stay. I can make an excuse."

"There is nowhere else I'd rather be. Besides, you promised me breakfast, and the five of us are going to Monroe and Legend's for Sunday dinner."

"They're going to tell us the gender of their baby." I slap my hand over my mouth.

"Wait a minute. You were already going, weren't you?"

"Sorry." I wince.

"Come here." He leans in, and I turn my head.

"I need to brush my teeth."

"No, you need to kiss me. Come on, woman. Pay your penance, and we can make breakfast."

I can't say no. I don't want to say no, so I lean in and press my lips to his. Who knew adult sleepovers could be so fun?

"Who lives here?" River asks as Forrest parks my car in Monroe and Legend's driveway.

"This is Monroe and Legend's house," Brogan tells her. She's sitting in the back seat with the twins. She wanted to drive separately, but I insisted she come with us. I'm not ousting my sister because I have a boyfriend.

"I don't think I know them," Rayne says thoughtfully.

"You've met them both," I assure her.

"What are we gonna do?" River asks.

"We're going to eat lots of good food and hang out with our friends and family," Forrest answers her.

River gasps. "We have friends and family?"

My chest tightens. The girls have only really known Brogan and me until Emerson and Monroe brought us into the fold of their lives, and now, Forrest.

"You do," Forrest answers her. "You ready to play with Lilly?"

"Lilly is here? We love Lilly," Rayne replies.

"She is. Come on." Forrest opens his door, and there is nothing left to do but follow him. He insisted he drive, and since the car seats were in my car, I compromised that we would take mine instead of his truck. He grumbled something about getting his own damn car seats. At least that's what it sounded like.

Brogan helps the girls unbuckle, and soon we're all striding toward the front door. Forrest doesn't bother knocking as he turns the knob and steps inside. He offers each of the girls one of his hands, and they jump at the chance to have his attention. "Ladies." He grins and nods at Brogan and me to go on inside.

"We're here!" Forrest calls out once we're all in and the door is shut behind us. He leads us down the hall to a large living room.

"We're here too!" Rayne says, making everyone laugh.

"Come on in. Make yourselves at home," Monroe says.

"Girls, do you want to play blocks with Lilly?" Emerson asks. She's sitting on the floor with Lilly.

I watch as my daughters look up at Forrest for his permission. He kneels. "Do you want to play with Lilly?" he asks them. They nod. "It's okay. Mommy, Aunt Brogan, and I will be right here."

"We want you to go with us." River juts out her bottom lip.

"Blocks are my jam," he says enthusiastically. Standing to his full height, he walks to where his sister is sitting on the floor with his niece, takes a seat, and the girls plop down on his lap. He reaches for a few blocks, and they start to play. Lilly comes walking over, and she, too, somehow manages to settle on his lap.

"Girls, let Forrest have some space."

"Mommy, he's our Forty," Rayne says.

"Yeah, Mommy." Forrest winks at me. "They're fine, babe."

I melt under his gaze, and I'm certain everyone in this room can see it. I'm terrible at hiding my emotions and right now, they're stronger than ever when it comes to this man.

"It's almost time to eat," Legend announces.

"Can we help?" Brogan asks.

"Sure, come on into the kitchen." Brogan follows Monroe and Legend into the kitchen. Maggie trails behind them.

"You coming, Briar?" Emerson asks me.

I glance back at the girls.

"I've got them," Forrest tells me. "Go have girl talk or whatever it is you ladies do."

"Are you sure?"

"He's sure," Maddox speaks up. "We've got a tower to build, right, girls?"

"A tower?" the twins ask at the same time.

Maddox moves to the floor and starts stacking blocks, and the girls climb off Forrest's lap to help him. Lilly curls up on his shoulder, and let me tell you, it's a sight to see these men so tender with my daughters and Lilly. I don't know what we did to bring these people into our lives, but I'm grateful.

"How much longer?" Emerson whines. "This is torture, Mo. Pure torture."

"Baby girl, she'll tell us soon." Roman tries to pacify her.

"I guess we can tell everyone." Monroe looks up at Legend, who is staring at her like she's his entire world.

"Whatever you want," he tells her.

"Let's do it." Monroe stands from where she was sitting on Legend's lap on the couch, and moves to the kitchen. She comes back holding a box. "Everyone gets a cupcake. Rayne? River? Would you want to help me with something really special?" she asks the girls.

"Yes!" they cheer.

"Em, how do you feel about Lilly getting messy with a cupcake?"

"I don't think she needs all the sugar. It's almost nap time," Emerson replies.

Monroe nods. "We'll send hers home with you." She motions for the girls to come to the coffee table. She places two small paper plates down and unwraps two cupcakes. "Okay, are you ready for the rules?" Monroe asks them.

"Yes," they say in unison.

"So, these cupcakes are very special. The insides are either pink or blue. If you have pink in your cupcake, that means my baby is a girl. If you have blue inside your cupcake, that means I'm having a boy." Monroe peels the paper off the cupcakes to make it easier for them to bite into.

"Where's your baby?" River asks.

"In my belly."

Rayne turns to look at me. "Mommy, can we have a baby?"

My mouth falls open. I don't know what to say. If I say yes, Forrest will think I want him to knock me up, and his friends and family are here. Also, the girls will keep asking. If I say no, it might crush them.

"Maybe one day," Forrest answers for me. He's sitting on the floor in front of my chair and gives my leg a gentle squeeze. His answer seems to appease my daughter, and she turns back to Monroe, ready for further instruction.

"Now, when I say three, you take a big bite of your cupcake and tell us what color it is. Are you ready?" Monroe asks them.

"Ready!" They wiggle in excitement.

"One. Two. Three!" Monroe calls out and the girls grab their treats and take a huge bite. They have icing all over their faces, pink and blue to throw us off, but there is no missing the blue crumbs that fall to their plates.

"A boy!" Emerson cheers and rushes toward her best friend, wrapping her in a hug. "We're getting a boy." Everyone takes turns passing out hugs, handshakes, and congratulations before we venture back to our seats.

"Em, it's not ours." Roman laughs.

"We're a family. It's ours. We need a boy. Three girls, he's going to feel outnumbered."

I freeze. Three girls. She included my daughters. Hot tears prick my eyes. I blink hard to push them back, but they're still there. I chance a look at my sister, who is watching me closely. She's sitting on the love seat with Maddox next to her. She also has tears in her eyes. She gives me a subtle nod.

This is where we belong.

"We need more babies," Rayne announces.

"What do you think, Brogan? We could get some practice in," Maddox asks my sister. She swats at his arm, and everyone laughs. Maddox catches my eye and winks. He could see the heaviness of the moment, and he eased the tension in the room.

I mouth a "Thank you," and he nods.

"All right, who wants a cupcake?" Monroe asks.

We eat cupcakes, laugh, and talk, the kids play, and I can't remember a day where I had more fun. It feels like everything we went through brought us here. To this town, these people.

This is where we were meant to be.

FORREST 17

"I T WAS NICE OF YOUR girl to have us all over," Lachlan tells me.

We're sitting in lawn chairs in Briar and Brogan's backyard. Today is July Fourth, and as it turns out, Ashby's fireworks are set off on the other side of the river. There is a clear view from their backyard. Instead of having our annual Fourth of July party at my place, Briar and Brogan insisted we have it here. In the past, we never cared much about the fireworks. We'd let a few off in my backyard. I'd take Emerson when she was younger, but it wasn't that important as she got older and lost interest.

That's about to change.

We have littles in the family again, and the girls have been stoked about this all week. We're unsure how Lilly will do, but we're all here to cuddle her if she hates them. Hopefully, she'll love them.

"Yeah," I agree with Lachlan. "The girls are pumped about the fireworks."

"How's that going?" he asks.

I turn to look at him. "What? The girls?"

"Yeah, you know, dating a single mom?"

"Good. Great, really. The girls are sweet as hell."

"Where's their dad?" Lachlan asks. "That jackass is missing out on seeing his kids grow up."

"Not in the picture," I say casually, hiding the anger that wells inside me when I think about what happened to Briar and Brogan that night.

"Good. You're a better dad than he ever will be. Fucking sperm donors," he mumbles under his breath.

Lachlan's biological father is a deadbeat. He gave up his rights to Lachlan before he was born. Two years later, his mom met and married his stepdad. That's the only father he's ever known, and you would never know Lachlan isn't his biological child. He's been there for Lachlan without fail his entire life.

"I hope to be."

Before he can answer, Rayne comes running over with tears in her eyes. "Forrest." Her lip quivers.

"What's wrong, Dazzle?" I ask, using her nickname, hoping it will cheer her up.

"I hurted my foot."

"Let me see." I lift her into my arms and inspect her bare foot. Sure enough, there's a big red spot on the bottom of her right foot. "What happened?" I ask her.

"A big, big rock," she says with a huff.

Leaning down, I kiss her foot. "There. All better."

"You made it better, Forty," she says, leaning back against my chest.

I wrap my arm around her, and my eyes find Lachlan's.

"You're a good man, Forrest Huntley."

If loving this little girl, her sister, and their momma makes me a good man, then I'm the best there is. There isn't anything I wouldn't do for the three of them. I'm itching to say the words. To tell all three of them that I'm here to stay and that my heart is split in three for them, but I hold back. I need her to tell me she's ready to hear it. Until she's ready to accept that I love her, saying the words will be empty. When I tell her I love her, I want to see it in her eyes. I want that total acceptance that we are each other's future. I want to be the girls' dad. Waiting is torture, but she's letting me in a little more each day.

"You want me to take her?" I look up to find Briar standing next to my chair.

"Nah, she's fine. Where's River?"

"She's with Brogan. They're around front, hiding from Maddox with a water gun."

"I want my water gun," Rayne says.

"You want me to take you?" I ask her.

"Come on, Rayne. Let's go sneak up on them," Briar says.

Rayne turns and hugs me. "Love you, Forrest," she whispers.

My heart stops. Briar freezes, but not me. I wrap my arms around her and kiss her cheek. "Love you, too, Dazzle." My voice is gruff as I say the words I've been dying to let free. I want to tell her sister and her momma too, but Rayne, she got to them first, and no way in hell am I not saying it back.

Rayne smiles and climbs off my lap. "Mommy, I hurted my foot, but Forty kissed it better." I hear her say as they walk off hand in hand.

Leaning forward, I rest my elbows on my knees. Damn, but my heart is melted into a puddle right now. Who knew a tiny four-year-old could bring me to my knees?

"Damn, bro," Lachlan mutters.

"Yeah. I'm toast." I laugh.

"Happy for you, man."

"Thanks." I sit back in my chair and let the moment sink in.

I have two daughters. I'm a dad.

"Forrest!" The girls come rushing over.

"Razzle, Dazzle." I bend and open my arms, accepting a hug from them. "What's up, ladies?" I ask them.

"Mommy said the fireworks are now."

"We're getting close."

"Who needs a gym when you have twin four-year-olds with unlimited energy?" Briar huffs out as she joins us. She holds up a blanket. "Grabbed one for us."

"Where are we doing this?" Monroe asks, her own blanket in her hands.

"I don't know, but I'm ready," Maggie says, also holding a blanket.

"Do you think we have time for popcorn?" Maddox asks.

The girls giggle. "Mad, we don't eat popcorn with fireworks," Rayne explains.

"Oh, we don't?"

"No, silly." River laughs.

"I don't have a blanket." He pouts. "And now I don't get popcorn."

"Aunt Brogan has a blanket," River says helpfully. "She'll share with you. It's nice to share, right, Aunt Brogan?"

"That's right, sweetie," Brogan replies. "Although, I think Maddox should ask nicely."

"Mad, you have to ask nicely," Rayne repeats helpfully.

"Brogan, can I please share your blanket?" Maddox asks.

"Hmm, I don't know. Was that nice enough?" Brogan goads him.

I know my best friend, and he's going to go over the top if for no other reason than to make the twins laugh. The little twins, hell, maybe even the older ones.

Maddox dramatically drops to his knees and clasps his hands together, peering up at Brogan. "Brogan, will you please do me the honor of sharing your blanket with you?"

"Maddox!" River and Rayne are in a fit of giggles.

Maddox winks at them and climbs to his feet. "What about now?" he asks Brogan.

"He was so nice, Aunt Brogan," River defends.

"Fine," Brogan grumbles, while Maddox high-fives River and Rayne. "Besides, I have a big blanket. Maggie and Lachlan can share with us too." She smirks at Maddox, and he shakes his head with a smile.

We all lay out our blankets on the lawn and sit back, getting ready for the show. Briar and I have the girls with us. Emerson and Roman are snuggled up with Lilly. Monroe and Legend are together, Maddox is sharing with Brogan, and so are Legend and Maggie.

The twins are lying between Briar and me, and I know this is another one of those moments with them that I'll always remember. We feel like a family.

We *are* a family.

The girls ooh and ahh over the show. Lilly does great, bouncing on Roman's belly. She seems to be scared at first, but when she sees we're all relaxed, she settles down.

Today has been a great day. Lots of memories, lots of love, and so much more to come.

Everyone has gone home, and the mess from the party is all cleaned up. The girls are nestled in their beds. Brogan and Maggie went to Get Hammered, the local bar in town, with Maddox and Lachlan. That leaves Briar and me.

"What a great day," Briar says, from her place beside me on the couch.

"It was a great day. Thank you for letting us invade your space."

She nods. "It was a lot of fun."

"You and the girls both seemed to be enjoying yourselves. You seem more... relaxed lately." I'd like to think it's because she's secure in what we have, but I'm not sure that's it. Something has changed over the last couple of weeks.

"I've been talking to someone. Brogan has too."

"Meaning?"

"We've been doing these virtual therapy sessions. It's still early, but I don't know, something about talking about it, not hiding behind that night. It's... freeing."

"Baby, I'm so fucking proud of you." Reaching over, I lift her from her place and set her on my lap. "I love to see you taking care of yourself. Brogan too. Am I allowed to tell her that the next time I see her?"

She snuggles into my chest. "Yeah, she'll be here in the morning when we wake up."

She can't see it, but there's a wide smile on my face. This woman has made leaps and bounds by trusting me with her heart. She's been through hell, and she's fighting to come out on the other side and not let her past define her future.

"Thank you. I don't know that I ever would have taken that step if you hadn't come into our lives. I never thought I would feel safe with a man. You changed that. You make me want to be better. Not just for you, but for me, and my girls, and my sister. I've realized that Brogan has put her life on hold for me and the girls. She was there that night, and she has survivor's guilt, and I don't want that for her. I want her to be happy and healthy. I want her to find someone... like you. Someone who will hold her in their arms, and just being there, she'll know everything is going to be okay."

"She'll find him," I say with confidence.

"Yeah, I think she will too," she says, covering a yawn.

"You ready for bed?"

"Yes."

"I'll lock up."

"Can you leave the light over the stove on for Brogan when she gets home?"

"Absolutely. Need anything?"

"Just you, Forrest."

"You have me, baby. All of me." I lean in for a kiss. One that was meant to be a quick peck, but she opens for me, and grips my shirt, pulling me closer. That's all the encouragement I need to deepen the kiss. I don't hide my hunger for her, and she gives it back to me tenfold.

Forcing myself to pull away, I rest my forehead against hers. "I'm seconds away from stripping you down, and I don't want to risk the girls waking up and seeing that." Standing to my full height, I take a step back.

Briar juts out her bottom lip. "Aw, Forty." She crosses her arms over her chest.

"Our girls have taught you well, Momma. Off to bed."

Her eyes widen, but a sweet smile is her reply.

I swat her ass and head to make sure the house is locked up, and to leave the light above the stove on for my future sister-in-law when she gets home later tonight.

In the bedroom, the lights are off, but that's okay. I know my way around. I strip down to my boxer briefs, and slide into bed. Briar immediately snuggles up next to me.

"Did you mean it?" she finally asks, her voice small.

"I don't say things I don't mean, baby. But did I mean what?"

"You said our girls."

"Are you mine?" I ask her.

"Yes."

I smile into the darkness. There was no hesitation in her reply.

"They're your daughters. You're mine. They're ours. You have to share with me, Briar. It's only fair."

She's quiet, and I know she's processing my words. "My therapist says it's important to talk, to be open and honest. Can you tell me what that looks like for you? When you say they're ours?"

"Are you ready?" I ask her.

"I—I don't know."

I nod. She's not ready to hear it, but I know she's getting there. She can take all the time she needs. In the meantime, I need to make her understand without freaking her out. "It means that I can see a future with the four of us. I can see me stepping up for them as their dad when you're comfortable with that. I promise I won't step over any boundaries that you give me, but you make me happy. Being a part of your lives, all three of you, is what was missing from mine. You chase away the lonely."

I love you. I want you and the girls to move in with me, and I want to have more babies with you. That's what I want to say, but that time will come. When she's ready, I'll have said the words so many times in my head that my confession will roll off my tongue with ease.

"They love you."

My chest expands because I speak Briar, and I know she's using the girls as a way to express what she's feeling. Yes, the girls love me. I love them, too, but this whispered confession is more.

So much fucking more.

"I love them too."

She lifts her head and through the light of the moon shining through the window, I watch as she leans in closer. Her lips find mine, and I let her set the pace. Slow and easy is what she gives me, and it's what I'll take.

"This is all new to me, Forrest. You've had ten years, and well, what feels like a lifetime's more experience than I have."

"You're forgetting one thing."

"What's that?" she asks.

I brush her hair back over her shoulder. "This is a first for me. I've never cared this much, Briar. I've never been this invested. Every touch with you feels like the first time."

"I don't know what I'm doing."

"Baby, there is no right or wrong way. You do what feels good. What turns you on?"

"What turns you on?" she counters.

"You."

"I'm being serious," she says, swatting at my chest playfully.

I capture her hand in mine and slowly guide it over my abs until we reach my cock. I'm hard as stone. She gasps. "I'm yours, Briar. There isn't a single thing you could do wrong when it comes to touching or exploring. You're safe with me, always."

"I'd like to try."

"Good girl," I husk. Lifting my arms, I lock them behind my head. "I'm all yours."

"This is embarrassing, Forrest. I'm twenty-three, a mom of two." Her voice is laced with what sounds like sadness and anger.

"Life has knocked you down, baby, but you're getting back up. I hate what happened to you. If I could find him, I'd make him pay. I would, but there's also a part of me that's excited that I get to be here with you like this. I get to be the man you get all your firsts with. Forget the past. The only part we want to remember are those two beautiful girls sleeping down the hall. The rest of you is mine. It's ours, and I'm all in."

I hear her exhale a heavy breath, and then her hand moves to my cock. She palms me through my boxer briefs. I keep my mouth shut. This is her time. I need her to know that she has all the control. I need her to feel safe to explore for the first time in her life.

"Are they all this... big?"

A huff of laughter leaves my chest. "If you're trying to inflate my ego, baby, it's working."

"Did you make it do that?"

"Do what?"

"That twitch, or whatever it was."

"Your hands are on me. I have no control over my body's reaction to you. In fact, I should probably warn you that if this continues, and I hope that it does, I might make a mess of both of us."

"Oh, you mean... get off?"

"That's exactly what I mean."

"Let's do that." There's excitement in her voice.

"You want me to get you off?" It's not where I thought this night was going, but if that's what my girl wants, that's what she's going to get. It's not like it's a hardship for me.

"You. I want to get you off."

My cock thickens, and she gasps. "Told you. It's you, and I have no control."

"Tell me what to do."

"Just touch me. Stroke me." I'm grappling with my control.

"What about my mouth?"

Fuck me. I pull in a slow, deep breath and exhale just the same. "You want my cock in your mouth, baby?"

196 | KAYLEE RYAN

"Yes."

Fuck. I pray that I can hold off to give her time to practice or explore or whatever in the hell we're calling this. Honestly, my brain is malfunctioning. I can barely remember how to speak.

Lifting my hips, I work my boxer briefs down over my hips. "The door."

"What?"

"Lock the door. I do not want the girls to walk in and see this."

"The door. Right. On it." She scrambles off the bed and rushes to quietly shut the door and turn the lock. I make a mental note, one that I hope I can remember, to unlock it before we go to sleep in case the girls need us in the middle of the night.

She bounces back to the bed and settles next to me. She wastes no time palming my cock and stroking. She's being gentle.

"Harder."

"I don't want to hurt you."

"You won't."

"Show me."

This woman, she's trying to kill me.

Placing my hand over hers, I stroke from root to tip, squeezing, showing her what feels good. After a few strokes, I return my hand to lock behind my head. She strokes me, going slow, then fast, applying a little more pressure, then easing up.

My eyes are closed as I enjoy the feel of her hands on me. However, when I feel her tongue—her hot wet tongue that licks my tip—I let out a low, deep groan.

"Is that a good sound?" she asks.

"Very good."

"What about if I do this?" She takes me into her mouth, and I see stars. "Is that good?"

"Are you playing with me?" I question her.

"No. I mean, I've never done this, but I've seen it done."

"Where?"

"Porn."

"You watch porn?"

"I'm a single mom of two with zero experience, as stupid as that sounds. So yeah, I watch porn."

"What do you like?"

"I don't really know. It's not like I sit up in bed with my laptop every night and watch. I've just watched it a few times here and there over the years."

"We'll come back to this later," I tell her. My mind is already going crazy with ideas of things we can try, or watch and then try. Fuck me, that's so hot. "Your mouth is heaven, baby. I like anything you do to me." That's all the encouragement she needs as she takes me back into her mouth. This time to the back of her throat. She holds there, then releases me only to repeat the process over and over again.

She's up on her knees and she's rubbing her thighs together. "Do you need relief, baby?"

My cock falls out of her mouth with an audible pop. "I'm aching. I don't know that I've ever been this turned on in my life."

"You want my mouth or my fingers?"

"I thought I had your cock?" she asks, stroking me.

"On your pussy, baby. You want my mouth or my fingers?"

"I want all of it. I want you to be my first." Her words are shy, a murmur into the darkness, but that doesn't make them any less potent to my heart.

I know what it took for her to say that. I know what a huge step this is for her, after being violated and not remembering it. I'm glad she doesn't remember. I think those memories would be even worse for her to battle.

"There's no rush."

"I don't feel rushed, Forrest. I feel free. I feel excited and turned on. I feel safe, and I know that if I freak out, you'll stop. I know that I want it to be you."

I love you.

I want to scream the words to her and to anyone who will listen. Instead, I swallow back the words and try to stay focused. "I don't have any condoms." This is the last thing I expected tonight. I should be prepared, but I know what she's been through, and I wasn't going to rush her.

"We don't need them."

"What?"

"I mean, if you don't want. I'm in the clear. Obviously, I was tested and, well, you know my history."

"I'm negative too. I was tested at my annual checkup. That was three months before I met you. There's been no one since even before that. But, baby, this is a big deal. Don't make this choice because you think it's what I want. We can wait. There's no rush," I say again. I need to know she understands.

"I'm in a rush, Forrest. I want this. I want you. I want to choose this time, and I choose you. I trust you, and I'm on birth control. I wasn't before because I wasn't sexually active, but I never wanted to make that mistake again should— So, yeah, I'm on birth control. I want this to be on my terms with a man I choose."

"Take what you need."

"What?"

"You're on top. You are in control. You take as little or as much as you need. You hold all the power here, baby."

"But I don't know what to do."

"You do what feels right. It's as simple as that. There is no right or wrong answer here."

"Will you help me?"

"Straddle my hips."

She does as I ask.

"When you're ready, rise up on your knees, fist my cock and slide down."

Briar is an excellent student. She does exactly as I say, and we both hiss out a breath when she guides me inside her.

"Oh," she moans.

I send up a silent prayer that I can hold off on my release until she gets hers. My hands are fisted, gripping the sheets as she slides lower. This time she doesn't stop until she's taken all of me.

"Wow," she whispers. "What now?"

"Now, you move. Rock back and forth, lift your hips up and down, rise on your knees. Just try it all. See what feels good to you." She rocks her hips, and her pussy pulses around my cock. She's so damn tight, and hot, and wet. It's unlike anything I've ever felt before.

"Never been bareback," I tell her.

"Really? I'm your first?"

"My only." I let the words hang between us. Her quick intake of breath indicates that she heard me.

"Am I doing okay?" she asks as she starts to find her rhythm.

"You're perfect."

"I really want to kiss you right now."

"Then come here and kiss me."

She does as I say, leaning in for a kiss. I raise my hips and slowly move inside her while she does.

"That's... damn." She lifts back up and quickly drops back down.

I'm barely hanging on, fighting the urge to take over, but this is her show.

"I need... I don't know what I need. Help me."

"Are you sure?"

"Yes."

Rising, I wrap my arms around her and flip us over on the mattress. She squeals with laughter, and her pussy squeezes my cock. "You tell me if this is too much, and we stop. Understand?"

"Please don't stop."

"Wrap your legs around me and hold on."

She does as I say. Once she's holding on, I pull out and push back in. I listen to the sounds she makes. I focus on the way her nails dig into my back. All my senses are on high alert.

"There," she moans, and thank fuck, because I'm close.

"Touch yourself for me."

"What?"

"Your clit, rub it gently, or whatever feels good."

"This feels good."

"I know, baby, trust me, I know, but I'm close, and I refuse to come before you do. So I need you to touch yourself for me."

Without needing further instruction, she slides a hand between us and rubs her clit.

"Oh."

"There it is," I say as I feel her pussy start to go crazy. "You're squeezing me so good," I tell her.

"It's—don't stop. Please. Please. Please," she chants.

"Not a chance in hell." I thrust harder. My hips piston in and out of her, and I bite down on my lip, hard, welcoming the pain.

"Forrest!" She calls out my name, and her body convulses around me. Her release washes over her, and her nails dig deep into my skin as she holds on.

I keep thrusting until her body relaxes into the mattress, and then I finally let go, spilling over inside her. Fuck, it's so different without latex. She's ruined me. I'll never want to have something between us ever. I've never come so hard in my life, and it's more than just no condom. It's the woman.

It's the fact that she owns every inch of my heart.

Bending, I rest my forehead against her chest, not willing to leave her yet. I already know I'll miss the warmth of my cock being nestled inside her. I would live inside her if I could.

I hear her sniffle, and my hackles rise. I lift my head and slowly pull out of her. No condom is a hell of a lot messier, but I can't focus on that right now. "Are you crying?"

"Yes."

"I'm sorry. Did I hurt you?" My voice cracks as panic sets in. I thought she was with me.

"No. No, of course not. These are happy tears. I never knew it could be like this."

"It's not. It's never been like this for me. It's us, Briar. It's who we are together."

"I like us together."

"Me too, baby. Me too." I kiss her softly, trying to show her that I more than like us together. I love us. I love her. "Let's get cleaned up."

We make quick work of cleaning up in the en suite. I slip back into my boxer briefs, and unlock and crack the door open in case the girls need us before sliding into bed and pulling her into my arms. Where she belongs.

I love you.

BRIAR 18

"**W**HERE ARE WE?" RIVER ASKS from her brand-new car seat in the back of Forrest's truck. It's the first week of September and we're headed to the county fair. Forrest picked us up, and the girls were thrilled to see they had their own seats in his truck. He got bonus points because there was a pink seat and a purple one. He knows my girly girls pretty well. I turn and smile at my girls, and my sister, who is sitting in the middle of the back seat between them. I offered to sit there, but she insisted she was fine.

"This is where I work, Razzle."

"You work here?" Rayne asks from her matching seat that's sitting right behind Forrest.

"I sure do."

"This is where you draw?" River asks.

"Something like that." Forrest laughs.

"Are we going to draw?" Rayne asks.

"Not today, Dazzle. Remember when I told you we were going to go to the county fair?"

"Oh, yeah." Rayne nods. "What are we gonna do there, Forty?"

"We're gonna ride some rides, play some games, and eat some junk food."

"Why are we going to eat junk?" River asks. I don't have to turn to look at her to know she's scrunching up her nose in distaste.

"Junk food is a way of saying food that's not super healthy," I explain to my daughters.

"Like elephant ears and deep-fried Oreos," Forrest adds.

"I like Oreos, but I don't think I've ever had any elephant. Have I, Mommy?" River asks.

It takes extreme effort to hide my laugh. "No, baby. But it's not an elephant ear for real. It's just called that."

"Sissy, junk food is weird," Rayne whispers.

"We're going with a bunch of people. Everyone I work with and their families," Forrest says.

"Are we your family, Forrest?" River asks, her voice small.

Forrest pulls his keys from the ignition, unbuckles his seat belt, and turns to face the girls. "You are my family."

"Where you been?" Rayne asks.

"I didn't know you until this year, but now that I do, we're family," Forrest explains. He looks at me, and I nod.

It's hard to make their four-year-old little minds understand, but they'll get it one day. I've been in therapy now for going on three months. I should have done it years ago. Brogan and I both have been making great progress, and for the first time in my adult life, I'm ready to move beyond my tragedy. I know I have Forrest to thank for that. He's... well, he's everything. My girls love him, and I love him.

No, I haven't told him yet. It's scary as hell to put yourself out there.

I know I have nothing to worry about with Forrest. He's proven himself over and over again. He's in this with me and my girls. I'm pretty sure he loves me. In fact, I'm certain of it, but he's never pushed me. He's given me the time I need to grow and process all these feelings.

I don't know how I managed to do so, but I met an incredible man who has captured all three of our hearts, and in turn, we've given him ours.

Brogan hops out of the truck, and she and Maggie ride with Maddox and Lachlan, while Roman, Emerson, and Lilly ride with Legend and Monroe. Then there is Lyra, Drake, and his girlfriend, Lisa, who also works at Everlasting Ink; they're all riding together. In a convoy, we pull out of the lot and make our way toward the county fair.

A family outing, as Emerson called it. I finally understand what she means. Family isn't blood, and this family—some blood related, most not—have chosen one another, and me, my girls, and my sister are lucky enough to be included in that label.

For the first time since our father passed, we have a family.

Our Everlasting Ink family.

"Which one do you want?" Forrest asks the girls.

"I want the pink one!" River says.

"I want purple!" Rayne calls out her request.

"Girls, don't get your hopes up. Forrest is going to try to win, but these games are hard. He might not be able to."

Maddox cracks up, laughing. "Briar, keep him in line."

"What? No, I mean, I'm sure you're great," I tell Forrest, grimacing at the fact that I pretty much just told the girls that he wouldn't win. "But these things are hard to win, right?"

"Your girl's doubting you, bro. You going to let that go?" Lachlan asks.

"Don't worry, girls," Legend says. "If Forrest can't win them for you, Uncle Legend will."

"Are you my uncle?" River asks.

"Yep. We're all your uncles," Legend tells her.

River looks at Rayne with wide eyes. "Sissy, we gots lots of uncles."

"And aunts," Emerson speaks up.

"You have Brogan, but you have me, Monroe, and Maggie, too," Emerson explains.

"This is the best day ever. Forty is family, and now we gots lots of aunts and uncles too!" Rayne exclaims, making everyone laugh.

"And what about me and Lisa?" Lyra asks.

"Oops." Emerson giggles. "Aunt Lyra and Aunt Lisa, too, and Uncle Drake."

"That's lots," River says.

"Don't worry, kiddo," Roman says. "We're not going anywhere. You have lots of time to remember our names. All you need to remember is that we're your family, and if you ever need us, you can come to any of us."

The girls nod, but it's Rayne who speaks. "We need those pink and purple bears." Everyone cracks up laughing as Forrest hands over his money to the game attendant.

"How do you win, Forty?" River asks.

"All I have to do is hit three balloons and make them pop."

"Oh, well, pop them all, will you?" she asks.

Forrest chuckles. "That's the plan, Razzle." He winks at her as he accepts his five darts.

"I want up." River holds her arms up for Maddox, and he scoops her up in his arms.

"Me too, me too." Rayne does the same to Lachlan, and he doesn't hesitate to place her on his hip.

"Go, Forty!" the girls cheer.

The smile on his face matches theirs. His first five dollars is a win as he points to the pink bear and hands it to River.

"Now I'll get yours," he tells Rayne. She wiggles around in excitement. I'm surprised Maddox and Lachlan can keep a hold of them with how much they're wiggling around.

It takes two rounds, but Forrest gets to hand Rayne her purple bear. "Lilly needs a bear too," Rayne says.

"My turn." Roman hands Lilly to Forrest as he steps up and passes over his five dollars for his five darts.

"Rome, you have big shoes to fill," Forrest goads him.

"Go, Rome!" the girls holler.

"Even your girls know I've got this, Huntley," Roman fires back.

"Prove it," Forrest taunts.

It takes Roman three tries, but he finally hands Lilly a green teddy bear. She snuggles it close to her where she's resting against Forrest's chest. Lachlan and Maddox declare it's Tilt-O-Whirl time. With my daughters on their hips, they head off to the rides, and we all follow along behind them. I don't know what I expected, but we're truly taking in this fair as a huge group. It's nice to be surrounded by good people.

I watch as my sister and Maggie laugh and cut up with everyone, and it's nice to see her happy. As if she's reading my thoughts, she winks at me and nods. She's thinking the same thing.

I move to stand next to Emerson and Monroe as we watch all the guys and my daughters climb onto the ride. Maggie snags Lilly from Forrest, and he joins them. "Thank you," I say, not looking at either of the ladies standing next to me.

"For what?" Monroe asks.

"Inviting us to girls' night." I finally turn to look at them. "You changed my life. All our lives. I will forever be grateful for that."

"You and the girls have brought him to life. He was struggling after I moved in with Roman. It all happened quickly, at least in Forrest's eyes. We were together a while before he knew. He was lonely, but he's not anymore. I should be thanking you," Emerson tells me.

"Let me tell you a story. I'll give you the condensed version." Brogan hears me and comes over to stand next to me. She takes my hand in hers. Maggie joins us, and I tell my story, which is also kind of my sister's story. The only other person I've told is Forrest and my therapist. By the time I'm done, I'm crying. Thankfully, the girls convince the guys to go another round on the ride, and they rush back to get into line.

"We've been talking to someone. A therapist the last couple of months," Brogan adds. "It's helping. We're healing."

"We are. However, I don't know that I would have taken that first step had it not been for Forrest."

"And me. When Briar told me what she was going to do, I knew that I needed to as well. We were young and didn't deal with any of it well. Then Dad passed, and we just kept pushing forward as best as we could."

Emerson looks at me with tears in her eyes. She doesn't say a word as she hugs me, then my sister. Monroe and Maggie do the same.

"Thank you for listening," I tell them.

"That's what friends are for. I can't even imagine what you went through, but we're here."

"All of us," Maggie adds.

"Thank you."

"Forrest knows," I tell Emerson, and she nods. "The others... can you all tell them? I don't want to hide anymore, but I don't know if I can face four gorgeous guys and tell them our story." I turn to look at Brogan. "Are you okay with that?"

She nods. "Yeah, we're living for the future." She hugs me tight, just as River and Rayne come barreling toward us.

"Mommy, that was so fun!" they say excitedly.

"It looked like you were having a great time." I smile down at them.

Forrest walks up behind me and wraps his arms around my waist. I don't hesitate to lean into his embrace, trusting that he's there for all the right reasons. He kisses the top of my head, and it feels right. This moment feels right.

"Girls, what about that one?" Lachlan points to the scrambler.

"Yeah!" they cheer. Rayne goes to Lachlan, and River to Maddox, and they rush off to ride the next ride.

I don't panic that my daughters are with them. I don't worry that they won't be safe. I've found my trust, and like my therapist likes to tell me: I'm not broken. I might be a little bent, but life is a trip of twists and turns, and it's how we handle them that matters.

I am stronger than my past. I am a mother to two incredible little girls. I'm a sister to the best person I know. I'm the girlfriend of an amazing man and a friend of an amazing group of people.

I'm not broken.

I am enough.

"Night, Razzle." Forrest leans in to kiss River on her cheek before he moves to Rayne's bed. "Night, Dazzle."

"Night, Forty. Love you," they chorus.

"I love you too." His voice is rich and husky as he passes by me. He leans in and kisses my cheek before stepping out into the hall and allowing me my time to say goodnight to the girls.

"Forty reads stories good," Rayne says with a yawn.

"He does," I agree. I kiss her good night, and make sure she's tucked in before moving to River's bed and doing the same.

"Mommy, can Forrest be our daddy?" River asks.

My heart stalls, and quickly starts again as it hammers in my chest.

"We don't have one, and he's real nice," Rayne adds.

"I—we can talk about this later. It's time to go to sleep."

"Love you," they chorus.

"I love you too."

My legs are shaking as I make my way out of their room. I pull the door but don't close it all the way. When I turn around, I freeze. Forrest is standing leaning against the wall.

"Yes."

"What?" I ask, swallowing hard.

"I want to be their dad." His swallow is audible. "I want that so much, Briar. I know you're not ready, and that's okay, but hearing those angels ask you if I could be their daddy, I need you to know where I'm at. They're your daughters, but I'd give anything for you to share them with me."

"Forrest." My heart is going haywire as it gallops in my chest. How can his words melt me on the spot and have burning desire rolling through my veins at the same time? I wish I could find the words. I wish I could tell him what him saying that means to me. However, I can't seem to find my voice, so instead, I use my body.

Stepping up to him, I place my hands on his shoulders and kiss him. I try to show him how I'm feeling, pouring all my want, desire, and hope into this kiss.

"I need you." My words are mumbled against his lips.

"I'm yours."

"Good." I pull back and step around him, going into my bedroom. I turn on the lamp on the bedside table. "I locked up while you were reading them a story."

"Look at my girl thinking ahead." He steps into my bedroom, softly closes the door, and turns the lock.

Tugging at my sweatshirt, I pull it off over my head, letting it fall to the floor. My leggings are next as I tear them down my thighs and kick them to the side. "You better catch up, Huntley."

"I'm so fucking proud of you, Briar."

"Stripping is tough, but I think I got it nailed down," I tease.

"Not that. You've come such a long way. Look at you stripping for me, not an ounce of hesitation."

"I'm safe with you."

"You're damn right you are." He makes quick work of stripping naked. "Now, who's behind?" he teases as he grips his cock and strokes.

"Maybe, but I'm really enjoying the show," I tell him.

"Naked and on the bed, baby."

Doing as he says, I strip out of the rest of my clothes and climb up on the bed. He crawls after me, but instead of lying next to me, he settles between my thighs on his belly. I automatically widen my legs, making room for him. He's right. I have come a long way, and it's him... the way he looks at me. The way I feel is not only safe, but cherished every time we're together, naked or clothed. It doesn't matter. He makes me feel beautiful.

"Grab the pillow, baby. You might need to hold in your scream." He winks before he takes his first taste.

"Oh, God," I say, my hands immediately going to his hair, and holding him in place. He's done this a handful of times since we've been intimate, and every time is better than the last. Who knew that a tongue could make you feel so much desire?

He sucks on my clit, and my legs clamp around his head. He's probably suffocating, but I can't help it. My hips lift off the bed, and he moves his hands to cup my ass and sucks harder.

"Forrest," I call out for him. "I'm close." He squeezes my ass, letting me know he heard me, but doesn't stop. Not that I expected him to. I learned that the first time. He wants my orgasm almost as much as he wants his own. Honestly, the way he's devouring me, I might be inclined to say more.

I feel the now familiar feeling as my release barrels through my body. Reaching for the pillow, I cover my face just in time to muffle my screams. After the last wave subsides, my legs fall open, and Forrest lifts his head. He wipes his mouth with the back of his hand, and why is that so sexy to me?

"This is going to be fast," Forrest says. He grips his cock and aligns himself at my entrance. "I'm sorry in advance. I'll make it up to you."

"Take me. However, you need me."

He pushes inside, and we both groan. "So damn tight. I'll never get over the warm, wet heat of your pussy choking my cock, baby."

His words have heat pooling between my thighs. He smirks when he feels it. "Hold on."

I do as he says, and he unleashes. He doesn't start slow; instead, each thrust is hard and fast as he chases his high.

"Fuck, fuck, fuck." The veins in his neck bulge, and I know he's trying to hold off. I don't want him to. I got mine, and I want him to get his. Tightening my core to help the process, he chuckles. "You keep using your pussy to milk my cock, this will be over."

"Good. Do it. I dare you."

"You want me to come, baby?"

"Yes." I squeeze him again.

"Fuck." He thrusts again.

Once.

Twice.

Three times, and he's smashing his lips to mine as he releases inside me. When he pulls away from the kiss, he opens his mouth but quickly closes it. "Let's get you cleaned up. I'm sure the girls will be up bright and early in the morning."

He's stayed over enough that he's learned that my daughters don't know the meaning of sleeping in. Forrest moves off the bed and offers me his hand. "If I wasn't so exhausted, I'd make you shower with me."

"There would be no making in that act," I confess.

"You need your back washed, baby, I'm your man."

"Another time," I assure him as we get ready for bed.

Once we're both ready, he turns off the bathroom light and we quickly find our clothes. He waits until I'm settled in bed before unlocking the bedroom door and cracking it open before returning. He turns off the lamp on the nightstand and settles in what I've come to determine as his side of the bed, and pulls me into his arms.

"Today was fun," I tell him.

"Yeah, it was. We'll do it again next year."

Next year.

I don't comment, but I fall asleep in his arms with a smile on my face thinking about the future.

FORREST 19

PULLING INTO THE DRIVEWAY, I smile, knowing what waits for me behind those doors. My girls. It's Friday, and my scheduled day off, so I decided to bring them lunch. I don't know how Briar does it, watching the girls and working from home, but she makes it look easy. I thought bringing lunch might give her a little break, and maybe I can spend some time with the girls and keep them occupied for a few hours while Briar tries to get some work done.

Climbing out of my truck, I grab the bag of takeout I placed on the back seat floorboard and make my way to the front porch. I probably should have told her I was coming, but I like to see her eyes light up when I surprise her. The girls, too, for that matter. I knock on the door and wait.

"Hey, you. This is a nice surprise." Briar leans in for a kiss, then steps back, allowing me to step into the house.

I lift the bags of takeout. "I brought lunch."

"You didn't have to do that."

"I know, but I'm off today. I have to meet Legend at the new build site later, but until then, lunch, and I thought I could occupy the girls so you could get some work done."

"They know Mommy is working, and it's easier with two because they have someone to play with and talk to."

"Well, now they get me." I kiss her again. "Girls!" I call out.

They come racing down the hall, their little feet padding on the hardwood floor, echoing throughout the house as they rush me. With a twin on each leg, yelling "Hello," I can't hide my smile, only to look up and find Briar watching us with a soft expression.

"Never gets old, the excitement they have over seeing me." I shake my head, still in disbelief that these three are in my life. I'll never take a single day with them for granted.

"What's that?" Rayne asks, pointing toward the bag.

"I brought lunch. Grilled cheese and french fries for my Razzle and Dazzle, and buffalo chicken wraps and Saratoga chips for your mom and me."

"Let's go." River pulls on my free hand, tugging me into the dining room.

Once we reach the table, I start taking food out of the bag, while Briar gets our drinks. Within a few minutes, we're sitting down having lunch together. I live for days like this. There is nothing I would rather do than spend time with my girls.

"How's your day going?" I ask Briar.

"Same old. Medical billing isn't the most riveting career, but it keeps the lights on."

"What would you do if you could do anything?"

"Honestly, this. I wouldn't change it for anything. I've been able to have a career and raise my girls. Sure, it's tough, and there are lots of nights I have to keep working once they're in bed, but I have that time with them, and that's what's important."

"What about next year when they go to school?" I ask her.

"It will be easier. I can be here to take them to and from school, and the entire day will be quiet. I should be able to get more done in that time."

I'm immediately thinking about building her an office in the basement at my house. A space just for her. I back away from those thoughts. She's not there yet, but she's getting there.

"We want to ride our bikes, but Mommy said we have to wait until later," River says, shoving a fry into her mouth.

"Why don't I take you out after we eat? That will give your mommy some time to work. I don't have anywhere I need to be until later in the afternoon."

"Can we, Mommy?" they ask.

"Of course," Briar answers.

The girls chatter on about riding their bikes and about how they're trying to remove their training wheels. Briar and I just listen to them and comment when they give us a chance to. They shovel in their food because they know I'll tell them that's gotta happen before we go outside and play.

"Done," Rayne says with her mouth full of her last bite of grilled cheese.

"Me too," River says, doing the same, only hers is fries.

"Go get your jackets and play shoes," Briar tells them. The words are barely out of her mouth before the girls are scrambling from their chairs and racing to do as they're told.

"You sure you don't mind taking them outside for a while?"

"Positive. I have to meet Legend later, but until then, I want nothing more than to spend time with the girls. Maybe you can get caught up on work, and we can take them for pizza or something tonight after I'm finished?"

"We can do that. Sounds like the perfect way to end the work week."

"Agreed. I do have to work tomorrow, but I don't go in until nine."

"I'll try not to keep you up too late." She smirks.

I love this side of her, the playful side. "Who needs sleep?" I ask, leaning over and sneaking a kiss.

"Forty! We're ready!"

"You better go before they come looking for you."

I start to gather our trash.

"Go on. I got this."

"You sure?"

"Yes."

I lean in for another kiss before going to find the girls. They're in the living room with their jackets and their play shoes on. "Are you ready?" I ask them.

"Yes!" They jump and cheer.

"Let's do it." I lead them to the garage and open the door, pulling out their matching bikes with training wheels. It's the beginning of October, so there's a chill in the air. Nothing I can't handle, and the girls don't seem to mind it, either, as they race their bikes up and down the driveway. I watch them closely and praise them when they show me how fast they can turn or pedal. I'm smiling so much my face hurts.

We play outside for an hour. Their little noses are red, and I know it's time to take them inside to get warmed up. "Girls, let's go get warm. I'll make you some hot chocolate before I leave."

"Okay." They easily agree, which tells me they're cold but didn't want to miss any playtime outside to say they were ready to go inside.

Fifteen minutes later, they're sitting on the floor in front of the coffee table, watching cartoons and sipping on their lukewarm hot chocolate.

"I'm going to head out," I tell Briar. "The girls are set up with their hot chocolate."

"Thank you. I got a good bit of work done."

"Good." I lean in for a kiss. "I'll see you soon."

"See you soon."

"Girls, I'm leaving," I tell them as I enter the room. I bend and kiss each of them on the top of their heads. "I'll see you in a few hours."

"Okay, Forty," they say as their eyes return to their cartoon.

"Damn, it's really coming together." I survey the building in front of us, and it might not look like much right now, but it's starting to take shape.

"I know. It's hard to believe our vision is coming to life," Legend replies.

"Thanks to you." Legend got an inheritance from his late grandparents who he never knew, and this was what he wanted to do with the money—make all our business dreams come true.

"Nah, we all worked our asses off to make a name for Everlasting Ink. I just got lucky enough to have an inheritance to help fund it, so we're all not strapped for cash."

"It's hard to think that one day, this will be left to our kids." He glances over at me. "You think the girls will want to take up the trade?"

"Honestly, I'm not sure. Whatever they want to do, I'll support them."

"Life's changing pretty damn fast. Monroe is thirty-six weeks. In a month, I'll get to hold my son. I can't say I'm mad about it, though."

"Yeah," I agree. "We have a lot to be thankful for."

"Who would have thought five best friends from the small town of Ashby, Tennessee, would have made a name for themselves in the tattoo industry? I mean, come on, where was this on career day?" he jokes.

I laugh because he's not wrong. "We're living the dream, man."

"Hell yes, we are."

"Mr. Raines, Mr. Huntley, it's good to see you," Terry, our contractor, greets us.

"Terry, good to see you." Legend greets him with a handshake.

"How's it going?" I say when he turns to shake my hand in greeting.

"Good. We're on schedule. Everything is going smoothly. I just like to touch base periodically, as you know, to make sure there are no changes or issues that might have arisen."

"None that I can think of." Legend looks at me, and I shake my head.

"Great. How about a tour? I can answer any questions you might have about the process, and you can pass them along to the others."

"Sounds great. Lead the way," Legend says.

We spend the next two hours walking through the build site. Every item on our wish list of what each of us deemed the perfect shop has been taken into consideration. We'll have a separate wing for guest artists. They'll have their own break room as well. That allows us to keep our side with our family and the break room, as well as the room for the kids. Not that we don't trust our guest artists. We have to in order to invite them into our space, but you don't trust just anyone around your wife and kids. It's overkill, sure, but we had the space and the capital to do it, so we did.

"Thank you, Terry," Legend says as we end the tour.

"Anytime. All right, I have another site to get to before the day's over. I'll talk to you soon." He shakes our hands and heads off to his truck.

"I got a mock-up of the sign. It's badass," Legend says, pulling out his phone to show me. "It's our logo, and it's going to be all lit up and massive right in the center." He points to the general location. "I'm going to have them make a smaller version for the waiting area too."

"Damn, that's sick."

"Right?" he agrees, shoving his phone back into his pocket. "Well, I'm going to head home. I should get home at the same time as my wife." He grins.

"You know, I'm gonna get me one of those."

"Yeah? You think she's ready for that?"

"She will be." I'm just waiting on the day for her to tell me. Once she does, there's no holding back.

I wave goodbye to Legend, climb into my own truck, and pull out of the lot. I honk as he turns from the stop sign and ease up for my turn. I'm looking right and left, getting ready to turn toward Briar's, which is why I don't see it coming.

Something slams into the back of my truck, causing me to spin. My head bounces off the airbag as my truck comes to a stop.

It takes me a few minutes to process what just happened. I blink a few times and look through the windshield. A man climbs out of a dump truck before jogging toward me. He pulls open my door in a rush, his eyes panicked.

"I'm so sorry. Are you okay? Of course you're not okay. I lost brakes. I couldn't stop," he rambles. "Shit, you're bleeding. I need to call 9-1-1." He places the call and tells them what happened. They told him to not let me move until the paramedics get here.

I'm queasy, and lightheaded, and my head is pounding, but other than that, I feel fine. I reach for my phone in the cupholder and wince at the stiffness my body is already feeling, but my phone's not there.

"Can I use your phone?"

"Sure. Anything you need." The man hands me his phone, but my vision is still blurry. "Can you call Everlasting Ink? Tell them Forrest was in a car accident." As soon as the words are out, the paramedics arrive on the scene. I hear them tell the man they're taking me to the county hospital, and for him to relay the message. I don't know who he reached at the shop, but I know they'll get ahold of Briar and then they'll all be there.

I'm loaded on a stretcher, even though I feel fine, and was able to climb out of the truck on my own. They're insisting that I go get checked out, and I know my sister and my girls will be pissed if I refuse, so I comply and stop complaining.

This is not the end of my day that I was hoping for, but at least I made it out with just a scratch or whatever the hell is making my head bleed, and from the stiffness of my neck, I suspect some whiplash. It could have been much worse.

I'M JUST FINISHING UP FOR the day when there's a knock at the door. The girls are sitting on the couch with their bears Forrest won them at the county fair last month. They've got them wrapped up in blankets, and they are pretending to feed them with bottles from their baby dolls. I smile because they love those bears and refuse to go to sleep at night without them.

Moving toward the door, I pull it open, expecting to see Forrest, but it's Roman standing there. "Hey, Roman. What can I do for you?"

"Are the girls here?" he asks.

"They are," I answer him cautiously.

"Okay, we'll take your car."

"Take my car where?" I'm confused, and Roman is being evasive, which puts me on edge.

He sighs. "Forrest was in an accident."

"What?" My heart drops to the floor. Fear and panic wash over me. "What do you mean? Where is he? Is he okay?" I ramble off questions, not giving him time to answer.

"I don't know much. I know he was awake and talking to the man who hit him. He asked him to call the shop to let us know."

The man who hit him!

"Where is he?" Fear slides over me. I can't lose him. I can't. Before Roman can answer, I call out, "Girls, I need you to put on your shoes and grab your coats." I rush around, pulling open the closet door, removing our coats, and sliding into mine.

"Where are we going?" River asks.

"Oh, hi, Rome," Rayne says.

"Girls, we're going to take a ride. Everyone will be there when we get there. But I need you to listen to your mom, and let's get your shoes and coat on," Roman explains.

"Can we take our bears?" River asks.

"You bet you can." He gets to work helping the girls into their shoes and coats while I race to get my phone and purse.

"Keys?" Roman holds his hand out, and I don't try to argue. I'm too emotional to drive.

"Come on, girls." I usher them out to the car, barely holding on to my tears, and get them strapped into their seats.

Once they're safe, I hop into the passenger seat and try to buckle myself, but my hands are shaking. Roman reaches over and does it for me. He places his hand over mine.

"He's going to be okay."

"He has to be," I say, my voice cracking as I lose my battle with my tears.

"Mommy, what's wrong? Why are you crying?" River asks.

"Mommy, I don't like it when you cry," Rayne says. Her voice quivers, and I know I need to hold it together for them, but I just can't do that right now. I'm scared out of my mind.

Roman glances over at me, and I shake my head. I can't tell them.

"Can I?" he asks, and all I can do is nod again. "Girls, there's been an accident. Forrest has a boo-boo, and we're going to go visit him."

"Is hims hurt bad?" River asks.

"He's talking, and I know he wants to see you." He evades the question.

"I'm scared," Rayne says.

"It's okay, sweetheart," Roman assures her. "Everything is going to be okay." His voice is calm and soothing, but I can hear it. There's some worry and fear of his own laced into his words.

I can hear the girls sniffling in the back seat, but I can't turn to comfort them. I know as soon as I do, I'll upset them even more, which will upset me even more. So, instead, I keep facing forward, while I send up a silent prayer to keep him safe.

Please let him be okay.

The drive to the local county hospital is the longest ride of my life. In reality, it didn't take us more than fifteen minutes, but my heart and my head are in disagreement about the length of time. My head knows the distance, and my heart feels a lifetime of fear.

Taking a deep breath, I wipe at my cheeks and turn to face my daughters. "We have to be sure to use our inside voices in the building, okay? There are people who are sick and trying to sleep."

"Like Forrest?" Rayne asks.

"Yeah, sweetie. Like Forrest."

"Let's get inside. Everyone is waiting for us." Roman steps out of the car, and I do the same. We each help the girls out of the car and hold their hands on the way inside the emergency department. As soon as we're through the automatic doors, I see a small crowd of people.

Our people.

Emerson comes rushing over, and I think she's going for Roman, but she bypasses him and comes straight to me. She wraps me in a hug and whispers in my ear, "He's okay. He's going to be okay."

I break. I don't know if it's her arms that are locked around me in a caring embrace or if it's the overwhelming relief after such intense fear that he's going to be okay, but I sob into her shoulder. It's only the scared voices of my daughters that finally has me pulling away.

"Where is Forrest?"

"I want Forrest."

"Briar."

I turn to find Brogan, with Maggie on her heels, rushing into the ER. "We came as soon as we heard. How is he?"

"He's going to be okay. He's asking for Briar and the girls," Lachlan explains.

"We want to go," River demands, crossing her little arms over her chest.

"I want to go too." Rayne mocks her sister's stance.

"You heard the lady," Lachlan teases. "Come on. I'll take you all back."

"Are you sure it's okay?"

"I've been back already, and so have Lachlan, Legend, and Maddox. He's going to want to see you three before the rest of us. Trust me on that," Emerson explains.

I nod, take one of the girls' hands in each of mine, and follow Lachlan down the hall. "I'm just showing them to his room, and I'll be right back out," he tells the nurse. "I know there is a two-person limit, but two little humans count as one, right?" He winks.

The nurse smiles and glances down at the girls. "I only see two, with one leading the way that's going to come right back out." She tosses back her own wink and goes right back to typing on her computer. She must be in her early sixties, and the wink, well, it suits her. I'm sure she's used to dealing with all kinds of personalities in her line of work.

"Thank you," I mumble.

"You're welcome, dear."

Lachlan stops at the end of the hall. "Go on in," he tells me as he holds the door open for us.

Quietly, we step into the room. Fresh tears are already coating my cheeks, and I'm certain I'm holding the girls' hands too tightly.

Forrest is lying in the bed with a bandage on his forehead. His eyes are closed, and it gives me a few minutes to take him in. His face is bruised, and there are a few scrapes.

"Forty," Rayne whispers.

His eyes pop open, and he smiles. "There's my girls."

My daughters pull out of my hold, probably due to my sweaty palms, and rush to his side of the bed. "You gots a boo-boo," Rayne says softly.

"I do, but I'm going to be just fine."

"You got hurted," River adds.

"I was in an accident, but I'm okay. Just a bad boo-boo."

"Mommy cried, and we did too," River says, trying to climb up on the bed.

"River, be careful. Forrest is hurt." I rush to stop her, but he grunts as he lifts her up on the bed, and she wraps her arms around his neck.

"I'm fine, baby," he assures me. "Dazzle, did you come here to give me some love?" he asks Rayne.

Her reply is to start to climb, and with another grunt, he lifts her up to the bed, and she, too, hugs him as if her life depends on it.

That leaves me.

"Girls, climb over here so we can make room for your momma." Rayne carefully climbs over and settles next to River. "Come here, Momma." Forrest pats the side of the bed.

Cautiously, I sit so that I'm facing him. I try to speak, but the words won't come. Instead, all I can do is cry. "Baby, I'm okay."

"Mommy, Forty is better," River says, trying to console me.

"I was scared," I finally say, more for the girls' benefit than my own.

"I can't imagine what you went through when you got the news, but I'm fine. I have a bump on my head that needed a couple of stitches, whiplash, and I'll be sore for a few days, and the bruising will get worse, but I'm okay."

"All I could think about was our lives without you in it. It's not a vision I ever want to have in my head again," I say, wiping at my cheeks.

"Knock, knock," Brogan says. "Hey, Forrest, I'm glad to hear you're going to be okay."

"Yeah, me too. Thanks," he says.

"Girls, guess what?"

"What?" they ask.

"They have this cool machine that dispenses hot chocolate, and you get to watch. Want to come get one with me?"

"We love hot chocolate," Rayne says.

Brogan chuckles. "I know you do. Come on, let your mom and Forrest talk, and we'll see about a hot chocolate and some snacks. You know what else?"

"What?" they ask.

"Maddox and Lachlan are out in the waiting room, and they're lonely. We better go keep them company."

"Oh, no!" Forrest gasps. "Girls, you better go keep them company. Those two might get into trouble if they get too lonely."

"Let's go, sissy!" Rayne says.

"Wait. I need another hug."

They oblige and give him another hug before Brogan helps them off the bed. "Thanks, Brogan," I call after my sister. She turns around and nods. She knew I'd need some time. Time to express my feelings without scaring the girls.

I love my sister.

Once the door closes, I turn back to Forrest. The tears start to fall again. No matter how many times I blink them away, they still fall.

"I'm okay," Forrest says soothingly.

"You're not okay. You're in the emergency room with a bandage on your head and bruises all over your face. That's not okay."

"I'm just fine. Nothing that won't heal."

"You can't leave us. You can't. I—I can't think about a life without you in it."

Forrest tilts his head to the side and raises his hand to cradle my cheek. He studies me for far too long before he gruffly asks, "Are you ready?"

I don't even have to think about my answer. I've known for a while now that I was ready, but I was letting lingering fears hold me back. I realized today that my fear could have kept him from knowing how I feel. I promised myself that if he made it through this, I would never hold back again.

"Yes."

A slow, sexy smile crosses his face. "Briar Pearce, you are the love of my life. I'm madly in love with you. I want to spend forever with you, raising our daughters and any future children we might have. I love you."

More tears. This time they're accompanied with a smile. "I love you, too, Forrest Huntley. I'm sorry it took me so long to tell you."

"I could feel it, Briar. I could feel your love in every look, every touch, every smile." He traces his thumb over my lips. "I could feel it. I didn't need your words, baby."

"I—me too. Every single day."

"And forever," he says. "Now come here and kiss me."

"You're hurt."

"I'll hurt worse if I don't get your lips on mine. Come here, baby."

Needing to feel his lips on mine, I do as he says and lean in close. I kiss him softly as he murmurs, "I love you." My heart is full, so full it could crack from how happy I am.

"I needed you. There was a reason I was compelled to raise the girls here in Ashby. It was more than just the connection to my dad. It was you. The universe knew I needed your kind heart, your strong hands, and your patience. You brought me back to life, Forrest."

"I could say the same. I needed you too. I had this big old house, and it was lonely. It was made for a family, and I wanted one of my own desperately. Then I found you and our girls. I can't wait until you move in with me."

"You want us to move in with you?"

"I do. I have the space for all of us, and any more kids we should have. My sister is next door, and Monroe and Legend are right across the street."

"I don't know if I can leave Brogan."

He nods. "I'm sure that's something the two of you will need to talk about, but I'm ready when you are. If you really want to live somewhere else, we can. I just assumed you'd move in with me."

"I love your house." I hate to think of leaving Brogan alone, but she's not alone anymore. We have a huge group of friends and a support system, and I'll just be on the other side of town. I know what Brogan would tell me. I can also hear my therapist telling me to fight for myself and what I want. I want us to be a family. I want to go to sleep and wake up with him every day. I want to have dinner together, and help the girls with their homework, and yeah, more kids when we get to that point. "Okay."

"Okay? Okay, you'll move in with me?"

I nod. "Me and the girls."

"Really?" I don't think I've ever seen his eyes this bright. Even with the swelling and bruising, it's easy to see.

"Yes. I'm ready."

"I love you."

"I love you too."

"Lie with me. I need to hold you."

I do as he asks and lie with him until the nurse comes into the room to tell us that he can go home. I help him get dressed into clothes that someone brought for him. It doesn't matter who, because I know they all were willing, no matter who it was lying in this bed from our family.

"Where are we headed?" Legend asks when he sees the nurse wheeling him into the lobby.

Forrest looks up at me. "Home. Take me and my girls home."

"Our home?" River asks. My nosey girl.

"How would you feel about you, your momma, and your sister moving in with me? You would live at my house?" Forrest asks her.

The girls gasp. "What about Aunt Brogan?" Rayne questions.

"Rayne, sweetheart, I'm a big girl," Brogan tells her. "I'll still see you all the time, and we can have sleepovers at my place."

"Won't you be lonely?"

"Nah, we won't let her be lonely," Maddox says, dropping his arm around my sister's shoulder.

River looks at Rayne, and something passes between them.

"You can bring all of your things and share a room or have your own rooms. Whatever you want," Forrest tells them.

Another look passes, and then they cheer. "Okay!"

Everyone laughs, including the nurse who is still pushing the wheelchair. Forrest pulls the girls up on his lap, and Roman takes over pushing duties as we all follow them out of the emergency room.

Brogan links her arm with mine. "And they lived happily ever after," she whispers.

"Your day is coming, Brogan. I can feel it."

"Well, at least I won't have to sneak him in the house past the girls."

We both toss our heads back in laughter.

This is our new life, and we're more than ready for what's yet to come.

FORREST EPILOGUE

THE LAST SIX WEEKS HAVE been the best of my life. The day of my accident, Briar and the girls came home with me, and they never left. This is now their home, and this big old house is no longer quiet and lonely.

Now, it's filled with the pitter-patter of little feet, lots of giggles, and love. So much fucking love. Those girls are mine. I couldn't love them more if it were my blood running through their veins. And their momma, that woman snuck in and stole my heart, and I have a strict no-returns policy.

Today is Thanksgiving, and it looks a little different. It used to be just Emerson and me today, and then tomorrow would be our Friendsgiving, but my little sister is married and a momma, and as for me, I'm a dad now. Sure, the girls don't call me that, but in my eyes, that's who I am to them, and no one will ever be able to tell me differently.

Emerson and I sat down a few weeks ago, and together we formed a new tradition. She has Roman's family to have Thanksgiving with now, not just me, and I have my girls, and Brogan. Roman's parents eat a late Thanksgiving dinner, so we're having our own at my place for lunch. That means I was up at the ass crack of dawn cooking. Briar joined me around seven. She made the girls breakfast and jumped right into helping me with the side dishes.

"Forrest, can I help?" Rayne asks.

I look down at her where she's tugging on my jeans. "Of course you can," I tell her.

"Me too?" River asks.

"You bet. Let's wash your hands and pull your hair back."

"I can do that," Briar tells me.

"Nah, I got it." I lead the girls to the bathroom and help them wash up, before pulling their hair up into ponytails. I practically raised my little sister, so this was a skill I learned long ago. Although, I'm better than I used to be. The girls should thank Emerson for that.

Back in the kitchen, I lift the girls to the island so they can help. "Okay, this is a really important job. Are you ready?" I ask them.

"Yes!" they say together with a loud cheer.

"All right, I'm going to give you each a cup of cheese and I need you to spread it over top of the broccoli."

Rayne wrinkles up her nose. "It's yucky."

"What?" I gasp as if she hurt my feelings. "This is my favorite. It's all cheesy goodness. You have to try it. But if not, that's okay. That leaves more for me."

"I like cheese," Rayne says thoughtfully.

"And then we have these crackers that are soaked in butter that goes on top. I'm telling you, this is the best."

"I guess I can try it," Rayne concedes.

I look up to find Briar watching us and wink at her. She smiles and shakes her head. I just convinced our picky eater to try her vegetables. Sure, I had to smother it in cheese and buttered crackers, but broccoli casserole is still better than no vegetables. Baby steps and all that.

A few hours later, my sister, Rome, Lilly, and Brogan all show up, each bringing desserts. They chat with the girls while Briar and I pull everything out of the oven. After I carve the ham, I call out, "Time to eat!" The girls come rushing in, and I get them set up with a plate while Briar gets their drinks. Everyone is seated around the table, and I can't help but get choked up.

This is what life is all about. The moments with the people you love. We eat and laugh, and it's a day I'll always remember.

Once our plates are empty, I stand from the table. "Thanksgiving hasn't always looked like this. It used to be just Emerson and me. We would celebrate the day after with our friends, and it was perfect for us. Life changed, and my baby sister went and fell in love with my best friend. Now they're married and have a beautiful little girl, and it isn't just us anymore.

"Now, here we are, and life has changed again. This time, it's me who is no longer alone. This time, I'm adding the love of my life, our daughters, and her sister to our family." I swallow back the lump in my throat, and it hits me.

Now is the time.

I wasn't planning to do this today, but the moment feels right.

Stepping away from the table, I kneel next to Briar, and she turns to face me. Her eyes widen when she sees me on one knee. "I love you. I love our daughters. I love my new sister." I toss a wink at Brogan, and she smiles, tears in her eyes. I glance at my sister, and she, too, is blinking back tears. Good. They know where this is going.

"You brought life back to this place, to me. I was lonely. I was happy for Rome and Em, but I missed having life in this big house. You and the girls, you changed that. Now there is the sound of little feet padding down the hall, giggles, so many giggles, and love. So much love.

"I never want that to change. I want this feeling to last a lifetime. I want all the holidays and all the moments just like this one." Reaching into my pocket, I pull out the ring I've been carrying around for weeks, waiting for the moment to feel right.

"I bought this the week after I came home from the hospital. I've been carrying it with me everywhere I go, just waiting for the time to be right. This moment, surrounded by those we love most, feels right to me. On a day that we give thanks, I need you

234 | KAYLEE RYAN

to know that I'm thankful for you. I just have one question, baby." I smile up at her and wink. "Are you ready to be my wife? Will you marry me?"

Tears coat her cheeks, and she nods. "Yes. Yes, I'll marry you." She smiles through her tears. Damn, this moment, it's the first day of my forever with my girls—all three of them. I don't think I've ever been this happy or this hopeful for what's yet to come.

I slide the ring onto her finger and kiss her. Knowing that the girls are watching, I pull back far sooner than I'd like.

"Forrest?" River asks.

"What's up, Razzle?" I ask her.

"Are you marrying me and sissy too?" she asks.

The adults laugh, and I smile, keeping my eyes locked on my little girl. "Forever," I tell her.

"Forrest?" This time it's Rayne.

"Dazzle." I smile at her.

"Can you be our daddy, 'cause we don't gots one?"

It's my turn to blink back tears. "Come here," I croak. The girls scramble out of their seats and come to me. I wrap them both in a hug, and just let the moment sink in.

I'm a father. The moment chokes me up.

I pull back and clear my throat. "I already am," I tell them.

They gasp. "You are?" River asks.

"I am, and I love you very much."

"I love you, too, Daddy," they chorus, and my heart is so fucking full it could burst from happiness. I hug them again, because I need to. I meet Briar's gaze and she's openly crying as well, but she's also smiling. My eyes scan the room and see that Brogan and Emerson are also crying, and hell, even Roman looks like his eyes are misty.

"Congratulations!" Emerson can't hold it in a minute longer as she comes over and hugs us all. Brogan is next, and then Roman.

This is definitely a day to give thanks. I can't wait to do it again tomorrow with the rest of our friends, and I can tell them and the world that I'm getting married to the love of my life and I'm the dad of two very adorable little girls.

BRIAR EPILOGUE

I KNEW THE MINUTE FORREST slid the ring on my finger that I didn't want to wait to get married. I wanted to start the rest of our lives together. The following Monday, I contacted a lawyer to start the adoption process. The process for a stepparent to adopt is three to four months on average.

When the girls each handed Forrest an envelope, on Christmas morning with the paperwork he would need to sign to start the process, I'd never seen him smile like that. In fact, the smile has not left his face since that morning.

It could have something to do with the fact that we're in Vegas for our wedding. When I started looking for places to get married, Vegas was always a top hit. When I saw they had a children's museum and other fun things for the girls to do, I was set. We considered Gatlinburg, but I wanted a place that had something for everyone.

I chose Vegas.

And here we are.

We decided on a New Year's Eve wedding. We're starting the new year off right as a family of four. Sure, it's cliché to get married on a holiday, but it feels right, so we're going with it.

Besides, that gives us an excuse to celebrate extra hard every New Year's Eve, not that we need an excuse, but we'll have it, anyway.

"It's my understanding the groom wants to say a few words," the officiant announces.

I give Forrest a curious look, and he just smiles and releases my hands, pulling a piece of paper out of his back pocket.

He scans the crowd. Then his eyes lock onto mine. There is a very important person missing today, and well, I have something I need to say. He clears his throat and begins to read.

"Mr. Pearce,

"My name is Forrest Huntley, and today, I'm marrying your daughter, Briar. It's painful to admit that I finally know what it's like to miss someone without ever meeting them. Although we've never met in person, you live on through your daughters and your granddaughters and now through me.

"I want to take this opportunity to say thank you. Thank you for raising such a strong, loving, incredible woman. Meeting Briar has changed my life in so many ways. I knew my life was incomplete, but I didn't know what I was missing until Briar and the girls walked into my life. They are everything I never knew I needed.

"Loving your daughter is an honor and a privilege and I promise you all four of your girls will be safe, loved, and cherished with me. You heard that right. Brogan is my new sister, and I vow to you that I'll watch over her too. We're all a family now.

"We're missing you deeply, especially today, but we know you're here in our hearts. Your legacy will live on through all of us. I'll be sure to remind River and Rayne how much you liked to fish, and that the fish bite better on the Ashby River when it's raining. I'll show them, all of them, what it means to have a man love them and support them no matter what, just as you did for Briar and Brogan. I'll carry that torch for both of us.

"Today, we stand before our family and friends and vow to love each other until death do us part. It is also my vow to you to honor, love, and cherish all four of your girls. Their hearts are safe with me.

"Your son-in-law, Forrest"

I'm sobbing. I can't see Forrest because my tears blur my vision. I can imagine how awful I look with my eyes red and my face blotchy, but I can't find it in me to care. This man, my husband, he's the most incredible loving man I've ever met, and for him to do this, to write that letter.

"Forrest—" My voice cracks.

"I love you."

"I love you too." I lean in for a kiss, and the officiant rushes to pronounce us.

"I now pronounce you husband and wife. You may kiss your bride."

"Fucking finally," Forrest breathes under his breath before his lips capture mine. The girls giggle and our friends and family cheer.

Pulling out of the kiss, Forrest bends and scoops both of the girls up in his arms. I step into him and wrap my arms around his waist. "My girls," he murmurs.

"Let's celebrate!" Lachlan cheers.

"We'll meet you all back at the hotel. They have a conference room reserved for us," Forrest tells everyone.

"Daddy, what's a cofence room?" River asks.

"A *conference* room is a big room with lots of tables and chairs and open space for us to dance and celebrate."

"Sounds like a party," Maddox says. He reaches for Rayne and plops her on his hip.

Lachlan does the same with River.

"You're going to spoil them," Briar warns, with no real warning in her tone.

"That's the plan." Maddox grins. "We're taking the girls with us. We'll meet you back at the hotel."

Before we can object, they're leaving. That's when I noticed everyone else has gone too. "It's just us," I say, turning back to Forrest.

"Remind me to thank them for giving me a few moments alone with my wife." Forrest tosses me over his shoulder and takes off down the hall. We end up in the room I used to get ready. All my stuff is gone, so I know the ladies must have grabbed it for me.

"I love our daughters, but I need you." He kicks the door closed and slides me down his body, only to lift me again. I wrap my legs around his waist as he pushes my back against the door. "I love you, Mrs. Huntley."

My face hurts from smiling so much. "I love you too."

"Thank you for this life, for our daughters. I have just one question."

"What's that?" I ask as he trails kisses down my neck.

"When can we have more?"

"W-What?" I huff out a laugh.

"More kids. I want more. The girls are going to turn five in a few months. We don't want them too far apart."

"You want more kids. Now?"

"I mean, I wasn't going to do it here, but I'm game," he says, reaching between us. His hand finds its way under my dress as he slips his fingers beneath my lace thong. "What do you say, wife? Want to make a baby with me?"

"Not here."

"Fine, our hotel room then. We'll call this practice or a warm-up." He kisses me just below my ear, and I shiver at his touch.

"Everyone is waiting for us."

"Fine. Emerson and Roman are keeping the girls in their room tonight with Lilly for a sleepover. We can start then."

"Is that really what you want?"

"You pregnant with my baby? To give the girls a brother or a sister? Yes. That's really what I want."

"Me too." Just when I think this man can't make me fall more in love with him, he does. I knew we both wanted more kids, but I never dreamed he'd want to start now.

"It takes time, right? Once you stop your birth control?"

"I think so. I mean that's what they say."

"So, we'll leave those in Vegas." He winks.

"Yeah, we'll leave those in Vegas."

He kisses me again, and I get lost in him.

"If I don't stop, we're not leaving this room."

"We have a lifetime," I remind him.

"A lifetime," he agrees.

"It was beautiful," Brogan says, resting her head on my shoulder. "I'm so happy for you."

"I'm happy for us. We're stronger than ever."

"We are."

"He can't take his eyes off you."

"We're going to try to have a baby," I admit.

"Really?" Brogan sits up and wraps me in a hug. "I love that for you."

"Yours is out there, Brogan. It's scary as hell, but it's worth it."

"One day." She smiles, and I'm glad she's open to finding love of her own.

"We're heading up to our room. The girls and Lilly are losing steam," Emerson says as she joins us.

"Thank you for keeping them."

"Of course. The way my brother has been staring at you all night, it's for their safety. We don't need them scarred for life," Emerson jokes.

"Mommy!" The girls come rushing over. "Daddy said we have to go now to spend the night with Lilly."

"That's right. You're going to have so much fun. In the morning, we're going to have breakfast and then we'll go explore."

"Yay." They hug me goodbye, and rush over to Forrest and do the same.

"I'll see you later. Welcome to the family. Officially." Emerson winks, and heads to where Roman, Lilly, and the girls are waiting for her.

"You ready to hit the town?" Maggie asks Brogan. She leans in and offers me a hug. "Congratulations."

"Thank you."

"Yeah, might as well see what the Vegas fuss is all about." Brogan stands. "Just us?"

Maggie shrugs. "I think Maddox and Lachlan are venturing out too. But yeah, just us."

"Be safe," I warn them. "Call us if you need us."

"I'll call Monroe or Emerson." Brogan smiles. "It's your wedding night."

My wedding night.

"I'm married!"

They laugh and give me another hug before leaving. I move to where Forrest is talking to the rest of our crew. Lachlan tugs me into a hug.

"You're good for him," he tells me.

"We're good for each other."

"Stop hogging the bride," Legend complains, pulling me into a hug.

"My turn." Monroe steps into a side hug because she's holding their seven-week-old son, Kane. "Congratulations."

"Thank you." I bend and kiss Kane on the head. "He's precious."

"You need one," Legend tells me.

"We're working on it," Forrest speaks up.

"My turn, and we're out." Maddox hugs me tightly, lifting my feet off the floor.

"Paws off, Mad," Forrest grumbles.

"We love you!" Monroe waves as the four of them and baby Kane walk away. Forrest and I make sure we're not leaving anything behind and head up to our room. Once there, I walk to the window and take in the view of the city that never sleeps. I hear him approach, and I turn to face him.

"Are you ready?" I ask him.

He tilts his head to the side. "For you? Always."

THANK YOU

for taking the time to read **Are You Ready?**

I hope you loved Forrest and Briar as much as I do.
Not ready to let them go?
Scan the QR code below to download a free bonus epilogue.

Want more from the Everlasting Ink Crew?
What About Now? is available for preorder.
Scan the QR code below to reserve your copy of Maddox's story.

Never miss a new release:
Newsletter Sign-up

Be the first to hear about free content, new releases, cover
reveals, sales, and more.
You can also find free reads and bonus content on my website.

CONTACT KAYLEE RYAN

Facebook:
bit.ly/2C5DgdF

Reader Group:
bit.ly/2ooyWDx

Goodreads:
bit.ly/2HodJvx

BookBub:
bit.ly/2KulVvH

Website:
kayleeryan.com/

Instagram:
instagram.com/kaylee_ryan_author/

TikTok:
tiktok.com/@kayleeryanauthor

MORE FROM KAYLEE RYAN

With You Series:
Anywhere with You | More with You | Everything with You

Soul Serenade Series:
Emphatic | Assured | Definite | Insistent

Southern Heart Series:
Southern Pleasure | Southern Desire
Southern Attraction | Southern Devotion

Unexpected Arrivals Series
Unexpected Reality |Unexpected Fight | Unexpected Fall
Unexpected Bond | Unexpected Odds

Riggins Brothers Series:
Play by Play | Layer by Layer | Piece by Piece
Kiss by Kiss | Touch by Touch | Beat by Beat

Entangled Hearts Duet:
Agony | Bliss

Cocky Hero Club:
Lucky Bastard

MORE FROM
KAYLEE RYAN

Mason Creek Series:
Perfect Embrace

Standalone Titles:
Tempting Tatum | Unwrapping Tatum
Levitate | Just Say When
I Just Want You | Reminding Avery

Hey, Whiskey | Pull You Through | Remedy
The Difference | Trust the Push | Forever After All
Misconception | Never with Me | Merry with Me

Out of Reach Series:
Beyond the Bases | Beyond the Game
Beyond the Play | Beyond the Team

Kincaid Brothers Series:
Stay Always | Stay Over | Stay Forever | Stay Tonight
Stay Together | Stay Wild | Stay Present
Stay Anyway | Stay Real

Everlasting Ink Series:
Does He Know? | Is This Love? | Are You Ready?
What About Now? | Can We Try?

MORE FROM KAYLEE RYAN

Co-written with Lacey Black:

Fair Lakes Series:
It's Not Over | Just Getting Started | Can't Fight It

Standalone Titles:
Boy Trouble | Home to You
Beneath the Fallen Stars | Beneath the Desert Sun
Tell Me A Story

Co-writing as Rebel Shaw with Lacey Black:
Royal | Crying Shame | Watch and Learn

There are so many people who are involved in the publishing process. I write the words, but I rely on my team of editors, proofreaders, and beta readers to help me make each book the best that it can be.

Those mentioned above are not the only members of my team. I have photographers, models, cover designers, formatters, bloggers, graphic designers, author friends, my PA, and so many more. I could not do this without these people.

And then there are my readers. If you're reading this, thank you. Your support means everything. Thank you for spending your hard-earned money on my words, and taking the time to read them. I appreciate you more than you know.

SPECIAL THANKS:

Becky Johnson, Hot Tree Editing.
Julie Deaton, Jo Thompson, and Jess Hodge, Proofreading
Lori Jackson Design – Cover Design (Guy Cover)
Emily Wittig Designs – Special Edition Cover
Michelle Lancaster – Photographer (Main Guy Cover)
Chasidy Renee – Personal Assistant
Jamie, Stacy, Lauren, Franci, and Erica
Bloggers, Bookstagrammers, and TikTokers
Lacey Black and Kelly Elliott
Designs by Stacy and Ms. Betty – Graphics
The entire Give Me Books Team
The entire Grey's Promotion Team
My fellow authors
And my amazing Readers